A
SWORD
IN HER

DISCARD

A SWORD IN HER HAND

JEAN-CLAUDE VAN RIJCKEGHEM

AND

PAT VAN BEIRS

TRANSLATED BY

JOHN NIEUWENHUIZEN

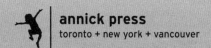

annick press
toronto + new york + vancouver

This edition first published in 2011.
First published in Belgium and the Netherlands in 2009 by Uitgeverij Manteau /
Standaard Uitgeverij, Antwerpen, with the title *Jonkvrouw*.
Text © 2011 Uitgeverij Manteau / Standaard Uitgeverij and Jean-Claude Van Rijckeghem
and Pat van Beirs
English translation © 2011 John Nieuwenhuizen

Annick Press Ltd.

Copy edited by Geri Rowlatt
Proofread by Tanya Trafford
Cover design by *the*BookDesigners
Cover photograph: © Jose AS Reyes / shutterstock.com

The translation of this book was funded by the Flemish
Literature Fund (Vlaams Fonds voor de Letteren—
www.flemishliterature.be)

Cataloguing in Publication

Van Rijckeghem, Jean-Claude, 1963-
        A sword in her hand / Jean-Claude van Rijckeghem & Pat van Beirs ; translated
by John Nieuwenhuizen.

Translation of: Jonkvrouw.
ISBN 978-1-55451-291-1 (bound).—ISBN 978-1-55451-290-4 (pbk.)

        I. Van Beirs, Pat   II. Nieuwenhuizen, John   III. Title.

PZ7.R54S96 2011   j839.31'37   C2010-907246-4

Printed and bound in Canada.

Annick Press is committed to protecting our natural environment.
As part of our efforts, the text of this book is printed on 100%
post-consumer recycled fibers.

Published in the U.S.A. by	Distributed in Canada by	Distributed in the U.S.A. by
Annick Press (U.S.) Ltd.	Firefly Books Ltd.	Firefly Books (U.S.) Inc.
	66 Leek Crescent	P.O. Box 1338
	Richmond Hill, ON	Ellicott Station
	L4B 1H1	Buffalo, NY 14205

Visit our website at **www.annickpress.com**

Mixed Sources

Product group from well-managed
forests, controlled sources and
recycled wood or fiber
www.fsc.org Cert no. SW-COC-001352
© 1996 Forest Stewardship Council

1

THE KNIGHTS OF FLANDERS AND BRABANT will swear allegiance to the infant in its cradle. The leaders of the free cities will welcome the child within their walls and wish him happiness, health, and wisdom. The traders from the East will present the young squire with gerbils and spider monkeys for his amusement. Even before his seventh birthday, the kings of France and England will offer him their loveliest daughters and talk to his father about arranging a marriage. The Pope, God's vessel on the sea of humankind, will bless the boy in his prayers.

My father's son will become Count of Flanders. He will be a leader, a warrior, and a diplomat. He will be admired for his knowledge of the world and its secrets. He will be able to sing in French, Flemish, and Latin, and to discuss the stars as if he had personally scattered them across the heavens. He will be able to bring down a wild boar at a full gallop and will never ask an unnecessary question. He will be hard in war and gentle in love.

He will be a man. A knight.

◻ ◻ ◻

ON THE LAST DAY OF THE YEAR 1347, my mother, the Duchess of Brabant, feels cramps in her sleep. She is lying in the women's room of the castle of Male, in a wide bed among ladies-in-waiting and washerwomen. The women lie together on sacks of straw, under sheepskin blankets. They're lying skin to skin, for in winter not a breath of warmth must be lost. The room is not quiet. The women cough and grunt and sneeze and snort. Their throats are as raw as butcher's meat and their noses blocked like the narrow neck of an oil bottle.

My mother suddenly feels a warm gush of water between her thighs. With a jolt she sits up and the cold grabs her bare back. She realizes instantly that I will be born on this freezing night. She has no idea how far the night has advanced. The world floats between compline and lauds, in a moment when time is vague and the night has no name.

A lady-in-waiting opens her eyes and asks what is going on. My mother shivers. Her breath is visible in the cold. She says the child is coming.

Someone groans, "At last." It is the midwife, Hanne, who, with her daughter, has been staying in the castle for the past month to take care of the confinement.

A moment later the whole bed comes to life. Ladies-in-waiting and washerwomen get up and, shivering with cold, pull shifts on over their bare bodies. They take my mother to the kitchens where the warm ovens still smolder. It's the only place in the castle where there's some warmth left. They kick the kitchen boys awake and send them off. They put red cushions on the long table and my mother lies down on them. One of the washerwomen runs across the inner courtyard to the main building. She hammers on the door of my father's room.

"The time has come, my Lord Count," she shouts.

Grunting and stumbling sounds come from the room. A moment later the door opens. My father is naked. The washerwoman averts her eyes.

"Get someone to wake up the surgeon," he growls.

The washerwoman looks up at my father in surprise. She hesitates. She wants to say that confinement is women's business, but she doesn't have the courage.

"What are you waiting for, woman, a sign from God?" my father snarls, grabbing his shirt from a chair and pulling it over his head. The woman runs to the men's sleeping quarters to find the surgeon.

My father, the Count of Flanders, smashes the ice in the washbasin with his fist. He splashes water over his face, feeling his cheeks tingle. He puts on a black robe, a belt, hose, and a cloak. He crosses the courtyard to the kitchens. He sees his wife lying on her side. With a grin he runs his rough fingers over her cheeks.

"I love you, my Brabant," he whispers in her ear.

She takes his hand, smiles, and says, "And I you,

my Flanders." Then she has a cramp so fierce that she scratches my father's arm open with her nails. She gasps for air and moans.

Midwife Hanne and her daughter Beatrijs both have muscular arms, thick fingers, and big heads with round cheeks. They are mother and daughter, but they are so like each other, people take them for sisters. Beatrijs starts a fire in the kitchen hearth. She breaks the ice in the water barrel, fills a kettle with water, and hangs it over the fire.

⊞ ⊞ ⊞

MASTER SURGEON WIRNT VAN OBRECHT enters the room. He's one of the best surgeons in Flanders, wise and old, at least forty, and exceptionally capable at treating a pierced shoulder or putting together a shattered cheekbone. But he has not the faintest idea what goes on inside the hard belly of a woman during childbirth. For him, that has always remained a divine mystery. During the pregnancy, Surgeon van Obrecht prescribed a calming poppy extract for the Countess every day, and now that the day of deliverance has come, he leaves the finishing touches to the midwife.

Meanwhile, Hanne slides her hand into my mother's belly. The wildly flickering fire in the hearth is the only light in the room, and the corners of the kitchen remain invisible in the black, eerily dancing shadows.

"I've consulted the stars this very night," Surgeon van Obrecht says to my father. "They are very favorable for the confinement. Very favorable. And furthermore, it is the new moon. The new moon!"

"A good omen?" my father asks hopefully.

"An excellent omen," the surgeon confirms expertly. "And just this morning my apprentices tasted the Countess's water, and it was sour!"

"Sour?" the Count asks worriedly.

"Yes, yet another good sign. And then there is the color, my Lord Count," whispers the Master Surgeon, "the color."

Wirnt van Obrecht lifts the sample book hanging on his belt. He unties the strings that hold the wooden covers together. In the book, strips of fabric varying in color from pale yellow to inky black are bound together. The surgeon chooses a strip of a deep orange color and triumphantly holds it under my father's nose, as if the color makes everything clear.

"Good?" my father asks nervously.

"It could not be better, my Lord Count," Wirnt van Obrecht nods wisely. "It truly could not be better."

That is when my mother screams. The midwives give her a wad of linen to bite on. Her cheeks burn from the heat of the fire and her face is beaded with sweat. She pushes the wad away.

"It hurts so much," she moans. "I can't stand it."

"That's how it's meant to be, woman." My father beams. "He will be a solid fellow."

Then Hanne withdraws her hand from my mother's belly and crosses herself. She turns to my father.

"My Lord Count," she says, calmly but seriously.

"I advise you to have Masses said. Right away. The Countess will need every bit of help she can find tonight—"

"What do you mean, woman?" the surgeon interrupts her. "All the signs are favorable. The new moon, the stars—"

"The child is lying crossways," Hanne interrupts. "And there is nothing the stars or the moon can do about that. Only God can help us."

My father looks at the surgeon, then at Hanne, and eventually at my mother. He sees the fear that wells up in her eyes. My father storms out of the room, runs down the stairs cursing all the saints who have walked the earth since Saint Peter, and all the saints who are still to come. He curses Heaven, Hell, Earth, and Purgatory, but when he enters the church he crosses himself, kneels before the altar, and asks forgiveness for his frivolous curses. He orders the bells to be rung, gathers up everybody—the knights, the pages, the soldiers, the washerwomen, the stable hands, and the shit scrapers—and sends them off to the chapel. He takes Chaplain Johannes van Izeghem to one side. The poor man is shivering. He has to look up at my father, who is two heads taller.

"I want to hear everyone praying," my father hisses, "till they have no spit left in their mouths. And make sure God hears you!"

The little man nods and runs back into the chapel, shaking with cold. My father climbs the stairs to the outer wall and marches along the battlements. The cold hits him like a blow to the nose. The wind snaps hairs from his beard. He pulls his hood over his ears, puts his hands under his cloak, and balls his fists. Why is God putting him to the test? In the moonlight, he stares over the marshy snowfield that stretches out around the castle. A feeling of fear tugs at his bowels. Is it true what people say? That God is punishing humankind for their sins with a perpetual winter?

Tomorrow will be Easter, the first day of the new year. And still there is no sign of the thaw. Winter ice holds the world tightly in its deadly jaws. Only last week, an iceberg as tall as a church tower rammed a ship in the port of Sluis. And supplies are running out. In the great barn of Lissewege, where one-tenth of the farmers' harvest is stored, the monks are selling the last, moldy remnants of grain at extortionate prices. In Kwaadkerken, a couple ate their own children out of sheer desperation. In Gistel, the bodies of hanged men were taken from the gallows for food. In Bruges, where the ice on the floodplains is so thick that carts can ride on it, people gather every morning at Saint Donatian's church, on their knees on the cold stone floor, to pray for forgiveness.

They all turn up: the clergy, the nobility, the guild masters, even the common rabble. At the *Hallelujah*, they raise their eyes to the vaulted roof with its keystones decorated with flowers to remind people of the biblical promise that after every winter there will be a spring. But no matter how fervently they pray, how firmly their shaking hands clasp the crucifix, or how many candles they light before the image of the crucified Christ, spring does not come.

Never has winter been so severe. Never has winter gone on for so long. Even Morva, the ancient woman whose age nobody knows, says so. Some of the oldest local farmers say they used to know Morva in their youth and that even then she was ancient. They say Morva has slept with the Devil and now has eternal life. But my father does not believe that. He knows that she has a rare understanding of things in Heaven and on Earth, and of the secrets of herbs. At this point, my father's breath catches in his throat. His thoughts freeze. *Why is he thinking of Morva? Is it a sign? Is it a thought God has put in his mind?* For a moment doubt gnaws at him, but then he knows for certain. Morva is the only one who can help his wife in her confinement. He crosses himself and hurtles down the stairs.

Morva lives in Plathoeke, a hamlet near Moerkerke mostly inhabited by rush cutters and duck hunters. The Count orders his best horses be harnessed to a coach to bring Morva to him. He is hoping his horses won't break their legs on the frozen tracks. Then he marches to the chapel, which is now full of people.

Tens of steaming mouths murmur prayers in the icy building where even the holy water font has frozen over. The chaplain vigorously swings the censer. But even in the chapel, the Count can hear his wife screaming, and with every scream it seems as if the child in her belly is tearing her apart.

THE WATER IS BOILING in the kettle over the hearth. Hanne hangs linen cloths on a stick, which she holds in the rising steam to cleanse them. Beatrijs lights the specially blessed candle of Our Lady. Even Master Surgeon van Obrecht knows that a confinement must be over before the candle has burnt down. If not, the child will be stillborn. Hanne gives the Countess a sprig of basil to hold in her left hand and a swallow's feather for her right. In the castle, doors and cupboards are left open to enlarge the opening in my mother's belly, the opening through which I must arrive in the world. In the courtyard, five archers fire arrows at the clouds to speed up the birth. It is all superstition and the Church disapproves of it, but, says Hanne, a child that is lying crossways needs every bit of help it can get.

◫ ◫ ◫

THE NIGHT DRAGS ON and Our Lady's candle slowly melts away. Beatrijs constantly dampens my mother's forehead with rose petal-scented water. At last, the opening is wide enough, and Beatrijs and Hanne press with all their might on the hard belly to push me out. My mother shrieks with pain. The only thing that appears is my bottom.

Hanne crosses herself—she knows I am doomed. She plunges a mug in the rose water and throws it over my backside, and my bottom is baptized in the name of the Father, the Son, and the Holy Ghost, Amen. So nothing more can happen to me. So my soul will not languish forever in the dark waiting room of Heaven and Hell called Purgatory.

At that moment, old Morva appears in the room. She has long fingers, a small mouth with five lower teeth, and a dark, festering hole where her left eye used to be. The midwives stare at her in bewilderment and even the Master Surgeon holds his breath. It takes Morva just a few moments to take in what is happening. Our Lady's candle tells her how long the confinement has been and when she observes my little behind sticking out, she realizes I am suffocating. In a rasping voice, Morva makes it known she wants to be left alone with the women. The sound of her voice grates throughout the room and makes the hair on my father's neck stand on end. And my mother, in the grip of sorrow and pain, moans and weeps.

Wirnt van Obrecht grips the Count by the shoulder and whispers to him that surely he cannot put his trust in that sorceress they call "the witch of the Marshland."

"She is the Devil's brood. Even if the child survives, it will be cursed," he whispers.

My father removes the Master Surgeon's hand from his shoulder. He looks at Morva with her one yellowish eye, and he tells her that his son's life lies in her hands. Morva repeats that she wants to be left alone with the women. My father takes the Master Surgeon by the wrist, propels him out of the room, and pulls the door closed. My mother hears the surgeon call out in the passage that the Count mocks his knowledge and he will speak to the master of his guild about this and that the child will be born into misfortune.

Suddenly, my father is in doubt. Has he done the right thing? Had it really been a sign from God? He, too, had been frightened by Morva's deformed appearance. Ten years ago, during the epidemic of the dreaded grain disease that turned healthy people into dying wrecks overnight, the people of Plathoeke had blamed old Morva for the disease. They said she had poisoned the grain. One night, at the end of the harvest period, they surrounded her mud-and-straw hut and set it on fire. Somehow Morva survived the fire, but she had become a terrifying sight. Her hair and part of the flesh of her scalp had been burnt away. The flames had melted her left eye. Yet, though her face had been disfigured, her hands had been spared.

And it is with those utterly capable fingers that she now pushes me back into the belly. Her lower arm disappears completely inside my mother's body. I am a plaything in Morva's fingers. She turns me around completely inside the warmth of my mother's belly.

The candle sputters, startling the midwives. Morva has noticed, too. Time is running out. She croaks orders at the women. They must cook onions and hang red linen cloths above the steaming water. My mother repeatedly loses consciousness. She groans and rambles deliriously in French.

And then, finally, Morva pulls her arm out of my mother's body. She produces a small flask from the purse that hangs off her belt and dips her fingertip into it. When she pulls the finger out, it is dripping with a red fluid. To the midwives' horror, she uses it to write strange heathen symbols on my mother's belly. With her bony hand spread over my mother's tightly stretched navel, she mutters something incomprehensible in a language that should have been dead long ago.

Hanne the midwife stands up and makes the sign of the cross on my unconscious mother's forehead. Then Morva hits my mother in the face. The old woman hisses that the child lives and that the Countess must now give her all.

And, with the last scrap of energy left in her body, my mother pushes. The small veins in her face burst with the effort, as the midwives press with all their might on the hard belly. My mother howls while my head finally slides into Morva's hands.

Morva is the first to carry me in her arms. She smacks my bottom. I gasp for air and squeak. But my squeaking is soft, far too soft. Morva bites through the navel string while Our Lady's candle dies. I have been born just in time, but I look like a hundred-year-old goblin. I am covered in wrinkles and so thin that the midwives think I might break in half at any moment. Morva takes a handful of the boiled, softened onion and rubs it over my body.

Time passes while the midwives wait patiently. The Countess falls asleep. Outside, day breaks.

Finally, Morva hands me back to Hanne and Beatrijs,

who rinse my body with lukewarm rose-scented water. Already I look a lot less wrinkly. I am yellow and green like any newborn. Beatrijs and Hanne wrap me in red sheets, which are to protect me from childhood illnesses and evil spirits.

The Countess wakes and asks if I will live. Beatrijs and Hanne look down at the ground. They have seen so many infants die in the first few weeks after they were born. Morva looks at the Countess with her yellowish eye, and on her hideously deformed face a smile appears.

Morva turns to the door. Everything has become quiet in the castle. She shuffles away through the passage and wakes my father, who is dozing on a bench. She tells him the child lives. My father asks how he can reward her for her services. She says that every year, with the first snow of winter, he should deliver a stack of dry wood to her so she can keep her chimney smoking through the cold months. Then she asks him to help her to her carriage. As Morva staggers away on my father's arm, my mother is wondering if Master Surgeon van Obrecht was right. If Morva really has slept with the Devil and her child has been born into misfortune. She crosses herself and reels off Hail Marys while Beatrijs hastily washes the heathenish symbols from her belly.

Before my mother cradles me in her arms, she anxiously examines my body. Somewhere there might be a sign of the Devil. A clubfoot, or a large birthmark in the shape of an animal's head. But all she sees is my gaping mouth, my little jaws, and my fingers trying to get a grip on her body. She decides I cannot be born for misfortune and whispers to me that everything will be alright, that I am a descendant of the counts of Flanders and the kings of France. I am blessed and, like her, will be protected by twenty-six angels. Nothing can befall me, my mother whispers into my ear, nothing at all. I have been born for love, good fortune, and happiness. Just like her.

My mother is startled from her thoughts when she sees her husband swinging into the room. He looks at my little face and at my little body, which his wife has covered with the red cloths. My mother smiles. My father glows with happiness.

"He looks like me," is all he says.

Then my mother's smile freezes and she lowers her eyes. My father worriedly lifts a corner of the red cloth. His lips tremble when he sees my lower body. He stares at my mother and his eyes fire a thousand reproaches at her. He can hardly speak with disappointment.

"It…it is…a girl," he stutters. Then he turns and leaves, slamming the door.

2

I **AM FIVE YEARS OLD.** I'm wearing a trailing red-silk dress stitched through with gold thread. It's my first real gown and my ladies-in-waiting are constantly telling me to lift my skirts so they don't drag on the ground and catch on the horse dung littering the inner courtyard of the castle of Male. I'm wearing a necklace with rubies from the ancient mines in Sicily. They're the color of doves' blood. My hair is braided with colored ribbons. I can't wait to show myself off to my father.

I run to the Great Hall where he is readying himself for the tournament. I walk into the hall and look up at the portraits of the counts of Flanders, painted on wooden panels. Grim and stern, they stare at me. They're all dead. Except my father.

He stands in the middle of the hall, surrounded by four squires who run back and forth feverishly. He's no broad-shouldered hulk who counts on brute strength to crush an opponent. He's a lean man with sinewy arms. His cheekbones protrude sharply; his hooked nose is prominent in profile; his short beard always forms a perfect triangle. He has reddish-brown hair and narrow-set eyes. There are those who call him "fox head," but never to his face. He smiles when he sees me in my dress.

I make a deep curtsy. My father smiles again and nods elegantly. He's wearing leather trousers and a leather vest, both of which are too small for him. One of the boys is lacing up the strings of the vest on my father's back, while another fetches a small bucket of pork fat that he rubs into the leather. My father never stands still. He always needs to be in motion, as if his bladder is full and he can't find a spot to pee. He moves even while he's eating, and during games of chess he constantly paces up and down, pondering his next move.

Now he keeps flexing his arms and legs to check that the leather is not too tight. Hurriedly, the boys grease a hauberk. My father goes to stand between two stools and each boy climbs onto one of the stools. My father lifts his arms up, and from their stools, the boys slowly lower the heavy chain mail coat over his body. The iron will protect his chest, stomach, and crotch. Next the boys lace up the armor. They fasten the four thigh plates around the leather trousers and hurriedly strap on the shin plates and the steel kneecaps. For a moment, my father's blue eyes look at me. They are set deep in his face and a scar curls around his right eye. The scar looks like a finger, and gives the impression that his eye is held in a clenched fist. I look at him and our eyes lock. Then my father turns away. He marches to the window and the boys are forced to crawl after him on their knees so they can fasten the last of the buckles. And still more steel appears: for the upper arms, the lower arms, the shoulders, the elbows. Now he puts on his armored gauntlets and ring-mail cap, the *coif* that covers his head. He picks up his tournament helmet with the narrow slits that restrict his vision but protect his eyes from his opponent's lance. The whole suit of armor weighs nearly fifty pounds. The sunlight reflects off the polished steel. My father looks like a warrior from some legend. The metal squeaks and clinks as he walks out of the room. The boys, though exhausted, run ahead to get his horse. I run to my mother, who is seated on a dais.

My father ties my mother's scarf around his arm. The people of Male cheer and throw flowers while my father and his opponent ride at a walking pace to their squires, who hand them the first blunt lance. The clarions sound. The warhorses snort impatiently and the knights push them into a fast trot. After about six feet, the horses swing into a gallop. They storm toward each other. Faster and faster. Each along one side of the wooden palisade. Mud flies and the knights lower their ten-foot-long lances. With an enormous shock, the lances shatter against the shields. Sharp splinters fly around. The people in the front row duck, shielding their eyes. My father stays in the saddle, solid as a rock, but his opponent is thrown and, with a dull thud, slams into the ground a long distance away.

He doesn't get up. My father is the champion. I break away from my mother, jump from the dais, and run to him across the field. I step on the hem of my dress and fall face down in the mud. People laugh. Someone shouts that I need more practice at being a lady. A lady-in-waiting helps me up, but I tear myself away. Proudly I stride toward my father, wiping the mud from my sleeve.

My father throws the remains of his lance away and rips off his helmet. He sees me standing before his horse. Holding on to the front of his saddle, he leans down sideways and lifts me up with his right arm, his sword arm.

I can't get a grip on the armor, so I throw my arm around his head and feel the iron ringlets of the *coif* against my cheek. My father smells of armpit, horse, wet earth, and pork fat. His face is drenched in sweat. I kiss him. His beard prickles against my cheek. People cheer. I untie the scarf around his arm and wave it at my mother. She gets up from the dais and her round belly is visible under her beautiful blue gown.

⊞ ⊞ ⊞

MY BELOVED MALE is the most beautiful castle in all of Flanders. Built from red bricks, it's a military fortress with turrets and fortified ramparts, but at the same time it's the palace of a count. Storytellers sing the praises of its sophisticated beauty. There are large gardens with cages full of birds from faraway places and tall towers above which our flags flutter. Its Great Hall is cleared of fleas every month, and then its floor is covered with a fresh carpet of dried flowers.

From the castle tower I can see the city of Bruges, and when the wind is westerly, I raise my nose to sniff the salty wind coming off the sea. The land surrounding the castle is so flat that the clouds seem to be caught in the treetops, and everywhere, as far as the eye can see, there are meadows and fields bordered by low dikes, with here and there a windmill. Along those dikes stand rows of pollard willows pushed awry by the west wind.

The lady-in-waiting who always braids my hair so reluctantly is called Constance Bouvaert. She's from Provence, the land of the troubadours, somewhere in the South. Her name is actually Boúúaert, but, following the latest fashion, she has turned her family name into Flemish to improve her chances with Flemish men in the marriage market. It isn't much use, though, because, as a child, Constance crashed at full speed into a Provençal wall, which knocked half her teeth out and left one of her eyes permanently half closed. So she is not bothered much by amorous noblemen and has all the time in the world to teach me the most refined manners: that I must always walk with my back straight and that I should wash myself every week.

She shows me aromatic oils of lavender, honey, and almonds, which I must drip carefully onto my neck so they slide slowly down my back. She teaches me that a woman's fingernails must never be allowed to grow too long, how to crumble scent tablets among the satin dresses in my clothes trunk, how I can bleach my brown hair with dove poo, and how slovenly it is to have wisps of hair falling over my forehead. Indeed, the higher the forehead, the more elegant, which is why my mother has my eyebrows and the hairs at the top of my forehead plucked out. It hurts a lot, but my mother says that real beauty is born from pain.

Constance also teaches me that I must kneel before God and bow before my parents. And how common people must greet me by kneeling, or bowing, or, at the very least, by nodding their head. She teaches me how to lower my eyes when a nobleman looks at me, how I must set an example at the table by spitting on the floor and not on the table linen—particularly if a priest is sitting next to me—and how I should pull a small piece of meat off a bone and lift it to my mouth between thumb and index finger. Ripping meat off the bone with your teeth is for the hungry rabble or for backward English noblemen who have only recently learned to walk upright.

Constance is under orders to keep me in her sight all day, and I make escaping from her into a contest. I often hang about the inner courtyard where life buzzes around me on all sides. There is a blacksmith called Ferre. Hair sprouts from his ears, and beneath his skin run cables that must pass for veins. Flemish pours from his enormous mouth in a thick stream.

"Look, little lady," he roars, pointing at the open

stoke hole of his forge. "You know what that is?" he asks me.

I look at the glowing coals and the blazing flames, which give off a fierce heat, and shake my head.

"Have a good look," he urges.

I take another step forward. I feel the scorching heat all over my body.

"It's Satan's arse," he hisses in my ear.

The fire growls. In a panic I take a step back and bump into Ferre's hard leather belly. To scare me, he lets go of the bellows that he's used to fan the fire. He roars with laughter. I am angry and pummel his belly with my fists. He catches them in his thick, fleshy hands.

"When you grow up, little lady," he says soothingly, "I'll make you a sword." He lets go of me and with two pairs of tongs pulls a red-hot sword from the fire. With a hammer, he slowly pounds it into shape. The forge seems to be full of thunder and lightning. Sparks fly in all directions. He shouts above the noise of his hammer blows. "That is what I do, little lady. I tame the lightning to make a sword for your father."

I nod and tell him I can't wait to grow up so I can hold him to his promise. He takes up the tongs and lowers the sword into the water. It sizzles and bubbles.

"What promise?" he asks innocently.

"Your promise to make me a sword," I remind him.

He snorts and says he was only joking. "Women and swords, they don't go together, little lady," he growls, bored now, and burns his fingers on the tongs. He curses a handful of saints and bellows, "It's your fault."

I grin.

⊞ ⊞ ⊞

I ALSO HANG ABOUT in the kitchens of the castle, where I talk with the kitchen boys who pluck the chickens, chop the vegetables, and knead the dough. They teach me to curse in Flemish, for if you have to curse, there's no language like Flemish.

Swearing is not allowed. For a swearword, or *maledictum*, you can burn in Hell. Yet everybody swears. The priests, the monks, the convent nuns, and, it's whispered, even the Pope—they all use the name of Our Lord in foolish and frivolous ways. There are actually severe punishments for swearing and cursing: Claes de Mollenpiepere from Dudzele was sent on a pilgrimage to Rome because he told my father that his taxes were "so exorbitant that even Our Lord would piss on them."

As for me, I try to swear as little as possible, except when it is really necessary—no more than ten or fifteen times a day. The kitchen boys call me "Little Lady Wiesterkapelle" because they think that, despite my fine manners and French accent, I don't look like a lady. A chapel, of course, always points to the East, and a chapel that points to the West—a Wiesterkapelle—is the wrong way round. They think I'm half a boy.

I call them the seven bleaters because one of them is always crying in the kitchens. These kitchen boys are so clumsy that they cut their fingers or burn their hands on the spit day after day. And to think this bunch of bunglers are going to be squires one day, perhaps even knights! Kitchen Master Aelbrecht is so busy looking after their little cuts with his special Apostle Ointment—so called because it has twelve ingredients—that he hardly has time to put together a menu.

▣ ▣ ▣

THAT SUMMER I AM LAZING near the water mill on the south side of our castle. I've got blisters on my right foot, so I soak my feet in the water, then pick some mugwort and stuff it into my clog to soften the pain. On the other side of the mill, I hear the tattling of the washerwomen. They laugh and chatter while they beat the rolled-up sheets dry on the stones along the bank. Then I hear that they are gossiping about "the Count."

I crawl toward them and see them at work. Some are rinsing tablecloths in the moat, others hold linen on their knees and scrub at stains with pumice stones. One of them cackles that, since "the Count" can manage to father sons with peasant girls, why can't he do so with his own wife. Another woman boasts that the Count often visits her and there is certainly nothing wrong with his equipment.

I jump up, shouting that they're lying. The washerwomen get a scare, and the wench who made the remarks about my father's equipment blushes bright red, all the way up to her scarf.

"You must have misunderstood, *Ma Dame*," the

woman called Greet stammers. She's so nervous that she lets the wet washing drip all over her lap.

I walk up to her and shove her in the chest with my wooden clog. The woman nearly topples over the edge into the water, and the next moment I feel Constance's arms pulling me away.

"You're lying about my father," I scream at the washerwoman. "You're lying." Tears roll down my cheeks. I turn to Constance and shout that the washerwomen are all nasty hellcats who spread lies.

The women quickly disappear while Constance calms me down.

"You must have misunderstood something, my sweet," she says soothingly. "Really, you must have. Why would those women say bad things about your father?"

I hiccup and blubber, my whole body shaking with fury.

I don't say anything to my mother about the incident. I can't keep my eyes off her. Everything about her is delicate. She has thin lips, gray eyes, a small nose, and skin that is almost milky white, with blue veins showing under it. She has slim fingers and small feet. She is all calm and elegance. The only thing about her that is not delicate is her belly. She is forever expecting a child.

⊞ ⊞ ⊞

WE'RE IN A COACH on the way to Bruges. The two ladies-in-waiting who accompany us are trying to wipe black smears off my face with a damp cloth. They whisper together in Flemish, saying they just can't keep me clean.

One of them sighs and says that it's a pity I'm not more like my mother.

I understand what she is saying, give her a kick, and hiss in French, "I am so like my mother."

My mother hears me and smiles. "Of course you are, sweetheart," she whispers, and the warmth of her hand caresses my face.

The coach slows down near the Holy Cross Gate, where the guards talk with the soldiers who are escorting us. A moment later we ride into the free city.

The sounds of Bruges wash over us—the clattering of horses' hooves on the cobblestones, the creaking of signs hanging outside the traders' houses, the lepers' rattles, the whining of stray dogs, and the moaning of the children who work the dockside cranes. The smells of Bruges seep into the carriage, too. Penetrating everything is the smoldering stench of the pigskins that the leather workers burn clean in the street and then scrape with sulfur on the banks of the canals. The stench of rotting animal fat in the water stings my nose every time we go over a bridge.

Finally, we stop at the Belfry Tower. My mother gets out. I feel the ladies-in-waiting holding me by the shoulders. I must remain where I am. My mother's blue gown nearly disappears into the teeming crowd. Then she turns to me and says, "Come along, Marguerite."

I push the ladies' hands off my shoulders and run to my mother. I look up and see her smile. I see the dimples in her cheeks, the teeth in her small mouth, and the merriment in her eyes. She pulls me along, for she hears the hawkers selling honey and spices, the quacks touting miracle remedies for carbuncles, and the town criers announcing who is getting married, who is being christened, who has died, which children have gone missing, and which houses are to be auctioned.

I hear donkey drivers calling each other "pig's head" and "ox-arse" because traffic in the alleys is completely jammed, and I hear the fishmongers calling out that their quivering pike and wriggling shrimp are alive and fresh. I see the Italians, with their huge moustaches, who work in the banks, the Portuguese sailors unloading cages full of wild animals, the Moors displaying their spices, the Russians carrying bags of salt from Riga on their backs, and the blind mendicant friar who insists that, far away in the East, he caught a glimpse of the Garden of Eden and so was struck blind by an angel.

And finally I see the women of Bruges in their brightly colored gowns, with their many-layered hats and their richly jeweled necklaces. They look like queens. The women of Bruges are the most beautiful in the world.

My mother drags me along through the narrow alleys, which are hung with signboards for bathhouses, rosary knotters, bow makers, candle molders, soap boilers, basket weavers, barbers, flax spinners, coopers, and Heaven knows what else. Nothing exists in the world that is not for sale in Bruges. We call in at our favorite spots: the workshop of Mattheus de Botereter, goldsmith and jeweler; the workshop of Isenbrandt Naeghel, the shoemaker; Cornelius Gillekin's hat shop; and the bookbindery of Augustijn van Ivorie, the man who covers his books in fabrics woven through with gold-edged clouds, wisps of silver, and teardrops of palladium, the noblest of the noble metals, shed by the wife of God himself.

We drink a jug of mulled wine in the Pregnant Seahorse tavern in the Egg Market, where you'll always find a singer accompanying himself on the lute, warbling sorrowful love songs about knights who perform grand deeds for the noblewomen they can't obtain.

I've barely sat down before I ask the ladies-in-waiting to redo my braids so they will look exactly like my mother's. One of the ladies sighs and says my hair is so unmanageable there is no point. I snap at her that she must do it. She gets up, undoes my coils of bristly reddish-brown hair, and carefully twists them into two long braids with green and blue ribbons. When it's done, I sit on my mother's lap. Now we look alike. She presses me against her belly. I can feel something pushing in her belly.

"This time, you truly are going to have a little brother," she whispers.

I feel her softness again. I smell her lavender scent. I smile at her and she smiles back. It's the last time I see her smiling.

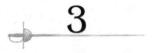

3

PRETENDING TO BE ASLEEP, I listen to the women talk about my mother. They're worried about the approaching birth. One of them says that my first brother was stillborn. He was strangled by the navel string.

"Not baptized in time," one of the women whispers, and I hear their hands rustling against their dresses as they cross themselves. Then they discuss the birth of my second brother, a year later.

"The Count sent for old Morva again," I hear Constance cackle. "This time, the soldiers only found her empty mud hut with a starving black cat inside. Morva had died that winter while she was collecting firewood in the village. She sat down by the side of the road, exhausted, and never got up again. Weeks later, she was still sitting there, on that fallen tree trunk, frozen stiff, waiting for spring. I saw her sitting there myself, just a scrap of a woman, all glazed over."

After Constance's jabbering, everyone falls silent.

The only candle in the women's room sputters out. It becomes completely dark. Someone clears her throat and spits.

"The Count didn't keep his promise to Morva," Gwenna, an old lady-in-waiting, lisps.

"She slept with the Devil," mutters another woman. "And God knows what sort of hellish circles she inscribed on the Countess's stomach."

"It may have been a good luck sign," old Gwenna suggests.

"A good luck sign!" shouts Greet. "Don't be such an idiot. The Count's line is cursed." Silence falls in the room again.

"I keep thinking of that second boy," sighs Constance. "He was jammed so tightly in his mother's belly that they couldn't get him out, no matter how hard the midwives pulled and tugged. The child tore apart like old rags. It was horrible. They had to baptize all the parts separately while they were still warm." The hands rustle again making the sign of the cross.

I feel my throat tighten and I desperately bite my lip to stop myself crying. My right hand feels for the cross that hangs around my neck. I grasp it tightly.

"And what now?" asks the washerwoman Greet. "The time has nearly come." Nobody dares answer.

"Nothing can go wrong this time," says Constance, but her voice is full of uncertainty. "The Countess has sat under the bell of Saint Donatian's church for an hour every day to protect the young life in her belly."

"Will that help?" asks Greet, who is now sitting on the chamber pot. The sound of her peeing clatters through the room.

"Of course, if that does not work, there is still the Holy Nail," suggests Gwenna.

And now, as the voices fade away in the darkness, I understand why my father spent an incredible amount of gold to buy one of the nails that was used to nail Jesus Christ to the cross.

"But is it a genuine relic?" Gwenna asks loudly, while she tips the contents of the pot out the window without looking. "Or just a rusty, flaky iron pin with a square head? They'll sell you anything these days. I once saw a Bulgarian in Bruges who was selling straw that was supposed to be from Baby Jesus's crib. Holy Jesus, what a swindler! He was being booed by the crowd and someone went and got the bailiff's soldiers. In the end, they had that Bulgarian's tongue ripped out because he was selling lies. The heathen bastard!"

"The nail is genuine," hisses Constance. "I was there when the courier brought it. The nail was wrapped in a silk cloth, and Chaplain van Izeghem said the nail came straight from Avignon and had been sent by the Pope himself. He showed the Count a letter in which the Holy Father wrote that the nail had been pulled from the wood of the only true cross, carried up the hill of Golgotha by Our Redeemer."

That silenced the women.

My father had the nail set in a glass sphere, which

was then mounted in the center of a golden cross. That is how the nail hangs above the altar in the chapel of Male.

"Every day of the pregnancy, the Count has prayed to the nail for a son," confirms Gwenna. "And seeing that the nail came from the true cross and is one of the most powerful relics in the world, his prayers must surely resound through Heaven. He will have a son. It cannot be otherwise."

▣ ▣ ▣

IT'S IN THE DAYS of the first snowfalls that my little brother is born. He weighs no more than a wet cloth, has a little face like marzipan, and looks like an angel. My father christens him Boudewijn, after the first Count of Flanders, who was called "Boudewijn of the Iron Arm." This ancestor was a game warden. He had been given his noble title by the German emperor because, so the story went, he had defeated the Vikings with a tiny army.

My father is already dreaming of the first suit of armor his son will buckle on, and of the moment when he and his son will stand together in the front ranks of an army of knights. Seated on warhorses shod with silver shoes, father and son will lower the visors of their helmets together and charge the enemy. The sight of their glittering armor and their fluttering banners will make the enemy scatter in panic. My father and his son will impale heretics, barbarians, and Englishmen on their lances like chicks on a skewer. After the victory, they will embrace each other, their armor dripping with heathen blood. It brings tears to my father's eyes. A son. A knight. An heir. It's his deepest wish.

But poor little Boudewijn doesn't live.

Even now, years after his death, I can feel the tiny fingers closing around my little finger. Little Boudewijn hardly drinks any of his mother's milk and seems to be forever asleep, between his sheets of finest silk in his cot shaped like a pelican, the divine bird that feeds its young with its own blood. My father orders the shutters of the delivery room to be kept closed for three weeks after the birth, to prevent the evil spirits from the Northern Sea from stealing the child's soul and spiriting it away to the other end of the world. My mother is worried because the child drinks so little and seldom cries.

And so Master Surgeon van Obrecht, the genius of the pierced shoulder and the shattered cheekbone, is called in. After thoroughly studying little Boudewijn's pee and consulting the positions of the stars, he ordains that the child should be fed cod-liver oil, celery mush, rosemary, and stirred egg yolks. The Countess pinches the little boy's nose and spoons it all into his mouth. Moments later, little Boudewijn spits it all out again. The Countess desperately presses the child against her breast, which is dripping with milk. She does so hour after hour, day after day. She gently strokes the boy's head and begs him to drink. And in that dark room with its closed shutters, in his mother's arms, little Boudewijn goes out like a candle.

Afterward, my father recalls the omens. Wasn't it

on Saint Thomas's Day that Bishop Lievin de Beveland died without any apparent cause? Two monks forced the door into his bedroom and saw his lifeless body, a bat in its mouth. Did anyone know how that animal of doom had got inside the sealed cell? And was it not on the feast of Saint Alexius that an enormous whale was washed up in the Zwin? The harbor master had the animal dragged to the market square in Sluis, where, watched by the inhabitants of the town, it was cut open by three fishermen. Dozens and dozens of eels, snails, and maggots slithered from the stomach of the gigantic beast. The people of Sluis screamed at the sight of all that devilish vermin. Children ran away in all directions and an old crone dropped dead on the spot. As the satanic brood crawled through the streets of Sluis, a crowd gathered in the church. People crossed themselves, rosaries slipped through fingers, and the scent of incense filled the air. Only when the day was close to its end did people gather enough courage to go home.

And now that they thought about it, hadn't everyone noticed how magpies had circled above the castle of Male during the days before the birth? The guards had tried to kill the evil birds, but no crossbow was powerful enough to bring them down. Hadn't my father noticed all those omens?

The shutters of the Countess's room are not opened again. For weeks, she refuses to emerge. The ill-fated pregnancies of the past years have exhausted her. One night she wanders about the castle, naked. The guards who see her in the moonlight think she is a ghost. She talks to herself, her forefingers raised, and is not even aware of the ladies-in-waiting who guide her back to the women's room.

Non compos mentis is the judgment of Master Surgeon van Obrecht. "Her mind is deranged."

"Why don't you just say she is mad?" shouts my father. "On the day she gives me a living male heir, the chickens will sing vespers and the monks will scrabble around on the dung heap."

"My Lord Count," the surgeon objects, "your wife's affliction is of a passing nature. She's tired and in despair and—"

"Why does God do this to me?" my father shouts at Chaplain van Izeghem, who is nervously studying the straw on the floor. "Don't I have a nail from the Holy Cross hanging in my chapel? Haven't I had enough Masses said? Haven't I been a friend to His Church? Do I give insufficient alms to the blind, the lame, and the lepers of Bruges? Do I have to go on a crusade and personally storm the gates of Jerusalem and kiss the yellowed bones of Saint Melisanda before I can have a male heir?"

There is a brief silence. The chaplain makes the sign of the cross three times and Surgeon van Obrecht, too, clasps the cross to his chest to ward off evil. I have listened fearfully. My ears are buzzing.

"My Lord Count," begins the chaplain, emphasizing the seriousness of his words by sniffing through his nose, which is as pointy as that of a mouse. "Mortals such as us cannot fathom God's ways. You must have patience. I will pray to God for forgiveness for your rash words."

"I do not deserve this," my father shouts and stalks off. Only then does he notice me in my usual spot among the blocks of wood next to the smoldering fire. My lovely dress is covered in black smudges and my long, unruly hair is sticking out in all directions. He glares at me. I can feel the powerlessness that wracks his body. I see the glow from the fire that spreads over his face. For just a moment, it looks as if he will say something to me, but in the end he just stares at me. I don't dare raise my thin body. I hardly dare look him in the eyes. My father turns to the chaplain and the surgeon.

"When God wants to destroy someone," he whispers, "he first makes him go mad."

The chaplain makes the sign of the cross. My father strides off. I make myself as small as I can in my corner by the hearth. So small that nobody can see me, not even God. I want to be as small as an insect and hide forever in the cracks between the stones so I won't have to be part of this life full of suffering, pain, and fear. The surgeon and the chaplain leave. They don't seem to see me. I am invisible.

The doctors try to heal my mother by putting leeches on her throat, which are supposed to suck away the mists in her head. They give her a broth of fox brains, which is to bring back clarity to her mind. They hang her upside down from the roof beams so the evil matter will drain out of her brain. Nothing helps. My mother has a flask containing an extract of the belladonna plant. She sometimes puts drops of it in her eyes when we have a feast. The drops make her pupils wider and on days like that she looks radiant. But one evening, she drinks the whole bottle.

In the middle of the night—I am sleeping in the women's room between Constance and the washerwoman Greet—I wake up suddenly when I hear my mother screaming. Or actually, it's not my mother who is screaming, it's something else. An evil spirit that has been locked in the bottle and has now settled in my mother and utters heartrending screams. My mother lies on the floor in convulsions and it takes four women to hold her. Constance claps her hands over my eyes so I cannot see my mother. I only hear her shrieking. Her terrifying shrieking.

The next day my father calls for me. His right hand is trembling, and he clamps it under his other arm so it won't show.

"There are holes in your mother's head," he begins. "That's what the surgeon says. You can't see the holes because they're too small. But they are there."

He coughs and looks down as if he's wondering whether he has already said enough. He gives me a sidelong glance. Is this it? Am I supposed to go now?

"Her spirit has become deranged," he adds impatiently. "But the monks of the monastery of Ten

Duinen will care for her. She will get the best care there. Do you understand, daughter?"

I nod, biting my lip to keep from crying.

"I will visit her," I say.

"The monastery is one and a half days' journey from here."

"Then I will stay with her, in the monastery, until she—"

"You cannot stay with her," he interrupts. I am silent. His words are too heavy for me to push them back.

"You will stay here. Surgeon van Obrecht says your mother needs six months of rest, isolation, and prayer. That will help her get rid of the mists in her head."

"Six mon—"

"She will stay in the monastery until Christmas. When she is cured, she will come back."

"I do not want it," I mutter.

"It's what I have decided."

I look at my father with his powerful body, his nervous hands, and his angular head. I feel thistles growing in my throat. I feel tears dripping down my face. I want my mother. *Mama*, I feel like screaming, *don't go away, please. Saddle my horse and I will trot to the magic forest where elves and kobolds live and breed blind lizards whose tails are made into potions that can cure the worst afflictions. Give me a ship and let me journey to the East, to the Garden of Eden, to find the pond where the unicorn quenches his thirst, because there grows the secret herb that clears us of all that is bad or evil. Bring me a pilgrim's staff and show me the road that leads to the Holy Grail, because whoever drinks from the cup from which Christ once drank becomes a new person and will never know illness or deprivation again.*

"Father," is all I can manage. I want him to take me in his arms the way he did at the tournament. But he doesn't.

"What wrong have I done God to deserve a creature like you in my life?" he hisses, and for a moment I can't breathe. He picks up a chair and hurls it onto the floor. The wood splinters.

"I'm not a creature," I hear myself say. "I'm your daughter."

My father takes a step toward me.

"You are my misfortune," he roars, looking outside at the sun, which is high in the sky. "If you hurry, you can just say goodbye to your mother."

"Goodbye?"

"They'll be leaving any moment."

I jump up, curtsy quickly, and run down the stairs. I find my mother in the women's room. They have laced her into a leather corset and put her on a chair. Her arms are tied behind her back. Her mouth is full of dried blood because she has bitten off a piece her tongue. She tries to speak and I put my ear close to her mouth. I feel her warm breath on my cheek. She speaks with great difficulty, as if she can hardly breathe. I want her to tell me not to worry, that we'll go together to the market in Bruges again soon. That we'll drink a glass of wine

again at the Pregnant Seahorse and clap for the singers. ·
But she doesn't.

"Make sure my little Boudewijn eats properly," she
says, slowly, with difficulty, in a voice I hardly recognize.
Her words aren't properly shaped because of her
mutilated tongue. "And see that he dresses warmly when
the leaves start falling and winter comes. You know that
fox-fur jacket I had made for you? It's far too small for
you now. But it'll be perfect for your little brother. You
won't forget, will you?"

And I nod, my head feeling as if it's underwater. A
moment later, Surgeon van Obrecht's servants carry my
mother away—my poor mother, with her warm voice
and her hands like precious silk. She sits in her chair like
a rag doll, her mouth crusted with blood. I swallow my
tears and feel my whole body shaking with anger.

⊞ ⊞ ⊞

IN THE CHAPEL OF MALE, I kneel before the cross above the
altar. The cross of the Holy Nail. I pray for my mother
to be cured. I beg Our Dear Lord to let her come back.
I beg my twenty-six guardian angels to help lift the fogs
in her brain. I say rosary after rosary, Our Father after
Our Father, Hail Mary after Hail Mary, all through the
afternoon. My knees are stiff and cramped when I get up
from the stone floor. I strap on my clogs and it is so quiet
in the chapel that even the sliding of the buckles seems
to echo along the ceiling. I wonder if anyone in Heaven
has heard me. If my prayer hasn't got lost in the howling
storm of prayers that always blows around Heavenly

Jerusalem—a whirlwind driven by the tens of thousands of desperate souls begging for mercy. Even God cannot cope with so many voices. There's no point, I think—no one can hear me up there. Which relic, which shrine, which sacred ground could be more powerful than the nail in the cross? I let my eyes wander around the chapel. Then I notice the image of Our Lady, and suddenly, I know where I must go.

About two miles' walk from Male lies the Marshland. It is a swampy, watery area with dikes and stretches of quicksand so large that one day a farmer sank into it with his cart and horse and was never found. The whole of the Marshland is soggy and often flooded with seawater. The farms are surrounded by pollard willows, which suck the moisture out of the ground. And everywhere you look there are reeds. I run along the dikes and the narrow footbridges. The wind roars over the flat country-side, making my sleeves flap. The soil is sodden with spring rain. By the time I reach my destination, puffing and sweating, my dress, my clogs, and my stockings are covered in mud.

Among the creeks stands an ancient chapel, badly damaged by wind and weather. In the chapel stands a statue of the Virgin, which has been completely black-ened by time. Its hands are missing. How that happened, nobody quite knows, but everyone thinks the Devil had something to do with it. The grass around the chapel is withered and dirty, as if it's ashamed to be growing in the shadow of the chapel. Every now and then, when it's getting dark, you can see a woman stealing into the chapel. Sometimes it's a young girl who has escaped from her tyrannical father for a few moments; other times, it is an older woman who has been beaten by her husband. They might be women of the people or ladies of rank. They all have one thing in common: with their Hail Marys, they are praying for the death of the man who makes their lives a misery and whom they hate from the depths of their dark hearts.

That's why people in this area call the statue "Our Lady of Hate." I stare at its disfigured face. Bits have broken off the hood and the halo. And, as night settles over Flanders and I'm shivering with cold and tiredness, I curse my father. I curse him because he doesn't love my mother and because he fathers children with farmers' daughters and servant girls. I curse him because he looks at me with cold blue eyes that show contempt. Give me back my mother, I implore Heaven, and take my father in her place. Nobody will miss him. I pray for my father's ruin.

And this time Heaven must have been listening, for a few weeks later, war breaks out.

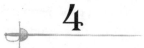

4

THE FRENCH HORSEMEN arrive during the harvest month. The month when the castle is deserted. The month when everyone is outside working together in the fields to bring in the corn. They're happy weeks. I resolve not to be happy and to spend hours in the chapel every day, praying for my mother's well-being. But I can't resist the laughter and shouting of the children as they run into the fields each day. I feel happy despite my misery.

With the other girls, I run after the farm workers, bringing them jugs of cool water from the well to quench their thirst. With scythes and sickles, they cut the stalks of corn in the full glare of the harvest sun. The women gather the cut stalks and tie them into sheaves. Larks climb into the sky with their trilling song and then, from the edge of a lonely cloud, let themselves fall like a stone. Everyone is nice to me. The farmers give me pieces of sweetwood; soldiers let me ride on their horses. On the last evening of the harvest, we all celebrate and I am crowned queen of the harvest. My crown is made of poppies and blue cornflowers. Squire Jan van Vere makes me a bundle of cornstalks intertwined with peacock feathers. That's my scepter, he says.

The farmers light bonfires. Someone gets dressed up as a straw devil to scare all of us children out of our wits, but I chase him away with my scepter. He runs into the forest, pursued by hordes of shrieking children. We laugh, we shout, we dance, and we drink. The harvest fires burn high and thousands of sparks fly up toward the stars. We dance around the fires while the harvest master plays his bagpipe.

We children are allowed to taste the honeyed wine. Squire Willem, one of the kitchen boys, empties his goblet far too fast, takes three steps, and falls flat on his face in the grass. I can feel the earth moving, too, when I've finished my glass. Like all the other children, I let myself flop on the grass. We hang on to each other's sleeves. We giggle. We look at the stars and see twice as many of them. For the first time in my life, I'm tipsy.

It's Constance who drags me back to the castle. I can see light in the Great Hall and look in through the open window. In the glow of a few candles, I see three knights surrounding my father. Their clothes are dirty and dusty and their chins unshaven, as if they've been on horseback for days. They must have come from Paris, because there are lilies on their coats of arms. They're on their way to war. They are going to defeat the English once and for all. And they've come to get my father.

The war is my fault. It must be so. My twenty-six guardian angels heard my prayers and put the case before God, Christ, and the Holy Ghost. And when They, the Holy Trinity, tackle things, They think big. *So the Count of Flanders is almost done for? Then let there be war! Don't let him perish in some stupid riding accident or from some common fever. We'll let him fall in war, like a hero.* That is what God, Christ, and the Holy Ghost, in Their infinite goodness, must have decided.

"But it is all a misunderstanding," I pray that night. "My father must not die at all. Yes, of course, he should get a good solid hit on his ugly head. But actually wanting him dead, that was perhaps going too far." That night I dream that Jesus Christ climbs down from His cross and asks me, "Listen, young lady, what do you actually want? Should he or should he not die, this father of yours? I've had about enough of you and your prayers! It's always the same with women! One thing today, another tomorrow. My Father got a little carried away when he created woman."

⊞ ⊞ ⊞

TWO DAYS AFTER THE HARVEST, my father gets ready to depart for the South. He crosses the courtyard with Knight van Sindewint—Squire Willem's father—and the armorer, Jan van Vere. They inspect the seven pages who will go to war with them. The youngest is twelve, the oldest fifteen. My father summons the blacksmith, Ferre, who arrives carrying seven swords. They are newly forged, one-and-a-half-sized swords that can be handled with one or both hands. The pages glow with pride as they each accept a sword. I ask Ferre when he is going to forge a sword for me. He smiles stupidly, saying a sword is so heavy and sharp that I would chop off my own toes. With a sigh, I slowly approach my father, my stomach in a knot. All I can do is tell him the truth.

"Father," I say loudly, "the war is my fault. I prayed for your downfall. Because of what you did to my mother. I ask you to forgive me."

My father looks at me in surprise. The pages in the courtyard stop talking. My father shows no emotion, draws his sword, and lays it against my throat. I feel the cold steel against my skin. Full of dread, I look into his cold eyes. Fear pierces my stomach. He grins.

"Then I thank you, daughter, because I'm in the mood for war. My sword is itching. It has been idle far too long and is thirsty for English blood."

The soldiers and pages in the courtyard laugh, but my father does not withdraw his sword. He holds it against my throat.

"I forgive you, daughter," my father says loudly. "Now kiss my sword."

He pulls the tip of the sword away from my throat and lays it along my cheek, so I can kiss the flat side of the blade.

"Kiss your sword?" I ask in horror.

"Yes, so I may have good fortune in the fighting."

"I thought, Father, that I was your misfortune," I stammer.

Suddenly the sword is gone and the next moment I feel the flat of the blade on my head. It can't have hit me very hard, yet I reel. The pages laugh. My father grins and turns away to a block of wood in which reed stems have been clamped so they stand upright in a row. This is one of the most difficult exercises the pages and future knights have to practice. They must learn to split one of the standing stems in half with a single blow of their sword. That takes great precision. Mostly, they stand in front of the reed for a long time in total concentration, holding their breath, before attempting to split it. Often, they manage to split the stem halfway, but almost never all the way. My father doesn't need to concentrate. He walks up to the reed, swinging his sword above his head almost carelessly, and then, with a wild movement, splits the reed in half all the way down to the wood. "You are still the champion of Flanders, Lord Count," shouts Jan van Vere. The knights and pages cheer. I don't cheer. I walk away.

"Where are you going, daughter?" my father asks.

"I'm going to learn English," I shout back.

▣ ▣ ▣

KNIGHT VAN SINDEWINT, Armorer Jan van Vere, and my father leave with the pages and six packhorses carrying armor and tents. The old knight Johan Craenhals van Wijnendaele, who always ties his hair in a Celtic knot, becomes Regent of Flanders. He accompanies my father as far as Bonen, where the county of Flanders once bordered Picardy. Autumn has started, and it's rapidly getting colder. I hang around by Kitchen Master Aelbrecht's fires. He often makes me taste his dishes, and I have to work out what herbs are missing, whether it's been on the fire too long or not long enough, and why the dish is well balanced or not. It's in the kitchens that Constance Bouvaert, enjoying the glow of the fire on her back, reads my father's letters aloud to the servants.

In his first letter, my father relates how twenty-three knights from Flanders, fifty pages, two hundred squires, and a caravan of carriages carrying everything an army needs were waiting for him and Knight van Sindewint at Sint-Omaars. In his next letter, he describes how they rode to Chartres, where, in the first week of September, they joined the army of the French king John the Good.

"The armor, the lances, and the battle helmets of the army of knights," Constance reads, "glitter in the brilliant glow of the late summer sun. Above the army, which probably numbers twenty thousand men, the banners of all the duchies, counties, and baronies of France flutter in the breeze. And, of course, the Lion of Flanders. This is one of the largest armies ever assembled in Christendom. This army will demolish the English, those tattooed peasants who pretend France belongs to them. It will squash them like dung beetles and kick them back once and for all to the scabby island they come from. The French army is invincible. The battle has already been won and the future decided."

❂ ❂ ❂

AND THEN WE HEAR NOTHING for a long time. Until one day a messenger arrives on a horse so exhausted that its knees crumple that very night and it never gets up again. The courier tells us that all is lost. Many Flemish knights and squires have fallen during the battle at Poitiers. The great French army has been defeated by the English. The defeat is so total, so scandalous, and so shattering, there are almost no knights left in France to govern the country. The French king and his youngest son have been taken prisoner and taken to Kales, from where they will be shipped to England. The Count of Flanders, reports the messenger, has been seriously injured but has managed to find shelter behind the city walls of Poitiers. Knight van Sindewint has been killed. And Willem, poor Willem, cannot believe it. He keeps insisting that his father will come back on his warhorse. "You'll see," he repeats, his eyes full of tears. "He is coming back. He is coming back."

❂ ❂ ❂

ON THE FIRST DAY OF DECEMBER, the feast of Saint Eloy, my father returns from the war. That evening I'm praying in the castle chapel, together with the squires, the maid servants, and the serfs. I pray for the salvation of the soul of Knight van Sindewint, friend of the Count of Flanders and father of Willem. And during the vespers, everyone in the chapel is disturbed by the sound of bugles and a commotion in the courtyard. I interrupt my prayer and get up off the floor. And then the oaken doors with their iron fittings creak open and I see my father come in. His face is deathly gray, his hauberk—a tunic made of chain mail—is rusted, and his leg guards are covered in mud. His spurs clink on the stone floor and his distraught eyes are directed at the cross above the altar. The nail that held Christ to the cross is still there, at the center of the cross, caught under its glass cover. My father looks like a living corpse, with his bloodshot eyes and the stiff and painful way he drags himself to the altar. His upper leg and right shoulder are wrapped in strips of silk covered in dark brown stains. Before the altar, he throws himself on his knees and then lies full length on the floor. With his face against the marble tiles, he stretches out his arms like a martyr. We hold our breath. The chapel becomes deathly quiet. The only sounds come from the hissing torches and the rain pattering against the chapel's one stained-glass window, an image of Our Lady. I thank her and my twenty-six guardian angels for bringing my father safely home.

After half an hour, my father stands and walks out past us. He doesn't even look at me. No greeting for his daughter. No rough, calloused hand brushing my cheek. Willem has searched in vain for his father, and one of the pages who survived the battle gives him his father's badly dented helmet. I take Willem to the kitchens, where Aelbrecht has lit the fires with bundles of blueberry branches, which make the air smell damp. Our armorer, Jan van Vere, who is from Zeeland, sits down by the fire. His face is bandaged across his nose. Aelbrecht has heated a dish of chicken in beer. The taste of cinnamon and the smell of burning berry twigs will always remind me of this evening. Willem sits clutching the dented helmet. I sit on Kitchen Master Aelbrecht's knee. And all the inhabitants of the castle of Male stand, sit, or squat, listening to Jan van Vere's account.

"The English had dug in on a hill a few miles from the gates of Poitiers," he begins. "Our army was awe inspiring. There were countless knights and commanders. There were French, Flemings, Scots, Swiss, and even some Irish. We were going to give the English a kick in their rear once and for all." Van Vere sighs, gnawing the meat from the roasted bird. He narrows his eyes while he swallows and gives the kitchen master a grateful smile. "The French king John the Good and his three sons spent days pondering how they should attack the English," he continues with his mouth full. "In the king's tent, the noblemen argued for hours about how the attack should be carried out. The scouts brought contradictory reports about how and where the English had entrenched themselves. It was clear there could not be more than seven thousand of them, with, at most, five hundred knights. The rest of their army consisted of foot soldiers and bowmen."

At that point, Jan van Vere produces two arrows from his saddlebag. We open our eyes wide. English arrows. It was the cursed English archers who had ensured victory in the sea battle off Sluis and in the battle at Crécy in Picardy. My own grandfather was struck down by English arrows in the forest of Crécy. The English are the only people in Europe who use the longbow. English serfs are taught from an early age how to handle the bow and arrow, and in England all sports are prohibited except archery. The longbow is less accurate than our crossbow but it has a longer range and is easier to use. Jan van Vere continues, "A number of knights, including our Count, felt we should starve the English out on their hill. Other commanders asserted that no honor was to be gained with that sort of tactic. They argued that they would mow down the first ranks of bowmen with a fast, unstoppable charge by five hundred knights in armor. A steel-clad knight mounted on a great warhorse breaking through the lines could bring about terrible slaughter, not to mention the panic that would result. Most commanders told the king that great honor was to be obtained in a charge, because a knight could show how courageous and invincible he was. The Scottish knight William Douglas added that a knight couldn't run away from a rabble of peasants with bows and arrows, especially when that knight sits fully armed on his warhorse, thundering toward those peasants at a gallop. Just one of those barbarians needed to turn and run at the sight of our monstrous charge, and all the others would run after him like rabbits. Then the slaughter could begin. The French knights cheered and the commanders decided there should be a charge. A charge by five hundred knights."

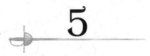

5

JAN VAN VERE LICKS HIS FINGERS. It has become very quiet in the kitchens. Everyone is trying to breathe as quietly as possible. Wine, spiced with thyme, sugar, and lemon peel, bubbles in the kettle over the fire. Jan van Vere is given the first cup and enjoys it. We can't keep our eyes off him. Nobody wants to miss the smallest bit of his story. He rubs at the bandage over his nose, looks up, and continues.

"The evening before the attack, they roasted deer and wild boar. They drained whole barrels of wine. And on the morning of the nineteenth of September, the five hundred knights mounted their horses. The knights all wore armor and rode great stallions covered in layers of protective leather. They carried long lances, which they would level at the last moment, as they approached their opponents. Their charge would break through the English lines and spread panic. Together with the pages, I brought out our Count Lodewijk's and Knight van Sindewint's horses. They both took part in the charge.

I held their saddle and reins while they climbed onto their horses, covered from top to toe in grating metal. Knight van Sindewint had his armor tied to the saddle, so the English couldn't lift him out of it, but Count Lodewijk did not. Then we led the horses to the front rank. It was an incredible sight. The sun was rising above the hill, and there stood five hundred knights in armor in a single line. The priests ran back and forth giving the knights a final blessing. Holy water splashed on each of the five hundred suits of armor. God was on our side. Then the charge began."

I feel my fingers clenching into fists as Jan van Vere tells us how the French banner with its golden flames was raised and the battle cry *Montjoie Saint Denis!* was shouted from fifteen thousand throats. My father and Knight van Sindewint rode side by side. The knights dug their spurs into their horses. By their sides hung great battle swords with magnificent hilts. Each of these five hundred hilts was set with some sort of holy relic from the East: one of Saint Joseph's finger bones, a stalk of straw from Jesus's crib, or two hairs of the Virgin Mary. The knights carried holy weapons, and that morning they had clasped the holy hilts in their hands and prayed for victory. Surely God must have heard them. God was on their side. The rising sun made the five hundred suits of armor glitter like mirrors.

First, the knights rode at a full trot, still in a single line, toward the hill where the English had hidden themselves like rabbits behind hedges of thorns and branches. The horses would break through those hedges effortlessly. Next, the horses were spurred into a gallop and thousands of pounds of steel came thundering down toward the English. Huge lumps of mud were hurled into the sky. Steel jingled and clanged ceaselessly. The knights saw the hilltop approaching through the slits in their helmets. Then the first English arrows whizzed through the air.

"At first, we didn't understand," says Jan van Vere. "I was standing with the rest of the army at the foot of the hill, and we saw how the English arrows were fired into the sky. The arrows did not seem to be aimed at the onrushing horses or at the knights. All we saw was a cloud of wood high in the sky. There were so many arrows that the sky seemed to be darkened by them. The arrows came down straight, right on top of the horse-men. At first, they had little effect. Here and there you could hear a painful whinnying because arrows had hit horses in their unprotected rear quarters. A few arrows had penetrated a knight's armor, but the valiant five hundred thundered on like snorting steel monsters from Hell. It was as if the arrows could not harm them. As if this line of steel was unstoppable. As if they were protected by Saint Joseph's finger bone, the stalks of straw from the Baby Jesus's crib, and the Virgin's hair. Then the second volley of arrows came down on the horsemen. The first horses fell. And the sky stayed dark, filled with thousands of arrows from the third and fourth volleys. And even before the third cloud of arrows hit the horsemen directly from above, a fifth volley whizzed off and the bowmen were fitting the sixth arrow to their bows."

Van Vere shows us an arrow. It has goose feathers tightly braided together at the end of it and a steel point shaped like a square nail. "These arrows are used to kill horses," Jan van Vere explains. "And those are used to pierce our armor." He shows us a similar arrow, but this one has a smooth, sharp tip. "This is the arrow that went through my nose in the battle." He rubs the bandage that divides his head in two. "The bows that fire these arrows are taller than a man."

I hold the arrow. It is easily three feet long.

"But how can an arrow like this go through steel armor?" asks Ferre the blacksmith.

"When the arrow is fired expertly," Jan van Vere explains, "and hits the armor at a right angle, it not only goes through the steel but also through the hauberk and the leather under it, and then through shirt, skin, flesh, and bone. That's why they fired the arrows up into the air. They came down on us like vertical spikes. I saw knights collapse on their horses. They looked like living pincushions. The feathered ends of dozens of quivering arrows were sticking out of their armor."

I slide my fingers along the arrow heads. We all cross ourselves. Kitchen boys are crying. Ferre is shaking his head. Chaplain van Izeghem prays silently. Nobody can even begin to believe it. So many invincible knights. Five hundred heroes. Felled by bits of wood with iron tips.

"It was the eighth volley that broke our charge," Jan

van Vere continues. "Palframand, the Count's war stallion, was hit in the neck. He crashed down. The Count was thrown from his saddle and fell on his face. The impact must have knocked the breath from his body. When he found the strength to lift himself up, all he saw about him was chaos. Knights lay crushed under their injured horses, who were kicking blindly in agony. Other horses, crazed with pain and trying to get away, trampled their own masters. And many knights who had landed on their backs could not lift themselves out the sucking mud because of the weight of their armor. All they could do was wait for Death, which, steered by feathers, was coming from the sky to nail them to the ground. The arrows kept coming.

"Three English arrows had pierced the Count's armor—one in his thigh, one a little lower down his leg, and one in his chest. This last arrow caused the greatest damage. His metal breastplate had slowed the arrow, but the steel tip was deeply embedded in his flesh. But he got up all the same, as did a number of other knights. Though they held fast to their shields, the impact of the arrows was so strong that some knights were knocked over by the force. Suddenly, the bowmen stopped. The Count wrenched off his helmet. Then he heard the war cry: 'For England and Saint George.' And the English emerged from behind their thorn hedges. A number of foot soldiers ran at the broken army, screaming curses in a language no one understood. They came to wound and capture knights. Each captured knight could be ransomed for pieces of gold. The Count had no time to break off the ends of the arrows sticking out of his body. He knelt and hacked the long toes off his armored shoes so he could move more easily. Pain roared through his body. He got up again and in a flash saw an overconfident English warrior coming toward him, wielding a spiked club. This was what he had practiced for since his early childhood. His instincts took over. It was a matter of taking a step back, raising the battle sword shoulder high, and swinging it from his upper right down to his left. The onrushing soldier didn't stand a chance. The Count chopped him in half. Blood spattered his steel armor."

I cheer for my father like everyone else in the kitchen.

"Then a handful of English knights on horseback came from behind the big hedge," Jan van Vere hurries on. "It was the English knight Geoffrey of Kent who caught sight of the Count and rode toward him on his stallion. I later heard that Geoffrey of Kent was very experienced in warfare. He wore a helmet in the shape of a dragon and was a veteran of the battle at Crécy. He knew that if he could capture the injured Flemish count, he could demand a fabulous ransom.

"The Count saw Geoffrey of Kent coming at him like a battering ram. The English knight dug his spurs into his horse's flanks and jumped over the dead bodies of horses and men. He was coming straight at our Count, who seemed as good as lost. There was no one to help him.

"But our Count had no intention of dying, and he did something the English knight wasn't expecting. He broke his lance in half and at the very last moment squatted down, ramming the shortened lance into the ground. A moment later, Geoffrey's stallion impaled itself on the leaf-shaped tip of the lance, with a heartrending cry. Its hooves had only barely missed the Count. Any other knight would have broken his neck in such a fall, but Geoffrey of Kent landed on his shoulder, rolled sideways, and got up again. He was seething and charged at our Count with raised sword.

"The Count looked at him full of awe. He seemed to have forgotten to draw his sword. Meanwhile, the trumpets blared, and together with three thousand foot soldiers, I ran up the hill. But we were too late. The fallen knights were nearly three quarters of a mile away from us. Count Lodewijk stood there with his little wooden shield. The reindeer skin that covered it had been torn in his fall. Geoffrey stepped toward him. And still our Count did not draw his sword."

Jan van Vere drinks his cup of spiced wine down in a single swallow. Someone blows his nose. Someone else coughs. The fire crackles. I feel my head glowing, my eyes popping. My whole body is screaming to know how it ended.

"A knight's shield," Jan van Vere explains, "is the most honorable part of his equipment. He must not let go of it no matter what happens. Capturing someone's shield is considered a great victory and brings shame to the loser. Geoffrey of Kent roared as he was about to knock the Count unconscious with the flat of his raised broadsword. And still the Count had not drawn his sword. But then he did something Geoffrey couldn't possibly have expected. Unseen by his opponent, he drew his arm out of the straps of his shield and then, as if it was any old round piece of wood, he hurled it at the onrushing Englishman's dragon helmet. The English knight managed to deflect the shield with his fighting arm, but the glancing blow was enough to distract him for a moment. When Geoffrey of Kent looked down again, he just had time to catch a glimpse of the Count grabbing him around the middle and twisting a long steel kidney dagger under his armor, where it did its terrible work."

The rest is not hard to guess. A look of disbelief must have spread over Geoffrey of Kent's face, and he must have felt a scorching, totally paralyzing pain.

"The Count is cunning itself," Jan van Vere grins. "There's a reason they call him 'fox face.'"

The people in the kitchen laugh, but not for long, because the rest of the story is drenched in sorrow.

"I was approaching with the foot soldiers and once more heard the trumpets blaring," the armorer continues. "Two battalions of a thousand knights each were marching up the hill behind us. The English soldiers hurriedly drew back to their fortified positions. Again, the knights who'd survived the charge shouted their battle cry *Montjoie Saint Denis!* and slashed at the

English as they ran back. But then the English arrows came. Again and again and again."

I listen breathlessly to the story of the rest of the battle, which was disastrous for the French troops. Every attack was checked by thousands of arrows, and when the English ran out of arrows, they used stones or ran to fallen horses and knights to pull the arrows out of the dead bodies and use them again. The Prince of England did not even have to draw his sword from its scabbard.

We hold our breath while van Vere tells us how he carried my father from the battlefield and brought him to Poitiers, and how, after the battle, he had to cut the body of Knight van Sindewint, struck down by more arrows than can be counted on two hands, loose from his dead horse. Knight van Sindewint was laid out in the cathedral of Poitiers together with hundreds of French knights. The clear light of thousands of candles brought out the colors of the brightly painted walls. And outside, at the foot of the honey-tinted cathedral walls, the town's inhabitants crowded together to lament the loss of so much noble blood. The French king and his youngest son had been taken prisoner, hostages of the English Crown. An immense ransom has been demanded for them, but ransom is demanded for all the other captured knights as well. The French people will have to bear ruthless taxes for many years to buy back the freedom of their king and his noblemen.

All the kitchen boys have tears in their eyes. Even that hardened hulk Ferre lets his tears flow. Squire Willem sobs softly over the dented helmet of his dead father. I feel Constance Bouvaert's hands on my shoulders. I hear Kitchen Master Aelbrecht spoon a final cup of spiced wine from the kettle. I hear the wood of the spoon scraping the iron.

"I'm going to my father's room," I whisper into Constance's ear, and she nods.

I cross the courtyard to the tower where my father's room is. I run up the spiral stairs and stop in front of his door. The flickering glow of the fire shines fitfully through the gap under the door. When I open the door, I see him sitting by the fire. Rufus, his great hunting dog, lies on the floor in front of him. He is a long-haired brown animal with crumpled-looking eyes. My father turns toward me, wincing with pain from the wound in his side. One of his knees is bent, but the injured leg is stretched out straight. His face is shiny with sweat because he is sitting too close to the fire.

I don't recognize the mighty knight who went off to the war. No longer is he the man of fire and strength and steel. Something in him is broken. The reddish-brown hair at his temples has gone gray, the raised flesh of the scars around his right eye seems more red and swollen, and a few of his teeth are missing. He is not even thirty years old, but I can see the old man he is going to be.

"What do you want, daughter?" He stares at me with screwed-up eyes, as if he is having trouble seeing my small figure.

I say nothing. We stare at each other. I'm on fire. I

want to go to him, but I can't move. Please let him say something. Please let him tell me to come to him. Let him take me in his arms. Let him press me to his chest. I want to feel his calloused hands. The prickling of his beard. The lumps of the scar on his face. I want to smell his scent of armpit, horse, wet soil, and pork fat. I want my father.

He turns his eyes away from me and pokes the fire with an iron rod. Sparks fly. The dog quickly changes position.

What if I make myself faint, I think. *Then he would have to take me in his arms. Then I can wrap my arms round his neck and...*

"I visited your mother on my way back," he says finally.

The breath is knocked out of me. My stomach sinks. I hardly dare ask my question.

"Is she coming at Christmas?" My voice nearly breaks.

"Yes, at Christmas. But then she's going back to the convent."

I feel myself go pale. The hair at the back of my neck stands up.

"What do you mean?" I ask.

"She's not going to get better."

I feel violently sick, as if eels are wriggling around inside me.

"I don't believe you," I stammer.

He doesn't react.

I burst into tears. "My mother," I stammer.

"It looks as if your mother will never bear me a son," my father continues. "Which means that you, daughter, will inherit my titles of Flanders, Rethel, and Nevers, and will pass them on to the prince or nobleman I will choose for you."

"I want my mother," I murmur, but my father is no longer listening.

"You'll also receive the Duchy of Brabant from your mother and no doubt a few other domains from your grandmother. You'll be Countess of more land and more territory than all of your ancestors."

"I don't care what I'll be," I screech, feeling my knees tremble. "You can keep your Flanders. I don't want it. Or your miserable Brabant either. I want my mother."

It's the first time I raise my voice against my father. He gets up and struggles toward me. He bites back the pain that throbs through his body. His face is right in front of me. He's wheezing. His words come in short bursts.

"My family," he says, "my father's fathers' fathers received this territory from the emperor himself. We are the Lords of Flanders. We defeated the Vikings, and with our own blood we built a boundary between the French and the German realms. We beat back the sea and we gained land. We passed on our title and our pride from grandfather to father, from father to son. During the last three hundred years, every count has managed to father an heir who in his turn produced an heir.

Except me. I have produced a daughter."

His words do not penetrate. They are only sounds that wash over me. I just stare at his body, which trembles with powerlessness and fury. He towers above me.

"What am I going to do with you, my little lady of Flanders? How are you ever going to be a countess? The world will tear you to pieces."

My ears are ringing. He is now standing quite close to me. I smell the wine on his breath. With his hand he brushes a braid of hair from my face. His crusty finger briefly touches my cheek.

"Every time I see you," he says softly, "I see God laughing at me. Because that is what you are. A joke. God's jest."

That's when I remember the chapel in the Marshland and the scratched statue of the Virgin with its hands missing, and anger rises in me like waves in the sea.

"Why didn't you die?" I shout, tears pouring from my eyes. "Why did the arrows miss you? Why didn't the English hack you to pieces on the battlefield?"

I turn and run outside.

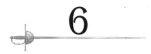

6

I SEE MY MOTHER AGAIN on the day before Christmas, and she is a mere shadow of the proud Lady of Brabant. She has become thin, and her eyes seem to be hiding in their sockets. She no longer smells of lavender, and she doesn't even seem to recognize me. She walks, eats, and rests like a ghost that, by some quirk of fate, finds itself left in the world of the living. I think her spirit is already wandering in Purgatory, waiting for her body, which must finish its journey here on Earth.

My father stays in his room over Christmas. In the Great Hall, the fires are not lit. Everyone thinks up an excuse to visit the kitchens, where the fires are always burning and it never gets cold. Master Surgeon van Obrecht cleanses my father's festering wounds and applies fresh bandages. He hopes the wounds will heal by summer.

I have little time to feel alone in the world. I am barely awake when Constance sees to it that I'm dressed and my hair is combed so I can go to chapel. Chaplain van Izeghem, who seems to shrink a bit every year, turns the pages of his Bible with woolly gloves. He reads in Latin in a voice that is so monotonous it could rock a werewolf to sleep under a full moon. The last words of his sentences fall apart like old dust. On top of which, he has a cold, so his sermons are interrupted by prolonged bouts of sneezing. Sometimes, when he interrupts himself to blow his nose on the sleeve of his habit, we have been known to break into a loud *Hallelujah!* even before the end of the sermon, just to get warm. Chaplain van Izeghem also insists that all girls keep their ears covered when they enter the church, for it has been positively proven that the impregnation of the Virgin Mary by the Holy Ghost took place through her auditory canal. If you want to make the chaplain lose his place when he is reading the Gospel, you just need to pull your cap off and have a good poke around in your ear.

The chaplain also has a truly biblical fear of the number thirteen. When we young women go to confession with him, we do our best to use the number thirteen, or a multiple of it, as often as possible. One girl tells him about a dream in which Christ had *thirteen* apostles. I tell him I have *twenty-six* guardian angels and ask him if that means I am blessed or cursed. Another girl points out that there are *thirty-nine* people present in the chapel. Every time he hears the cursed number, he turns himself to the East and offers up an Our Father. Our stomachs hurt from trying not to laugh during confession.

The loveliest moment of the morning Mass is Holy Communion. I love the body of Christ laid on my tongue; I love feeling the cold floor under my knees and closing my eyes and ears. I love talking with Him inside me and wondering why I am being tried so severely by a mother who is a living corpse and a father for whom I don't exist.

Then the final blessing, *In nomine patris, et filii, et spiritui sancto.* We leave the chapel in peace and struggle through the snow and the mud in the courtyard. The boys follow the armorer or the chaplain for instruction. The girls follow the ladies-in-waiting. We barely get inside a room before we hoist up our heavy skirts in front of the fire. We feel the warmth on our cold legs and bottoms. There is no more pleasant feeling. Each young lady has a governess who follows her around like a shadow.

I drag myself through the winter with lessons in music, poetry, arithmetic, geometry, and drawing. I learn to play the harp and I learn embroidery. From my ladies-in-waiting, I learn lovely French and ancient Latin. Spicy Flemish I pick up from the serfs in the castle.

It isn't till late in the afternoon that I begin to feel lonely. It's as if I can breathe in but not out. I see the servants setting off back to Bruges in a covered wagon. The first of the torches is lit. I stare at the closed shutters of my father's room. I go into the stables, climb up to the rafters, and sit under the roof among the empty swallows' nests. The pages feed and groom the horses. They leave me alone. I think about all that's happened. The snorting of the horses, the scraping of their shoes over stone and straw has a reassuring effect on me.

It is on such an evening that Jan van Vere comes to find me. He dismisses the pages.

"What is making you unhappy, Lady Marguerite?" he asks.

"I'm not unhappy," I reply, offended.

He nods. Jan van Vere is much older than my father. He has always remained a squire because he doesn't have enough money to buy armor. He tells me he is a real Zeelander because blond hair grows from his ears. He is proud of his origins. Everyone in Flanders respects the Zeelanders because it was the warlord Jan van Renesse from Zeeland who, more than fifty years ago, led the citizens of Flanders and a handful of knights and cut a whole French army to ribbons in the Battle of the Golden Spurs.

"They've brought back your father's horse," he says. "It was being looked after in Poitiers, after being hit by five arrows. I tried to ride it, but I can't get anywhere with it. It will not tolerate a rider on its back."

I finally notice the great stallion Palframand. I see the hole in his neck where an arrow had been embedded. There are spots on his flank and on his rear quarter where the hair was shorn so the wounds could be sewn up.

"Never again will he fight in a tournament or a battle," says van Vere. "A war horse only rides in a charge once. It's not seeing so much steel and so many dead men that is most frightening for horses. It's the scent of horses' blood that stays with them forever. It makes them go crazy. The Count never wants to see the horse again. I will have it slaughtered."

"No," I shout. "I want him. I'll look after him."

I clamber down from the rafters and jump to the ground, landing just in front of Palframand. The animal shies. Jan van Vere keeps a firm hold on the reins.

"I'm not sure that your father—"

"I don't care what my father thinks," I shout.

Jan van Vere nods, hands me Palframand's reins, and turns away. He crosses to the stable door but doesn't step outside.

"He's ashamed," van Vere says. I look up but only see his back. It is as if he is speaking to the door.

"He's a knight, and a knight can only prove his honor in war," he continues. "It's better to die on the field of battle or even to be taken prisoner than to come back half crippled, the pitiful remnant of a warrior."

For a moment, it's quiet. The words ring in my ears. The horses snort. Van Vere thumps a beam with his fist and walks out the door.

I carefully feed Palframand every day. First, I give him a week to get used to me being there. I sing to him and tickle his coat. Then I spend the whole winter working with him. Two months later, I ride him for the first time. From then on, he changes rapidly. The way he moves changes. The way he rests changes. The way he trots and jumps changes. He becomes an elegant horse, a beautiful horse, and by Easter time, he completely surrenders to me. All I need to do is stand in front of him and he bows. I love him, and he loves me.

Jan van Vere is always busy training the pages. He curses them for being spoiled mother's boys, dried-up nuns, and cowardly field mice. He shouts that they fight like country bumpkins. At the end of their winter training, he marks off a square with ropes. In the snow, the boys have to fight duels with their chests bare. I see the young pages shaking—and not just with cold—as they brandish unsharpened steel swords. They hardly dare cross swords, afraid of being hit. The armorer spurs them on and throws snowballs if one of them draws back too far.

Squire Willem thinks he is the best. He wants to be his father, Knight van Sindewint. At first, he manages, too. He maneuvers Squire Hendrik, son of the Knight of Ostend, into a corner of the fighting area and knocks his sword out of his hand. Then he tackles Godfried, who is from Sluis. Godfried is a taciturn fellow with a dark face. He is very cautious, parrying blow after blow without attacking. Willem becomes impatient and tries to break through Godfried's defense with wild swings of his sword. Suddenly, Godfried lets himself buckle at the knees and slams the sword sideways against Willem's unprotected shins. Willem tumbles onto his side in the snow and falls with his bare chest against one of the posts that mark out the square arena. The post breaks and Willem ends up with a huge splinter in his side. Blood gushes from the wound, making red patches in the snow.

Van Vere curses and wants to know who drove those bloody posts into the ground. He calls for the surgeon. Then he takes a sponge that has been soaked in healing herbs and poppy seeds. He holds it against the wound. Willem is crying, and Jan van Vere tells him it will be alright. He speaks to his pages, pointing out that this fight shows that force is not everything and that Godfried won through cunning and patience. Surgeon van Obrecht arrives. He pours wine over the wound to cleanse it. Willem screams. Then the surgeon sews up the wound with a needle and catgut. The pages' winter training is over.

That evening, Jan van Vere comes to the stables to check on my stallion.

"Master van Vere," I say, "if sword fighting is not decided by brute strength, why can't I learn it?"

He looks surprised and searches for words.

"I have no time for dreaming girls," he mutters. "But if you really want to…"

In one single movement, he pulls his sword from its scabbard and grips the blade close to the hilt, where it is not sharp. I grasp the hilt with both hands. He lets go. The end of the blade immediately hits the floor. I try to lift it from the floor, but can't manage. I spin around. The tip of the sword drags along the paving stones. Sparks fly, and for a very brief moment, thanks to the spinning motion, I lift the sword off the ground. Jan van Vere jumps aside.

"Careful," he shouts.

I spin around a second and then a third time, and the sword swishes through the air.

"Stop, don't let go!" shouts van Vere.

My foot catches on the floor and I stop twisting. The sword pulls on my hands, my wrists, my arms, throwing me to the floor. I scrape along the tiles, but I don't let go of the hilt. My chin scrapes along a stone mounting block. I feel my whole mouth throbbing with pain. Jan van Vere gives me his hand and pulls me up. Blood drips from my chin.

"You are meant to become Lady of Flanders, not Hippolyta, Queen of the Amazons," he grins, pressing the sponge against my chin. I feel the pain slowly drain away.

"The boys practice with wooden swords, so why can't I?"

Jan van Vere sighs.

"The Count doesn't need to know," I insist. "It'll be our secret."

He takes a deep breath and looks at me. We hear the bell for the evening meal. He smiles. I push the sponge aside and kiss him on his deformed nose. Then I run outside as though I had wings.

Jan van Vere teaches me fencing at daybreak, just before the first church service, when only the kitchen boys, the washerwomen, and the monks are about and the nobles are still asleep. Nobody will know about it. He lends me a sword made of whalebone. It has been polished and rubbed with oil and is as hard as stone. He teaches me attack and defense, thrusting and slashing. The whalebone sword is much lighter than a real sword, but not too light, so I can still practice the movements with speed and precision. As soon as there are signs of life in the castle, the lesson ends.

◫ ◫ ◫

THE DAYS ARE LENGTHENING. I can almost taste spring in the air. I'm learning to paint on a panel with oil paints. Every young lady has to paint a portrait of someone who poses for her. I paint my father. He's seated in front of the open window and he's not allowed to move. He's constantly attacked by flies and mosquitoes. He swats at them with a bundle of hard young reed canes. He looks straight at me and I study every line in his face. I realize how much I look like him, not very feminine with my narrow face, my big nose, and my reddish-brown hair. I know what they whisper in the kitchens of Male and in the streets of Bruges, that I haven't inherited my mother's beauty, that I'll marry a man who only wants me for my inheritance. That I'll be living proof that money doesn't buy happiness. For who will ever love a failed boy with her father's fox head? I'm not beautiful like the lady-companion Alaïs, who is staying at the castle. Even the sparrows fall silent when she makes her way through the castle in all her beauty. I'm thinking about all those things while I paint my father's surly face. I've only just finished a charcoal sketch when he strides toward me.

"Which hand are you sketching with?" he asks.

"My left hand," I stammer.

He glances at Constance, who immediately bends her head.

"Why do you let my daughter draw with her left hand, Lady Bouvaert?"

Constance is deeply upset and does not venture a reply.

"I write and draw with my left hand because that's how I want to do it," I say in a challenging tone.

"Show me your left hand," my father says.

I hesitantly hold out my left hand. He instantly strikes me with the canes. I feel the dozen twigs cut across my fingers and scream.

"You write, you eat, you embroider, and you paint with your right hand," he commands.

I clamp my left hand under my armpit. It is still throbbing with pain.

"Show me your hand!"

I hesitate.

"Your hand."

I stretch my trembling hand out again and another cutting blow swishes down. This time I don't scream. I hold my hand against my breast.

"From now on, Lady Constance, if ever she picks up a pen, a brush, or even a stick with her left hand, you'll make good use of this cane."

He throws the bundle of reeds onto Constance's lap.

"And you can find someone else's portrait to paint."

The next moment, he's gone.

❑ ❑ ❑

SOON AFTER EASTER, we're taught for a few days by Father Zannekin, under the strict supervision of our governesses. He's a traveling Franciscan friar. He wears the habit of a mendicant monk and a beard down to his waist. He also stinks like a pigpen. The girls think he's awful, but I find him interesting. He teaches us astronomy, the noblest of all the sciences. He tells us that a falling star is a knight killed in battle riding across the sky to his last resting place. He teaches us that the earth is a sphere with the stars moving around it. You can travel around the earth the same way a fly flies around an apple.

We have trouble believing it, and some of the girls laugh.

"I've seen it myself," Zannekin exclaims angrily, coming toward us. His beard moves up and down so vigorously that bread crumbs fall out of it. For a moment we step back because of his very unpleasant smell.

"I was standing on the deck of a ship when I was traveling to England," he explains. "From the rear deck we saw the mainland disappear from view, but the sailor who sat at the top of the mast could still see the land! That is the proof that the earth is round, not flat!"

It silences the girls for a while.

"How far away from us are the stars?" I ask.

"If you stood on a star and dropped a stone, it would take that stone a hundred years to reach the earth."

"A hundred years," I murmur.

"Yes, that goes for every star," he confirms.

"But where is God?" I ask next. "Is He still farther away than the stars?"

"No," he says, and now he seems to be speaking just to me. "God is here."

"Here?"

The girls sigh. Father Zannekin grins.

"Life, my dear young lady," he says, combing out his beard with his fingers, "is not just a journey through the world of people. It's also a journey into our innermost selves."

I stare at him. He blows his nose on the sleeve of his habit. One girl giggles foolishly.

"God is not to be found on a cloud beyond the stars," says Zannekin. "And his beard is not as long as mine. God is inside you."

Zannekin points at his heart.

It has become very quiet. The girls are no longer giggling.

"There's only one person you have to be able to look straight in the eyes," he whispers.

You could hear a pin drop. He turns to a small table. There's something on the table covered with a cloth. He brings it over to me. I can't see what it is.

"There's only one person to whom you are responsible. One person you dare not look in the eyes."

I feel my heart thumping against my ribs. I wonder if he has hidden my father's portrait under the cloth. I move closer. I can feel the edge of the chair under me. Then Zannekin removes the cloth. And I'm looking at myself in a silver mirror. I see my reddish-brown hair, my thin lips, my blue eyes, and my nose that is far too big. I feel myself go red and the girls staring at me.

"You look at the world and the stars, but not at yourself," Zannekin mutters in his beard.

I don't want to see myself. I don't want to look into the mirror. No one says a word. I'm burning with embarrassment and look for a way out. The silence is making me feel sick.

"There's one thing that's still not clear to me," I manage eventually.

"And what is that?" asks Father Zannekin.

"Is it true that the Holy Ghost impregnated the Virgin Mary through her ear?"

The girls laugh. But not Father Zannekin. He looks at me and after a while he smiles.

"It is a nobleman's duty," he replies, "to whisper the sweetest and loveliest words into the woman's ear hoping that she will give herself to him."

The girls giggle and the ladies-in-waiting think enough is enough. Like chickens, we are pushed outside.

And outside? Outside, it's nearly summer.

7

I**T'S THE END OF MAY**. The boys take off into the fields. The castle empties out. The adventure begins. I'm nine years old and have only one problem: my governess Constance Bouvaert, who screams if I'm more than fifty steps away from her.

"You must understand, Lady Marguerite," she's forever groaning. "Your father depends on me. He would never forgive me if anything happened to you. And nor would I forgive myself."

One brilliant June day, I sprinkle half a pound of dried peas in the stairwell. As expected, Constance is the first person to come down the stairs and, as always, she's in a hurry. The effect is better than I had hoped. Her legs shoot up and with a dull thud she lands on her shoulder. Her arm, which is completely dislocated, hangs limply by her side. Her wails would raise Heaven and Hell. I try to look concerned and assure her that I will immediately go to find Surgeon van Obrecht. He is, after all, second to none for repairing a smashed cheekbone and, *in casu*, a dislocated shoulder. I promise to be right back.

A moment later, I grab my whalebone sword and run out of the castle, in search of adventure. I stomp on ants, kick the yellow heads off dandelions, and climb trees. After a while, I meet the three boys who come to the castle for lessons. There is Willem, the son of Knight van Sindewint, who died in battle; Hendrik, the son of the Knight of Ostend; and Godfried, who comes from Sluis. They're collecting fresh cowpats, which they use to fill pigs' bladders with the help of a funnel.

"What are you doing?" I ask.

The boys say nothing. They look up briefly and carry on as if I don't exist.

"Can I come with you?"

"What for?" Hendrik, who has the loudest mouth, replies. "You ought to be at home making lace."

"Making lace gives me the shits," I shout, sounding as tough as I can.

They're a bit surprised by my choice of words.

"Please go back to your castle, Margriet," Willem says in a conciliatory tone. "We're on a secret mission."

"Yes," Hendrik grins. "A very secret mission."

Godfried from Sluis, who's constantly digging around in his nose, nods to indicate he totally agrees with Hendrik and Willem. You'll never catch him putting more than four words together if he can help it.

"A very secret mission," I laugh. "I suppose you're

going to steal a chicken from some farm."

"No," says Willem. "We're setting up an ambush for—"

"Girls are not allowed," Hendrik barks. "You would only cry when you see the first drop of blood."

Godfried grunts some gibberish to indicate he's in total agreement.

"That first drop of blood will be yours," I retort. "It'll come from your nose when I've smashed it in, little Knight of Ostend!"

"Quiet," says Willem, trying to calm things down. "It's just something we have to do on our own, Margriet."

"Yes, this is men's work," boasts Hendrik. "Unless you're a man and can pee against a tree standing up, we don't want you."

"So if I can pee against a tree standing up, I can come?" I ask.

"Yes, if you can do that, you can come," Hendrik blusters, far too confidently.

Willem looks at Hendrik angrily, as if to say, "Did you really have to promise that?

"What?" Hendrik asks, his hands spread in certainty that I won't be able to perform his task in a hundred years.

But I've already turned around. Standing in front of a tree, I use one hand to hoist up my skirts, while with my right hand I do something the boys can't see. And in a beautifully curved stream, I pee against the tree. I dry myself with my undershirt and walk over to the boys, beaming. The expression of amazement on their faces is priceless. Willem and Hendrik will wonder for the rest of their lives how I managed it. The truth is I once saw the washerwoman Greet do it.

And so it is that I go with them. With the boys. On a secret mission.

The boys have collected enough cowpats to fill a dozen pigs' bladders, which two of them carry in a fishnet. They are heading for the Reie, the river along which ships are towed by horses to the estuary at Sluis. The boys watch the ships' flags and wait patiently until the ship flying the flag of Genoa arrives. I realize the ship belongs to an Italian bank that lends money to the traders and nobles of Bruges and the surrounding area. I have heard that Hendrik's father has large debts with the bank. As the ship slowly floats past, pulled by a horse on the bridle path along the riverbank, we jump up and wave enthusiastically to the crew who, in their innocence, wave back. Then the boys fire their arsenal of cow manure at them, the juicy dung splattering all over the deck. For a moment, the sailors are too surprised to find cover. And if there is one thing the boys are good at, it's aiming missiles. The sailors, dressed in red-and-yellow-striped hose, don't stand a chance. Their clothes are soon covered in the gunk.

One of the soldiers, his green-and-red tunic dripping with slushy cow dung, is so furious he jumps overboard and climbs up the bank. The man is shouting in Italian. We don't understand any of it, but I suspect his vocabulary is a little crude. We run away. He runs after us through the fields and manages to catch Godfried, pushing him face down onto the ground. The boy screams bloody murder, and the Italian has already drawn his long dagger.

The man has pale blue eyes and is wearing a black hat with red feathers. He's about to cut off one of Godfried's ears when I yell at him to stop. He looks at me. Me, a child barely twenty apples high, in a red dress. He can see I'm not just a peasant girl. My dress is too expensive, my reddish-brown hair too carefully braided, and my fingernails too carefully looked after.

"I am the Count of Flanders's daughter," I hear myself say in Latin, trying hard not to tremble. "This boy is under my protection. My father will consider it a personal insult if you harm him."

The Italian looks at me. He's a short man. He strokes the long black goatee that reaches a long way below his chin. His forehead is furrowed. He can't be very young. He still has Godfried's neck in his grip.

"I'm not afraid of the Count of Flanders," he says in French, sliding the blade of his dagger along Godfried's ear.

"Mercy, noble Lord, mercy," Godfried shouts, his nose still pressed into the grass. I have never heard him say so many words at one time.

"My father," I shout, "will not forgive you if you hurt—"

"I fear no one," the Genoese interrupts rudely.

"Nor do I," I hear myself hiss. "And I demand that you release Godfried."

But the Italian tightens his grip on the boy's neck. Godfried howls. His arms are twisted against the ground.

"Please," I shout suddenly, feeling tears coming to my eyes. The Italian looks at me. And I repeat my plea, "Please."

Then the Italian lets go of Godfried. The boy shoots away like an arrow from a bow, never looking back at the Italian. He runs at least a hundred yards into the field, toward Hendrik and Willem, who are hiding in the bushes. I stand still. My heart is throbbing in my throat.

The Italian brushes the dirt from his tunic and slides the dagger into a red leather scabbard on his belt. He looks at me.

"Thank you, my Lord," I say courteously, bowing lightly.

He nods curtly, turns, and walks back toward the canal.

I cross the field to the three boys. They stare at me wide-eyed.

"He's gone," I say, rather unnecessarily.

The boys breathe again and I glow with pride.

"So," I ask, "what's the next very secret mission?"

▣ ▣ ▣

THAT SUMMER, the three boys help me discover the whole area around Bruges. The wide, flat polder land, the windmills, the dikes, the cornfields, the great grain barns, and the little villages on top of the sand hills. The grass whispers under our feet. We run through the shallow water of the Zwin, where salt is harvested. We swim in the inlets. We dip our feet in the silt. We chase sea gulls, herons, and magpies. We set fire to hayracks and overpower Farmer Ronselaar's huge red rooster, which we pluck alive so it doesn't dare show itself in the barnyard for the rest of that summer.

Sometimes, we wander all the way to Sluis to see the galleons moored in the harbor. Often we go into the town of Bruges, especially on days when an execution has been announced. All four of us love executions. All of Bruges seems to pour into the town on those days: rich cloth merchants and poor eel skinners, noble ladies and brothel keepers, graybeards and children, all swarming around the wooden scaffold where the executions are to take place. It's often a long wait, so we fly a kite or buy sweets from the hawkers who sell honey cakes, candy sticks, and sugar-coated apples. When the pickpockets and purse snatchers are finally brought down in a cart, the crowd gives a deafening cheer. It's better than a fair, and Hendrik, Godfried, Willem, and I compete to see who can shout loudest so that by evening we have no voice left. If we happen to be near the front of the crowd, we hurl lumps of mud or rotten turnips at the unfortunate men and women. Of course, we have to make sure we don't hit the priest who leads the condemned to the scaffold. The priest has heard their last confessions and pardoned their sins so that even they, poor wretches that they are, will be admitted to Heavenly Jerusalem. Whatever you've done wrong in this world, the priest can forgive you, unless you've robbed a church, raped a nun, or murdered a priest or a friar. In that case, the arch-devil Lucifer will personally skin and salt you and roast you on the spit in his oven forever and a day.

The condemned men and women don't usually cry when the executioner fits the noose around their neck and puts the white hood over their head. They're thinking of the children, parents, or friends who have died and with whom they'll soon be reunited in paradise.

The bailiff nods at the executioner, who pulls the lever that makes the trapdoor drop from under the victim's feet. They fall six feet, but their necks don't break. The noose slowly squeezes their throats shut and their legs thrash about in empty space while they soil their clothes with their own excrement. People say they perform the Saint Vitus dance, and it can take minutes before the rope finally strangles them and their legs stop thrashing about. Some of the condemned have given the executioner money, and for those, he climbs down the rope and squats with his knees on their shoulders so their suffering is considerably shorter.

When the first one is dead, the executioner steps across to the next victim and does the same thing, as if he's some sort of Good Samaritan, relieving people of their suffering or, as some say, Death's good ferryman. The bodies are then hung outside the walls, near the gallows field, where, for weeks, they are the prey of magpies, crows, rats, and slugs.

And then we're on our way, talking for hours about

the hanging, what we know about the unfortunate ones, who they were, who struggled the longest, and why they deserved the rope. But an execution becomes really spectacular when an arsonist is broken on the wheel, when a counterfeiter is thrown into a cauldron of boiling water, when an adulterous woman is hit on her bare bottom with a red-hot frying pan, or when a murderer has to chop off his own hand before being drawn and quartered.

And so, we're never bored on execution days. After all, justice is served and the condemned, relieved of their sins by that final confession, are already in Heaven, eating from a golden spoon and drinking wine from a jug that will never be empty.

◫ ◫ ◫

IT IS ON AN EXECUTION DAY that we cross swords with Roderik, the son of Guild Master Slicher van Rijpergherste, who is considered to be the leader of Bruges. Roderik asks Willem if he is going to be a lapdog of the French king like his father, the late Knight van Sindewint. Furiously, Willem turns to Roderik, who, of course, is not alone. He has two friends with him, also sons of guild masters.

"Say that again," Willem challenges.

"Just watch out," Roderik says quietly. "Here in Bruges, it's not all that safe for France-lovers."

He's referring to the Red Night, the massacre at Bruges more than fifty years ago, when a group of guildsmen drank themselves stupid until they felt like lions. Then, late at night, they dragged the pro-French nobles from their beds, asking them if they were "with the guilds." Before the nobles could reply, they were attacked with dozens of axes and battle clubs. Their heads inflamed with drink, the guildsmen kept hitting their victims until the ground was slippery with blood and guts. There were so many dead bodies that the streets had to be cleared. The corpses were thrown onto carts and then tipped into the canals. So many dead bodies floated in the canals that boats couldn't turn at the Minnewater, and for months people joked that in Bruges, the fish spoke French. The pro-French nobles who survived fled to the castle of Male that night and sought refuge there. But that didn't save them. The guildsmen pursued them and, at daybreak, set fire to the castle. The last of the nobles threw themselves off the sixty-five-foot-high fortress to escape being burnt alive. I'd heard this story several times. It's every count's greatest fear that the guild masters and the cities of Flanders will rebel.

Roderik is the grandson of one of the guild masters who led the Bruges massacre. He detests the nobles but is only too happy to have people address him as *Messire* in French.

"Why don't you drop in at the castle, Master Roderik?" I shout. "Our manure shoveler needs an assistant."

Roderik snorts. "Lady Marguerite," he says politely, "I don't want there to be trouble between us."

"But there already is," I reply. "These are my squires."

He goes pale. He knows I'm bluffing, but he wants to avoid a fight with the Count of Flanders's daughter. There is great tension between his father and the Count, but in reality he needs my father as much as my father needs him.

"I repeat, Lady Marguerite, I don't want there to be trouble between us."

"Are you scared of me, guild puppy?" I tease him.

Willem interrupts and proposes we settle the matter in a fair fight. Three young noblemen against three sons of guild masters. Tomorrow, by the creek near Rabauwenborg, a village where no one has lived for the last ten years, ever since the plague spread its dark shadow over the land. Rabauwenborg is a ghost village.

I'm so excited I can hardly sleep that night. We've kept the fight secret so no one can interfere. Roderik and his two friends are going to bite the dust, that much is certain. They're no match for Willem, Godfried, and Hendrik, who have had training for years. Although I won't be allowed to fight with the boys, I have brought my whalebone sword and my small round shield covered in sheepskin. You never know.

We run through the fields to Rabauwenborg. The closer we get, the less noise we make. We creep nearer through the tall grass. We can see the little village.

Willem crawls on his stomach ahead of us to reconnoiter. Godfried, Hendrik, and I stay back in the tall grass. The village looks dismal. The straw roofs of the little houses have collapsed and parts of the mud walls have been scoured away by wind and rain. The oak door of the small church, the only stone building, is hanging by its hinges. An emaciated black cat walks into the church, and I cross myself because it is well known, as Chaplain van Izeghem keeps telling us, that a black cat is the Devil's creature.

In the fields, overgrown with weeds, lie the carcasses of sheep, cattle, and other animals that had been infected with the plague. So many people perished in that year, the year of my birth, that everyone thought the world had come to an end and the final judgment had begun. But when winter came, God made the plague stop. Chaplain van Izeghem announced that God had given humankind a warning. He had shown us a glimpse of the Apocalypse. Humans would be given one and only one more chance to show they were worthy of Christ's sacrifice. If they threw that chance away, the Apocalypse would take place.

"There's five of them," Willem whispers, jolting me out of my thoughts. Hendrik and Godfried look at each other, a bit uncertain.

"Five against three," Willem repeats. He's always been the smart one. The boys hesitate. I spot a bull's skull in the weeds, scrape the vermin out of it, and put it on my head.

"Against four," I say, standing up and nearly giving Godfried, who had almost dozed off, a heart attack.

The boys follow my example and adorn themselves with sheep skulls. Godfried even ties a cat's ribcage into his hair. It rattles as we creep forward. We see Roderik van Rijpergherste and his four friends sitting near a tent made of animal skins. They're equipped with stones and sticks.

"What's the plan?" Willem asks no one in particular.

"The usual," I whisper. "We rush them."

Willem looks at me uncertainly. He's afraid he'll get a beating if anything happens to the Count's daughter. Then I grin. And the boys grin back.

The next moment, we jump up, hurl leap across the creek, and hurl ourselves at Roderik and his four cronies, the animal bones rattling on our bodies.

Roderik doesn't know what's happening. He is so amazed to see me with a bull's skull on my head that he doesn't even react when I ram my shield into his stomach and then knock out one of his teeth with my knee. The others smash into each other. Willem drags two opponents into the creek. We fight like lions. Without mercy. For honor, creek, and fatherland. We bash each other over the head with wooden swords, shields—anything we can find. We roll around in the mud, flinging ourselves about and shouting. Roderik and his mob take to their feet. We pursue them through the village, jeering and hooting, spurred on by the hot glow of victory. The three squires and I are black with blood and mud. My skirts are torn and the tip of Roderik's wooden sword has gashed my forehead. Blood pours onto my dress. But I don't cry. I say it's not so bad, I'll live, and I've hit Roderik so hard he'll remember it for the rest of his life.

So there we sit, the victors in the Battle of Rabauwenborg. Willem grins at me and I grin back. Like him, I am a warrior. The scar that will split my right eyebrow in two from now on is proof.

⌗ ⌗ ⌗

IT'S ON ONE OF THE LAST DAYS of summer that our rambles take us to the mill at Vierweeghe. Who will ever be able to forget that day! There, we come upon a stallion tied to the steps that lead into the mill. The sails aren't moving and there's no dog around. We know the miller's wife is beautiful and blonde and always wears a corset laced up so tightly that her breasts spill out of it like ripe fruit. Perhaps the miller's wife has a rendezvous with the master of this magnificent horse.

Willem, Godfried, Hendrik, and I climb the steps and silently push open the door to the mill. Giggles and grunts are coming from the first floor. We look at each other, and in our eyes, dripping with malice, the same thing can be read four times over: what mad joke can we play here?

The answer comes faster than we expected, because from the trapdoor to the first floor hangs a gentleman's stockings and dark green breeches, embroidered in gold thread. Within seconds, I've climbed the steps and grabbed the stockings and pants. I haven't given it a single thought, but acted purely on impulse. Willem, Godfried, and Hendrik are finding it hard not to laugh out loud when I come down the steps with my booty. A moment later, as we're cutting the pants into ribbons, the grunting from the first floor gets louder and louder and we burst out laughing, and then run helter-skelter down the outside wooden steps. We can hear someone cursing loudly inside the mill.

At the bottom of the stairs, we suddenly realize there's one thing we haven't thought about: how do we get away? If we run through the fields, the man, who must be a knight, judging by the gold-thread embroidery on his stockings, will overtake us in no time and give us a hiding from here to the Holy City of Jerusalem.

We look at each other, all thinking the same thing, then rush toward the great stallion tethered to the rail of the steps. The beast neighs and stamps its feet. Godfried unties the reins while the stallion twists around uneasily, surprised by the four creatures clambering onto its back.

And then the door of the mill is hurled open and a man in a white shirt and bare knees comes thundering down the steps. But by then I have a firm grip on the reins. Holding on tightly to each other, we shout "Giddyup, giddyup!" and poke our wooden swords at the flanks of the stallion, which thunders away.

The nobleman is cursing and yelling. I feel the wind whip through my hair and Willem's arm round my waist as we race away. Then I see him standing there—screaming, half naked, with his white shirt blowing up and his noble parts swinging around—my father!

That evening, I am ordered to the Knights' Hall of the castle of Male. I stand facing my father.

"You are nine years old, and it is time you started behaving the way a young lady of rank should behave."

I don't reply. I remain standing very straight in the middle of the room, my hands crossed behind my back like a man-at-arms standing at ease. I know I should lower my eyes, but I don't. I lift my chin and look straight at my father without blinking.

"There has to be an end to all this mischief. It's normal for boys to behave like that. It's in their nature. They have to become knights. Playing pranks, sowing their wild oats...it's all part of it. But for you to be involved in that is inexcusable."

I remain silent. My father barely looks at me. The straw crackles under his feet as he paces to and fro in the Great Hall.

"You can play tricks on peasants, serfs, or market vendors, but not on your father. Or on poor Chaplain van Izeghem, the way you did last week. How in hell's name did you get it into your head, daughter, to saw through the seat of the shithouse by the Ghent gate? He nearly drowned in shit. It took four men to pull him out."

"Five," I mutter.

"What did you say?" my father shouts.

"I heard it took five men to get Chaplain van Izeghem out of the hole."

"I don't give a damn if it took five men or ten men

to drag him up from the muck! It was your idea. It's always your idea. You stir those boys up. They'll never make knights at this rate! You turn them into clowns. You shouldn't be sawing through planks in shithouses, or putting dead rats in your governess's bed, nor should you set badgers free in the courtyard and send my hunting dogs after them so the whole castle, my castle, is in an uproar!"

"Yes, that I am sorry about, Father," I mutter sincerely. "Particularly when I think of poor Rufus."

"Poor Rufus, indeed!" the Count shouts. "He was my best hunting dog. A magnificent animal. A real killer. Rufus chased that badger up the chimney, and that bloody badger bit his nose to pieces. Rufus hardly dares to go outside now. He's even terrified of a robin! All he's good for now is to warm my feet. And this was an animal from the best breed of hunting dogs in Normandy. But today, daughter, you've gone too far."

"What were you doing in that mill, Father?" I retort. "The sails weren't moving much."

"You brat!" he shouts, marching toward me with his hand stretched out flat. I instinctively take a step backward, pulling my head back. He hesitates.

"You're a nail in my coffin, a boil on my—"

"Backside?"

His hand hits my cheek with such force that I'm hurled backward and fall to the floor. I taste sweet blood. I scramble up and turn to my father, my chin raised. Blood drips from my lips. I look him in the eyes as haughtily as I can manage, cursing the single tear I can't keep back.

"I forbid you to have anything to do with those boys," he shouts. "From now on, you will knit, embroider, and read the Bible. If I hear just once that you're behaving like a stupid boy or if you get up to anything that so much as smells like a prank, you're going into the convent of Ter Dullen until your wedding day!"

My throat contracts. The words "convent" and "wedding" feel like icy drops of water sliding down my back.

"Am I not making myself clear?"

I am silent.

"I am waiting for an answer," my father mutters in a controlled voice.

"You are making yourself very clear, Father."

"Lady Bouvaert is waiting for you in the corridor," my father concludes. "It's time you started wearing a corset."

"I don't want to wear a corset," I whisper. "I can't breathe in one."

"You'll be wearing a corset for the rest of your life," my father says. "You may as well get used to it."

He looks at me and nods. It is a signal for me to leave, but I don't move.

"Are you still here, daughter?" he shouts impatiently.

I turn and walk into the corridor. The whole castle smells of the September rain. Summer is over.

8

MY FATHER IS RIGHT. The years pass. England and France sign a peace treaty in Brétigny and I get used to wearing a corset. I have my first period. I become a woman. I become marriageable.

And as for my father, he becomes despondent. The hard, sinewy muscles that made him a feared fighter slowly waste away. His hair becomes gray and his face slack. The world has defeated him. He's away a lot. He often stays at the Gravensteen in Ghent to supervise the striking of coins bearing his image. He fritters away his days with expensive trips to London and Paris, because the future is England and the past is France. Flemish prosperity depends on England and the English wool that is woven into cloth in Flanders. That cloth is dyed, cut, and sewn into magnificent dresses, trousers, shirts, cloaks, tablecloths and bed linen, and even horse blankets. It is the best cloth in the world. It's sold all over Europe and even transported to the East, past the Great Wall, which cuts the world into two and where

China oranges grow. The cloth that makes Flanders rich is made by Flemish workmen, who have united in fifty-four powerful guilds. There are the tanners, the leather curriers, the fullers, the flax weavers, and many more. They each represent one step on the long road to the finished cloth and the wealth that flows from it. The guilds of Bruges are led by Slicher van Rijpergherste and those of Ghent by Frans Ackerman. They are the real masters of Flanders, for they will only pay taxes to the Count as long as he does what they want. Of course, he once forced them to their knees in battle, but they still have him in their power.

When my father is in Male, he often goes to Sluis to watch for the ships that bring him exotic animals. He has them transported to Ghent, to his zoological garden in the new Prinsenhof. But most of the animals do not survive their first winter here, because the winters are getting more severe and the summers ever shorter.

My father and I avoid each other and when we do meet, we hardly speak. At Christmas, I see my mother, which becomes more painful every time. Why doesn't God gather her up into Heaven? Why does he keep putting me to the test by showing me again and again the shadow that once was my dear mother?

❖ ❖ ❖

IN THE YEAR OF MY THIRTEENTH BIRTHDAY, the first snowfalls come in the second week of September. We don't understand it. Snow has never fallen so early. It certainly makes Chaplain Johannes van Izeghem very irritable.

People whisper that he whips himself every day as punishment for his own sins. And during early morning Mass, he can't stop talking about the evil that people commit and about the Day of Judgment, which he says is near. Everywhere, he sees signs of the approaching end of the world.

The young Lady Alaïs stands next to me, anxiously listening to the chaplain's passionate rant. He calls on us to repent before it is too late, because on the world's final day, the pure of heart will be called to the Lord while the others will scorch in the vaults of Hell. I tell Alaïs in a whisper that when the end of the world is here, I hope I won't be a virgin anymore. She giggles and I smirk. It's contagious and we struggle not to laugh out loud.

Suddenly, Chaplain van Izeghem stops talking. I turn my head to face him and see his wild eyes glaring at us.

"Wipe those smiles off your faces, young ladies!"

I instantly stop wanting to laugh. Blood rises to my face. Everyone is staring at me.

"You in particular should set an example," he shouts from his pulpit, spit flying everywhere.

"It's my fault, Chaplain van Izeghem," I stammer nervously. "I didn't mean…"

"You, women, are the Devil's plaything," he roars.

I look at him aghast. No one says anything. Everyone is staring at the floor. A clog scrapes along the tiles.

"Woman," the chaplain pontificates slowly, puffing out his narrow chest to get enough air for his words, "leads man into confusion. She is an insatiable beast.

She is a perpetual state of war, a daily devastation, a house filled with storms."

I dare not look at him. Lady Alaïs is about to burst into tears.

"You, Marguerite of Male, are the slippery slide into the abyss. Women like you impede the moral and material regeneration of the world. God is punishing us, and you are guilty, too."

I scrape up all my courage and take a step forward.

"I am the daughter of the Count of Flanders and I forbid you to speak to me like that."

"I am God's Church on Earth and your father has permitted me to reprimand you when I deem it necessary, woman."

My head is on fire. My knees buckle with embarrassment and my face glows with indignation.

"You speak about women with contempt," I finally retort. "But have you forgotten, Chaplain van Izeghem, that you yourself were born from a woman's belly and that you too have suckled a woman's breast?"

"Woman, the Bible teaches, was created from a floating rib of Man," van Izeghem growls. "She is no more than a useless appendage. And now, Lady Marguerite, I have heard enough obscenities from you in this house of God. I ask all of you to pray that the frivolity of the young Lady of Flanders may be forgiven."

As one, the people of Male kneel on the cold church floor, their eyes cast downward. I am the last to kneel, but I do not bend my head. I look at the Virgin Mary in the stained-glass window and see the sunlight illuminate her image. It's a sign from God, I realize, and I can almost feel the warmth of the delicate ray of light on my face. Now I know that God does love women and that the chaplain is not a man of God, but an ordinary mortal and a liar.

The Mass drags on and during Holy Communion, while Christ's body dissolves in my stomach, I beg Heaven and Mary for real love.

I open my eyes, get up from the cold stone floor, and see Willem standing there. He grins at me because I dared to defy the chaplain. And I grin back. Just like that time after our victory at the Battle of Rabauwenborg. No one grins quite like Willem. The dimple in his cheek, the light spot in his green eyes, and his short blond hair. He is almost a knight.

▣ ▣ ▣

A FEW DAYS LATER, when everyone is shivering under the first gusts of autumn, I seek out Willem in the stables. He's busy grooming my father's stallions. Apart from the horses, we are alone. I ask him to kiss me. Willem stops his brushing and looks at me with utter surprise, and I can see in his eyes that he's wondering if he has understood me correctly.

"I've never kissed anybody," I say. "And I think it's time I did. Let's say as a scientific experiment. I can write French, Flemish, and Latin, and I know all about arithmetic, geometry, and astrology, but I know nothing yet about kissology."

"Kissology," Willem repeats.

He looks at his horse brush, as if he isn't sure what he should do with it.

"But why me?"

"Well, if I think of Godfried, Hendrik, and you together, it occurs to me that you are the only one who has the manners not to break wind when I'm around. I think that's, let's say, knightly of you."

That, at least, produces a little smile on Willem's face.

"I'll have to think about it," he says eventually, then turns back to the horse.

"How long do you think that will take—the thinking?" I ask. "The end of the world is coming."

"Why are you always so impatient?" he asks.

"Why do you always talk so much, Willem?" I shout. "I ask you something and…and—"

That's as far as I get. Willem comes close to me and bends his head toward mine. He smells of horse, sweat, and sour milk. I have to stand on tiptoe to reach his lips and he holds me firmly by the waist (I can feel the horse brush on my behind) to keep me from falling over. It's a cautious kiss. We press our cold lips together and share the warmth of our breath. It lasts for a moment and then it's over. He looks at me, waiting for a reaction. It all went so quickly. I even forgot to shut my eyes.

"Well?" Willem asks.

"Hard to say."

"My beard wasn't too prickly?" he asks, rather forcefully.

"Do you mean that little bit of fluff on your chin?"

"You should talk! You want to kiss and you don't even have breasts yet."

"What have my breasts got to do with kissing?"

"Nothing, but…"

"Come on, then."

I stand on Willem's feet, stretch, and kiss him again. My teeth bump into his. Our lips curl around each other. I shut my eyes. Time stretches. Then our tongues touch. I push him away.

"What?"

"It was interesting, Willem. See you next time," I say, starting to walk to the door.

"Marguerite!" he calls after me.

I turn at the stable door.

"Shall we do this again?" he asks.

"I'll have to think about it." I smile, and then I'm gone.

▣ ▣ ▣

I LOVE THOSE FIRST DAYS OF WINTER, when the hours between sunrise and sunset are shortest and the days so gray they change seamlessly into night. When the winter night falls and it's pitch dark, the doors are bolted, the shutters are closed, and prayers are said for a safe night's rest. On the Marshland, you can see ghosts wandering among the pollard willows and every countryman who wants a safe night's rest hangs dogs' skulls on his shutters. Only in the castles, where we can afford candles, can the days be stretched a little.

By the light of a candle, I search out my stories. On the second floor of the new, west-facing tower in our castle is the small room of Saint Anne. It was she who taught the Virgin Mary to read, according to the Bible. In the room of Saint Anne, there are no fewer than seventeen books in a cupboard, which is kept locked and to which there are only three keys. I have one of them. Opening the cupboard is an almost solemn moment. Each book is wrapped in red silk to guard it from calamity and locked with an iron lock to protect it from strangers' eyes. The books have been written by hand and cost a fortune. Years ago, my mother gave me the seventeen keys to the books, and on these winter days, I wrap myself in a horsehair blanket and sit down to read.

The book's lock creaks as I open it and the parchment crackles. The pages are made of lambskin. The muddy ink, which has eaten deep into the parchment, is made from sour oak sap and colored black with ground insect shells. I shiver. With excitement, rather than cold. I drink in the graceful letters and the miniatures with their warm colors. I love the stories. About the wise wolf Izegrim who teaches an abandoned child how to survive in the wild forest. About the Amazons who burn off their right breasts so they can fire arrows more easily. About the knight Everard with his cloak of salamander hair that makes him invisible so he can take revenge on the knight who has stolen his wife. Or about the young Druid's servant Finn MacCool who has to roast the salmon of wisdom for his master, Finegas. Finn wants to make sure the salmon is cooked and pushes his finger into the pink flesh. He burns his finger, puts it into his mouth to relieve the pain, and so sucks up all the wisdom of the world.

Or about the sailor Hodde who follows the sirens' song all the way out to sea. When, after forty days on the northern sea, he finally manages to overtake the mermaids, they tear off their feminine skin and show their true, monstrous faces. They grind up Hodde's body with their marble teeth and drag him into the depths of the sea. Until this very day, his cries of terror resound through the night on the cold sea of the North.

My favorite story is that of the enchantress Hellawes, the loveliest of all women. No knight could resist her. But Hellawes shows not the slightest interest in the many nobles who court her. For seven years, the young woman has harbored an all-consuming love for Lancelot, the bravest of all knights. She hopes that Lord Lancelot will one day honor her with a visit and then she will seduce him with her magic arts. She asks the fairies to lure him to her.

One day, Lancelot and King Meliot of Brittany wage a fearsome battle with the giant Filborg, who is said to be invincible. Filborg is nearly seven feet tall and has yet to lose a fight, thanks to his sword, Govannon, which was forged by lizard-men using the poisonous spit of the gods. He wears armor made from the scales of a sea monster, so no sword in the world can pierce it. And there, on a beach strewn with rocks, with the surf roaring and the seagulls screeching, a great fight takes place. Filborg is stronger than Lancelot and Meliot. For hours, they manage to parry the mighty blows as Filborg tries to kill them. The giant never tires, and his blows become more and more powerful. But Lancelot lures Filborg close to a granite boulder and tricks him. Right in front of the boulder, he pretends to slip on the sea moss and lets himself fall backward against the rock. Filborg gathers all his strength for the final blow, but just as the sword comes down, Lancelot rolls away and Filborg's sword strikes the boulder with so much force that it gets stuck. The next moment, Lancelot knocks Filborg's helmet off and, with a mighty blow, splits his skull. The giant drops dead by his feet and his blood stains Lancelot's armor red.

But Meliot has been injured in the fight. A splinter of Filborg's poisonous sword is stuck in Meliot's thigh and is slowly sucking all life from his body. Meliot is dying, and Lancelot is desperate. The fairies whisper in Lancelot's ear that the king can be saved by the ravishingly beautiful enchantress Hellawes. She lives deep inside a magical forest, in a tower on a small island in a lake called the "fairies' mirror." In a small ivory casket, she keeps three dragon's teeth, which, when ground fine and dissolved in water, can bring a dying knight back to life.

The fairies, giggling among themselves, show Lancelot the way to the tower, which is forever shrouded in mists. The knight persuades a goblin in a small boat to row him across. The goblin warns Lancelot that the beautiful enchantress will seduce him and daze his senses so he will never want to leave the place again. On hearing this, Lancelot uses his dagger to make a cut in the palm of his hand, so that the constant stinging pain will stop him from giving in to any bewitchment. But once he enters the tower, he reels, for he is overwhelmed by the scent of burning sandalwood and salty sea. He has difficulty standing. The floors are covered in aromatic flowers that make him think of fields of corn ripening in the summer sun. Dried herbs hang from the rafters, and the long oaken table is loaded with fragrant fruits that remind him of the green apple orchard of his youth. But his hand burns with pain and Lancelot perseveres. Then Hellawes appears. The enchantress has swathed herself in gorgeous robes of gold brocade, which make her beauty blossom like a bouquet of wildflowers. She has splendid, curly hair, red as a sunset. Her eyes are like liquid gold, her lips are full, and her breasts are hidden like treasures under her gown, which is a vivid red on the inside and forest green on the outside. A leopard skin is draped around her middle. She is the most beautiful woman Lancelot has ever seen, but he must not betray his duty.

Hellawes prepares him a feast of eagle's meat with spices no mortal has ever tasted. She gives him warm love-wine to drink, pressed from grapes grown in a valley where no human has ever set foot. And Lancelot yields. They kiss. They kiss so passionately their lips bleed without them even noticing. Lancelot feels as if he has been engulfed by the green forests of Brittany, dripping with spring rain. But suddenly he becomes aware again of the pain in his hand and remembers his duty. He asks Hellawes if it is true that she has magical dragon's teeth that can bring the dying back to life. She nods and leads him into a room where a bed is spread with sheets of finest silk and the air is perfumed with mint and jasmine. She opens the casket that holds the dragon's teeth and shows him. Lancelot hesitates. He looks into Hellawes' golden eyes, but he can only see his dying king. The enchantress surrenders herself to her beloved knight and closes her eyes. Time stands still, the night is silent, and the angels laugh.

When Hellawes falls asleep, Lancelot steals the dragon's teeth. He swims across the lake, creeps past the sleeping goblin, and rides off on his horse with all speed. His head is spinning with the memory of the scents and tastes that had clouded his senses. Exhausted, he arrives at the stony beach where he grinds the dragon's teeth to a fine grit with the hilt of his dagger. He dissolves the grit in rainwater and gives the drink to the dying King of Brittany. King Meliot improves by the hour, and Lancelot whispers to himself that the enchantress Hellawes was only an illusion. An apparition that didn't really exist. A mirage in the magical forest. A false love whispered into his ears by the fairies. Only the dragon's teeth are real, he repeats to himself for hours. And so, with Meliot, he rides back to the tip of Brittany, past the River of the Specters, to his castle that guards the Forests of Joy.

Hellawes wakes up in a cold bed and realizes her love has been betrayed. As the memory of the enchantress fades from Lancelot's mind, Hellawes dies of sorrow. The fairies are so sad they mourn their beloved mistress for a hundred years.

For a long time, I stare at the lovely miniature of the enchantress with the golden eyes and the curly red hair. Hellawes may be the loveliest of all women, but true love escaped even her. She reminds me of my own mother, sitting in her convent room, abandoned by her Lord and her mind, in the little room with the trunk full of clothes, the bed, and the mural of the Holy Virgin Mary. Men are deceivers. They court one woman and are already thinking of betraying her. Like Lancelot. Like my father. But not Willem. Willem is true.

◫ ◫ ◫

THAT WINTER Willem sneaks through the castle to come and kiss me in the room of Saint Anne. If my governess, Constance Bouvaert, or one of the servants knocks on the door, Willem hides inside the seat of an old wooden bench. The bench is the favorite spot of the cats, who protect the books from mice who like nothing better than to gnaw holes in the old parchment. To make sure Constance doesn't open its lid and poke around in it, I sit on the bench with the Book of Hours on my lap, reciting the Latin prayers with an ardent devotion that must surely charm my twenty-six guardian angels. And after the interruption, I open the lid again and kiss Willem back to life. I wonder who invented kissing. There is nothing about it in the Bible. But then, as Father Zannekin has explained, the Bible is not complete. Some parts of it have been lost. Maybe Noah and his wife, who used to only rub noses, saw that girl and boy monkeys kiss each other on the lips. And that gave them ideas. Maybe Samson and Delilah invented the kiss in their shattering love. Or was it Solomon and Sheba who were the first to give each other scorching kisses? Or was it King David who committed the sin of the first kiss with Bathsheba? Who can tell? Tristan and Isolde, Abelard and Heloise, they may have been the greatest kissers of their time, but compared to us they were amateurs. For in all the history of mankind, no greater passion has existed than ours. Willem and I become masters of kissology. We look into each other's eyes as we press our lips together. And with each kiss, waves of warmth wash through me.

"Willem," I whisper in his ear, "when you become a knight…"

He stops kissing my throat and leans back against the wall. His face is downcast.

"I'm not going to be a knight," he says. "The lands my father left me don't make enough money. A knight has to keep squires, buy a suit of armor, keep horses. I will always be a squire."

"So suppose you're a squire and I have to marry some prince or duke, will you stay my squire? Will you do great deeds of courage for me?"

Willem smiles.

"I'll be your squire," he says, kissing me. "And write you letters (kiss) about my adventures (kiss) and my travels (kiss) and my grandest feats (tongue kiss)."

"And I will sew your letters into my loveliest dress right over my heart."

Willem looks up at me.

"Do you really love me that much?" he asks.

"More," I reply. He laughs, a triumphant look in his eyes.

I'm sure I love Willem. Every morning, I'm barely awake before I'm dying to kiss him. I cross the courtyard, wander into the chapel, or get something from the kitchens, hoping to catch a glimpse of him. And when, in the evening, he sneaks into the room full of books, I hurl myself at him and press my lips on his. I am addicted to our kisses. They never last long enough, and I hope the evening bell will never sound. Because that's when the dampers are put over the fires and Willem slips hurriedly through the dark passages of the castle to the dormitory where all the men sleep on wide beds. When he has gone, I lock away the books. Carrying a candle, I float through the passages. When I arrive at the women's quarters, Constance is already snoring. I slide into the bed next to her. The straw is old and the sheets feel damp, but I don't care. I hug myself and kiss the pillow as if it is his face. Troubadours, I dream, will sing about our love in seven thousand verses, and storytellers will describe it in their books. Our passion will be part of the history of our land.

It lasts precisely twenty-eight days.

When, on the evening of the twenty-eighth day, Willem enters Saint Anne's room, I know right away something's wrong. His eyes look empty. His fingers tremble. But I think I'm imagining things and kiss him. He keeps his lips pressed stiffly together. I look at him. My Willem, my young Lord of Sindewint, my squire and my master in the art of kissology.

"Marguerite," he says, his voice cold and hollow.

"Willem," I whisper, and I feel disaster crawling on my back like a cold slug.

"It isn't all that bad," he says.

"What do you mean?" I snort. I breathe in deeply to calm the sea of fear inside me. Why does he keep standing? Why doesn't he grasp my hand? Why doesn't he stroke my hair? Why don't his lips come closer?

"It couldn't last. You understand that, don't you?" he coughs, showing great interest in the straw on the floor that he's pushing apart with his feet, as if he's curious about the shape of the stone under it.

"What should I understand, Willem?" I hear myself ask, while a stabbing pain starts in my head.

"Well, your father, he…"

"What has my father been telling you?"

"He says he wants to make me a knight. He wants to give me armor and a horse. He's lending me a dozen craftsmen to restore my father's castle at Ruddervoorde. He wants to knight me before this week is out."

I stare at him.

"You've accepted?" My voice cracks.

"You know how expensive it is to become a knight. A suit of armor costs a small fortune, a warhorse even more. My father is dead, and I own nothing. Only a noble title."

"My father must have found out about our meetings. He wants to buy you. He—"

"Marguerite," Willem interrupts. "This is my chance to become a knight."

He must have been practicing his words all day. It sounds like he's learnt them by heart. I don't know how hard to bite my lips to prevent the tears and the sniveling. I've been Willem's friend for as long as I can remember. We've kissed for hours at a time. I've hidden him in the bench the cats sit on. I've sewn a lock of my hair into his velvet tunic. I've seen Heaven and Earth in his eyes, and his fingers have been entwined with mine for so long there was no feeling left in them. And now, Willem stands before me looking at the floor and telling me he wants to end our love for the sake of a few bits of iron and a war nag.

"When are you leaving?" I ask, no longer able to hide my anger. Willem is startled by the change in my voice.

"Next week probably, as soon as the weather improves a bit."

"Go then," I say, turning away.

"Marguerite, it couldn't be otherwise. You know that. Your father would never have allowed you and me."

"Of course I know that. I'll marry the man my father chooses for me. But like every noblewoman, I want a knight who travels all over the world performing great deeds for love of me, and who writes me letters with a passion so intense it will make my twenty-six angels weep. So I know that whatever happens there is a knight who loves me." I look at him. Willem is that knight. He has no choice. My head thunders with it: he loves me, but he has no choice. And now there should be a farewell kiss. The kiss that surpasses all previous kisses. A kiss for the history books. I go to him, grasp his clammy hand, and close my eyes.

"Actually, I've been wanting to break it off before now," Willem ends the silence. "It couldn't go on. You know, my friends are joking about it. You have to see it like that, Margriet. We've had fun, but it's over. It's time to stop. I was worried about telling you. I was afraid I might break your heart."

I keep looking at the wall so he won't see my lip, which I've bitten to a pulp. I try to breathe, to get control over my voice. "I'm really sorry if I've hurt you," Willem says softly, and I find my voice.

"Ah well, it's not that bad," I hear myself say. "I've been wanting to break it off myself."

"Oh." Willem sounds worried.

"Yes," I reply, pleased to have found an icy calm in

my voice. "You kiss like a beginner and you smell of sour milk. I don't like sour milk."

Willem looks at me, wide-eyed.

"Well, I suppose I'd better go, then," he mumbles.

"Yes, do. I won't miss you."

He coughs, turns to the door.

"But, Margriet—"

"Lady Marguerite to you," I rasp, turning to him so he sees my red, tear-stained face. He stares at me with his beautiful green eyes and his gorgeous boy's face of which I have kissed every square inch.

He bows and nods.

And so Willem, Knight of Sindewint, disappears from my life.

9

I NO LONGER GO INTO SAINT ANNE'S ROOM. I avoid the kitchens, where the boys are always laughing. I throw my whalebone sword into the fire. I even neglect my stallion, Palframand, who's kicking the wood of his stall to splinters because no one rides him. Constance asks me what's wrong, and I tell her to leave me in peace. Lady Alaïs is the only one I can confide in. But not completely. I'm jealous of her. She's engaged to the Knight of Gavere, and she's so beautiful that every man in the castle looks at her just a little too long when she wanders past. She reminds me of my unruly reddish hair, my nose that's far too big, my thin lips, and my breasts that are no larger than two peas on a board.

In November, when the cold west winds rip the last of the leaves from the trees, I sit by the fire with the ladies-in-waiting. We are each embroidering a scene from the story of the dreary Knight Parsifal. That is what I call him. The other women talk about the *noble* Knight Parsifal. I hear this story so often that winter that just hearing the name Parsifal is enough to make me want to puke.

Time and again, I must listen to the story of how the noble Knight Parsifal bounds around half the world in search of the King of the Holy Grail. When he finds the king's castle in the forests of Brittany, it turns out that the good man is in bed with a persistent sweating fever. He has been lying there for years, so the stench in the room is overpowering, but our Parsifal, being a well-brought-up nobleman, says nothing about it. Nor does he ask what is making the king ill. After all, a knight never asks unnecessary questions. Parsifal just stands by the poor old king's bedside for most of a day, rooted to the ground, and because he doesn't say anything, the king sends him away. Then Parsifal wanders around half the world once more, wondering all the time what he's done wrong. He certainly hasn't said anything wrong.

After five years or so, a little bell finally starts ringing inside Parsifal's hollow skull. He digs his spurs into his nag, manages to waste another few years traveling from Paris to Brittany via the Caucasus, and arrives, a little worse for wear, back at the king's castle. The poor man is still deathly ill, and Parsifal rushes to the king's room. Pinching his nose against the unbearable stench, Parsifal asks the king what is making him ill. The knight-errant has barely spoken the words when, ups-a-daisy, the king leaps off his sickbed. Cured.

There you are: the story of His Serene Dreariness, the Knight Parsifal. For months we embroider that story, and I swear each time I hear it I prick my finger with the needle. And on one of those dark December days, as I'm working on the noble Parsifal's dreary countenance, there's a knock on our door. It's Ferre, the blacksmith. He's still the same mountain of flesh and muscle, but his shoulders have become round and slumped. He has aged. He takes off his leather cap and greets all the ladies with a bow. We nod. A visit like that, so early in the evening, is unusual.

"*Ma Dame* Marguerite," he begins shyly, scrunching up his cap nervously. I see the lead badge of Saint Eloy, patron saint of blacksmiths, stuck on the cap. I offer him a seat. He sits on the edge of the chair, throwing nervous glances at the ladies, who are busy embroidering. He wrings out his cap as if it's a wet cloth.

"As you may know, your father no longer uses my services," he whispers. "I am going to live in Bruges, in the Proveniershof. I will get an annual payment for my years of service." I nod. At the Proveniershof, there are houses for elderly servants who receive a yearly allowance for their lifelong, faithful service. No man could deserve it more than Ferre.

"I'm sorry to see you leaving, Ferre," I say sincerely. "No one swears as beautifully as you do."

He smiles and Constance coughs, because I have once again said something unbecoming.

"You came to me once, *Ma Dame,* and I promised to make you a sword. You said you would remind me of that promise…"

"But of course I have forgotten," I reply. "And anyway, it was just a little girl's joke. I'm a woman now."

He looks at me as if I've hurt him.

"Almost," I add under my breath.

Ferre smiles and scratches his white hair. Then he undoes the cord around his cloak and puts it down on the chair. He stands up. A bundle is tied onto his back. He takes it off and, sitting down again, sets it on his knees. He undoes the three cords that hold the bundle together. The ladies-in-waiting whisper among themselves. They're dying of curiosity. They can barely stop themselves getting up and eagerly looking over my shoulder. I grin. Now Ferre puts aside the cloths covering the bundle. He does it slowly, almost solemnly. Gradually, the sword he has made me is revealed. It's not a knight's sword. It's not heavy and large and hard. It's a narrow sword. Light. A sword a woman can handle.

"It's a thrusting sword," Ferre explains, "which I've designed after an Italian model. This kind of sword is fashionable in Venice and Genoa. The Italians call it a *rapier.*"

Strips of leather have been wound around the hilt of the sword, and the pommel has been forged in the shape of a marguerite daisy. All the ladies-in-waiting have stood up to see the sword, but they don't dare come closer. For a moment, they've forgotten Parsifal and the King of the Grail.

"You must give the sword a name," whispers Ferre.

"I shall call it Ferre," I smile, and he blushes all

over. "But I thought you told me once that swords and women do not belong together."

"The best thing for a sword is to rest in its scabbard and never be used," Ferre says wisely.

I smile and nod gratefully.

A moment later, he puts on his cap, gives me a final greeting, and leaves the room.

The ladies-in-waiting approach to inspect the sword. I slide my hand along the steel. It's strong, but compared to a knight's sword, it's fragile. I clamp my fingers around the hilt. The sword weighs hardly more than a pound. I jump up and raise the sword high. The ladies-in-waiting recoil. Someone drops a piece of embroidery. I slowly lower the sword. I feel the pressure in my arm, but I can hold the sword horizontally almost without trembling. For the first time since Willem left, I smile. One thing I know for certain: this sword will not rest in its scabbard.

I seek out Armorer van Vere. He is pleased to see me.

"I heard you exchanged my whalebone for something harder," he says.

"I want to take lessons from you again."

Jan van Vere sighs.

"I know someone who can teach you better than I," he says. "There's a new school of swordsmanship in Bruges and the Count sends the squires to have lessons there twice a week."

"A school of swordsmanship," I say, my eyes sparkling. "Can I go with the squires?"

"Well, that depends," van Vere replies. "Even if the fencing master were to allow it, you couldn't practice with the squires. The fellows would complain to the Count. But it can't do any harm to meet the fencing master. Who knows what sort of agreement you can reach with him?"

I smile.

"But," warns van Vere, "the fencing master is not exactly a cheerful character. He's very choosy about who he accepts as a student. He's even sent some of the squires back. So don't get your hopes too high."

"I understand," I say. But I already feel the leather of the hilt in my palm. I already see the tip of my sword sliding through the air, and I already hear the clatter of steel on steel.

◼ ◼ ◼

ON LOST MONDAY, the first Monday after the feast of the Epiphany, Jan van Vere takes me to meet the fencing master. All the cloth workers have the day off and the streets of Bruges are unusually quiet at this early hour. It snowed during the night and everything looks pure and white. Plumes of smoke rise from the chimneys and long icicles hang from the gutters. The winter air tingles in my lungs and makes me impatient. The sun shines from a cold, blue sky, and the snow crunches under our carriage.

The school of swordsmanship is located behind the Bruges Exchange. There, the Italian trading houses of Genoa and Florence flank the stately mansion of the powerful banking family Van der Beurze. Bruges is being flooded with Italians who are making their fortunes in the cloth trade and in banking. Hardened Italian soldiers protect the ships against robbers and pirates. One of those soldiers, Andrea Tagliaferro from Genoa, set up the school in Bruges to instruct knights and squires in sword fighting.

Godfried and Hendrik are in the carriage with us. Hendrik is really irritated by my presence, and he tells van Vere that he has no intention of practicing in the fencing school if I'm going to be there. Van Vere tells him to mind his manners. He grunts. Godfried, as usual, doesn't say much.

The carriage takes us past the covered shipping hall, where there's a terrible smell. The city's garbage is piled in great heaps on the wharf, and from there, the workers dump it into barges with pitchforks and shovels. Jan van Vere urges the coachman to hurry past.

Soon after, we stop behind the Exchange, near what used to be the infirmary of the Black Sisters. Thirteen years ago, the year I was born, the plague wiped out every one of the Black Sisters, who had cared for its victims, and the Italian community bought the infirmary from the impoverished order. A very young groom admits us to the former hospital. The Italians originally turned it into a warehouse for spices, and you can still see the stains left on the slightly sloping wooden floor by the oil vats.

The empty hall echoes like a church. Between the

four arched windows hang colorful tapestries showing hunting scenes. Those tapestries are there to dampen the clattering and cursing of the fencing lessons. Against the west wall stands a rack that is a veritable ironmonger's shop, with everything from the smallest daggers to the largest battle swords.

Godfried and Hendrik join four other young squires. An elderly knight, whom I immediately recognize as Knight Craenhals van Wijnendale, walks toward the middle of the hall. By his side is a tiny man, hardly taller than I am. "That is the fencing master Andrea Tagliaferro," Jan van Vere whispers, quite unnecessarily.

The two opponents wear thickly padded leather tunics to protect them from sword thrusts. Knight Craenhals carries his sword on his back, at the level of his kidneys, like most of the older knights. He pulls it from its scabbard and raises the hilt in front of his nose. The fencing master, whose scabbard hangs by his side, goes through the same movements. Craenhals towers over his opponent. They both swing their swords sideways, and then bring them together until the sword tips touch. The fight has begun.

Craenhals has a one-and-a-half-size sword and a small shield. The fencing master has a rapier and a dagger. The weapons aren't sheathed in leather. It's strange, seeing a fight with such unequal, naked weapons. The Italian's fighting style is very unusual, completely different from what Jan van Vere teaches his pupils at the castle.

Craenhals forces his opponent back with great

sideways swings. The fencing master dances around the knight. The weapons cross only very rarely. They're feeling each other out.

The tall man tries to exploit his strength and wide reach, but his small opponent is too quick for him. The fencing master repeatedly jumps back, only to leap far forward, pointing his sword straight in front of him. Craenhals barely manages to evade those attacks. I am surprised, because I know Craenhals is a highly trained man-at-arms. He fights with fast, powerful swings, but he never really endangers his opponent. Finally, Craenhals, sweating and annoyed, goes all out. He drives the fencing master into a corner with mighty blows, but the one time he misjudges his swing slightly, the fencing master easily parries the great sword and has his dagger pointing at Craenhals's navel.

The little man smiles into his defeated opponent's flushed face and lisps, "Once upon a time, your mother gave you life through this little hollow, Knight Craenhals. One prick, and it would flow out again."

At first, Craenhals looks angry, but then he realizes that this is only an exercise and that a knight should always acknowledge a superior.

"In my mother's name, I gladly surrender," he says. "Her name was Bathilde and she would be grateful to you. I'm glad we're allies and not enemies."

Craenhals takes a step back and bows to the master. Tagliaferro acknowledges the bow.

"Our way of fighting is history," Craenhals sighs,

packing away his sword. "The English bowmen, the cannon from Mechelen, and the crossbows from your own city of Genoa make warfare a different thing. I don't know how we knights fit into all this."

The fencing master says nothing. Knight Craenhals stumbles away tiredly.

The squires change clothes silently, putting on hose under short tunics. They put on heavy chain-mail coats, made of metal rings braided together. The coats reach just above the knees and protect them against the flashing steel. They take one-and-half-size swords from the racks and start practicing with them.

The fencing master approaches Jan van Vere, and I am able to get a good look at him. He's a small, lean fellow with light eyes, a frowning forehead, and a long, black goatee, its point low under his chin. And suddenly I recognize him. He is the Genoese who nearly cut off Godfried's ears. He looks at me with contempt, but doesn't recognize me. He addresses van Vere.

"What's this child-woman doing in my hall?" he snarls with a thick Italian accent.

The boys laugh out loud. The fencing master turns on them and his glance is enough to silence them instantly. I see Hendrik clam up. And I smile. Jan van Vere hoists himself up and is about to introduce me, but I don't give him a chance.

"The child-woman has come to see if you give her squires proper lessons and if their Lord, my father's money is well spent on you."

"Your father?"

"The Count of Flanders."

The fencing master looks at me silently. If he recognizes me, he doesn't let on. In just seven steps—his feet seem to float over the boards—he stands before me. I look into his cold eyes. He nods briefly. He ought to bow, but he's proud, so he just nods.

"*Contessina,*" he says, not very respectfully. It's the first time I've been called "little countess." I look angry, but that doesn't scare him.

"For a game of fives or tennis, you need my brother Raffaello, in the school of the Friars Minor. You'll be able to practice there as much as you like. Here, in this school, your presence is not conducive to the boys' concentration. All sorts of things can go wrong with a woman nearby."

"You're afraid of women, Signor Tagliaferro?" I ask him viciously, and he grunts with repressed anger.

"I am not afraid of anyone, *Contessina,* except God the Father," he says calmly, kissing the golden crucifix around his throat.

"So you can give me lessons?" I whisper so only he can hear.

The color drains from his face. Jan van Vere coughs. The boys grunt impatiently. They let their swords scrape together and the sound irritates the fencing master. He looks at Jan van Vere.

"She has learnt the basics from me," van Vere says.

"What do you mean, *Signor* van Vere," he replies.

"You have taught her stick fencing for a few weeks?"

"A few years," he corrects.

The fencing master sighs and looks me in the eyes. He's barely taller than me. His voice is softer now.

"*Contessina,*" he whispers. "I have to turn these children into knights. They must become strong and proud. And they'll carry swords you would have trouble lifting. If you can't lift them, you're a danger in this hall. The worst thing that can happen to a student is to have to practice against someone who has not had instruction."

"I've had instruction. I can prove it to you."

"Even if I taught you, it would not benefit you. What do you hope to achieve with it?"

"I'll pay you, Master Tagliaferro. I'll give you three times the amount my father pays you for each of the squires."

He looks at me, his blue eyes a sea of contempt. I should lower my eyes, but I don't.

"Do you think, *Contessina,* that you can buy me with money? I am Andrea Tagliaferro, Knight of Genoa, a cavalier of the pearl of Liguria, and what you need is a good beating from your father."

"My blacksmith has given me a rapier," I keep trying. "You could teach me the new style."

"A rapier? You can use that to open your love letters."

"I don't receive any love letters," I reply fiercely. "My father sees to that. All I'm allowed to do is pray, embroider, study Latin, observe the stars, and taste my personal cook's dishes. I'm dying of boredom."

The boys giggle. One of them drops his sword. It clatters on the floor. Master Tagliaferro turns and is about to shout something at the boys, but controls himself.

"*Contessina,* you will have to solve your own problems," he says, raising his voice. "Every afternoon I have to teach these impatient young cocks how to most efficiently relieve their opponents of their earthly lives without cutting off their own fingers. A woman nearby is the last thing I need. I'm asking you to leave."

I hear Hendrik laugh. The fencing master turns.

"Squire Hendrik," he calls. "You can start by polishing all the one-and-a-half swords with your own spit. And you can be pleased I'm not making you practice wearing a sixty-pound lead vest!"

Hendrik groans. I hear the shuffling of his leather slippers. The fencing master accompanies me to the door. Van Vere starts to follow, but Tagliaferro gestures to him to stay where he is.

Andrea Tagliaferro walks through the passageway to the gate. He slides aside the bolts.

"I do not greet you, Master Tagliaferro," I say without looking at him.

"Tomorrow morning," he replies coolly. "At dawn. You'll get one single lesson from me. Without witnesses. After that lesson, I will consider whether I'll give you a second one. And only after the second lesson do I decide if I allow you a third. And so on. If there is even the smallest thing that displeases me about you, I stop. And you'll pay me per lesson. Five times what you pay for the squires."

"I thought you weren't for sale."

"I am not. You have earned your first lesson. But not yet your second. I do not greet you, *Contessina*."

The gate falls shut. I see the snow whirling around me. I hear the fencing master slide the bolts on the inside.

I smile.

For I shall learn fencing.

10

THE **NEXT DAY**, the feast of Saint Gudula, Jan van Vere takes me back to Bruges. I've hardly slept, I'm so worried about my first fencing lesson. The sun is hiding behind a gray sky. Our carriage is the first one admitted into the city. We drive to the hall of the Black Sisters. Jan van Vere lets me out and drives the carriage away.

Shivering with cold, I'm standing alone in the deserted street outside the fencing school. I raise the iron knocker and it thuds on the school's gate. Some fish sellers come past and give me a strange look. It is unusual for a lady in a long black cloak to venture into the streets on her own. One of them slows down. He looks at me and seems to wonder whether to bother me or not. My fingers clasp the hilt of the sword I keep hidden under my cloak. Then I hear noises inside. The fish seller looks away and moves on. A moment later, Andrea Tagliaferro pulls open the gate. He greets me with a brief nod, and I hurry inside. He's wearing a black tunic and precedes me into the fencing hall. I hang my cloak over a chair. It's biting cold in the hall.

"You can get changed in the side room," he tells me, his breath visible in the cold air.

"I'm already dressed," I reply. He inspects me. I'm not wearing a corset, but a padded soldiers' tunic, which is too big for me. Because it hangs loosely around my body, I can move freely. I undo the clasps on my clogs and put on leather slippers. The leather squeaks on the wooden floor. The slippers don't slide. The fencing master hands me a box of talcum powder, which I sprinkle over my hands to prevent sweating. I take the rapier in my right hand.

"*Contessina,*" he begins. "Have you always practiced with your right hand?"

"Of course," I reply.

"Of course, *Maestro,*" he corrects me coolly.

"*Maestro,*" I repeat nervously.

"So you know which is your master eye?"

"My master eye?" I am confused.

"Everyone has a master eye, *Contessina,*" he replies. "Do you see that large battle sword hanging on the back wall? It was my father's sword. He was a captain of mercenaries and made his name in the fight against the Venetians. He was killed at sea by a cannon fired from the cursed lagoon of Venice. Cowardly Venetians. *Veneziani di merda!*"

For a moment it looks as if the *Maestro* is about to spit on the floor, but he regains control of himself.

"*Contessina,* please point one of your index fingers at that noble weapon, and then close your eyes one at a time. Which eye stays focused on the sword? And which eye seems to move sideways?"

I point my left index finger at the enormous sword and close my eyes one by one, looking at the mighty weapon. When my left eye is open, my finger stays fixed on the sword. When I open my right eye, my finger jumps to the left.

"My finger moves when I close my left eye."

"Then your left eye is your master eye, *Contessina,* and therefore you are left-handed."

"But I'm right-handed," I protest.

"One more lie and you can leave, *Contessina,*" he shouts severely.

I stare silently at the sloping timber floor, ashamed of my left-handedness.

"I was once left-handed, *Maestro,*" I admit. "But my father made me see my error. He forced me to become right-handed. So now I am right-handed."

"You are the way God has made you, and that means left-handed, *per la Madonna,*" Tagliaferro curses. "And there is nothing to be done about it."

"So you refuse to teach me because I'm left-handed," I say, holding my head up high. We look straight into each other's eyes. He strokes his beard.

"In sword fighting, being left-handed is an advantage," he says.

"An advantage?" This is a surprise. "But everyone is

set against it. According to the Church, it's even a sign of the Devil and—"

"Yes," he interrupts me. "But as a left-handed swordfighter, you always put your opponent on the wrong foot. Of course, you have learnt to fight right-handed and I will teach you right-handed fighting. But, assuming you make the fifty lessons, I will teach you to use both arms. You must always use the opposite of your opponent to defeat him."

He comes and stands next to me with his rapier. He indicates that I should follow his slow movements. He bends his right knee and puts all his weight on it, stretching his left leg behind him. I imitate his movement. Then he does the same with his left knee. I try to follow as best I can. The movement is slowly warming me.

"Shall I tell you something?" Andrea Tagliaferro says suddenly. He no longer seems surly and moody.

"Before he joined the Friars Minor here in Bruges, my brother Raffaello traveled a lot in the East. There, everything is reversed. The dragon is a good-natured animal, the color of mourning is white, and writing goes from bottom to top and from right to left. The left side is considered the divine side. At the court of the Emperor of Cathay, in the land beyond the Great Wall of the Mongolians, poets must paint their poems on rice paper with their left hand."

"That's all very interesting, *Maestro*," I remark impatiently. "But what good is it to me in a fight?"

Tagliaferro quite unexpectedly turns toward me and

the tip of his sword hovers in the air, a mere thumb's breadth from my forehead. Frightened, I drop my sword. It clatters onto the wooden floor.

"Here," Tagliaferro points with his sword, "between your eyes, is where you are most vulnerable. Half a thumb's length of steel in this spot, and you are freed of all earthly concerns. But this is also the spot where a fight is decided. It is not force that is most important in a fight; it is cunning."

He pulls back his sword. I pick up mine.

"Next time you drop your sword, you'll polish all the weapons. You'll get the same punishment as the young cocks from your castle."

I nod.

"You're holding your sword like a shepherd who's about to hit his sheep on the bum," Tagliaferro continues. "That doesn't matter much if you're fighting with a broadsword, and that's what the knights want me to teach their sons: slash, parry, and hack. But with a rapier, you have to fight a different way. You have to lay the hilt along your wrist."

He stands behind me and puts my fingers, one by one, over the hilt. The pommel of the rapier's hilt now lies on my wrist. The sword seems heavier, and I have more trouble balancing it. I feel the fencing master's breath on my neck. Tagliaferro is now practically stuck to me. His arm is around my waist. I wonder if it is proper for a man to rub so closely against me.

"A rapier is not a weapon to batter armor with."

His voice is like a blast of wind in my ear. "It is fragile. It could even break."

I nod nervously. I feel his right knee pressing into mine and his right hand clasped around mine. He carefully pulls my sword arm back and then pushes it forward, while he presses his knee into mine so that we both bounce onto our right knee. The tip of the sword splits the air of its own accord. I nearly fall forward, but with his arm around my waist Tagliaferro stops me. He pulls me up straight and takes a step sideways.

"A rapier is made for thrusting, not for hacking," he concludes. "Now you can put your sword away."

For the rest of the first lesson, I'm not allowed to use my rapier. I have to step in strange ways and constantly bend at the knees. I have to move sideways along a chalk line. It's absurd. Reluctantly, I pay him his five pieces of silver, feeling swindled. I put on my cloak. At the gate, we look at each other.

"What have you learnt, *Contessina*?" he asks, and I flush. I realize I'm being tested, but somehow I don't care anymore. I'm not at all sure I want more lessons like this. I look at him, and all I see is a little Italian man with a goatee.

"Well," he snarls. "You're not usually so quiet."

"For years, Master van Vere has taught me fencing with a whalebone," I say proudly. "He said I was becoming good at it, really good, nearly as good as the squires. Now I come here, and you make me do the exact opposite of what I've always been taught. I don't understand."

He looks at me with a grin.

"You have earned your second lesson," is all he says before shutting the door.

Walking through snow-covered Bruges, I slowly start to feel happy. I look at the houses, their shutters closed tight against the cold. Gilded sunflowers have been painted on the outsides to make us think of spring. I watch the warmly wrapped people, their noses red and dripping, and the children running through the streets with their sleds. I watch the fishermen cutting holes in the thick ice of the canals and a coachman covering his sweating horses with blankets. I remember how I walked through Bruges with my mother. In the middle of the street, I bend my right knee and take a few rapid steps to the left and the right along an imaginary chalk line. Two children look on in amazement from under their thick woolly caps. I smile and can barely stop myself running to the tavern where Jan van Vere is waiting for me.

"And what have you learned today?" he asks me a moment later, stirring what's left of his spiced wine.

"That it's possible to write from bottom to top and from right to left," I reply.

A conspiratorial smile appears on his freckled face.

◻ ◻ ◻

FOR THE REST OF THAT DAY, I'm floating. I feel ready to tackle the whole world. I hang around near the fires in the kitchen where Aelbrecht has been ordered by my father to prepare a *blamensier*: chicken breast cooked in almond milk and rice flour, flavored with sugar, saffron, and, the greatest delicacy of all, crushed violets. It's my favorite dish and I wonder why my father has ordered it. I go to the women's quarters, where we're putting the final touches to the epic of Knight Parsifal and the Grail king. I've only just sat down when Constance comes in carrying a long dress, which she hands me with a flourish. It's a gift: made of blue silk, adorned with deep purple sapphires from the East that give off a white glow. The neckline and sleeves are lined with fox fur. It's a gorgeous dress.

"It's your father's wish that you wear this dress tonight," Constance tells me. Lady Alaïs and the other women gape at the dress, filled with jealousy. *For once, I think, I will look more beautiful than Alaïs.* I don't understand why my father is giving me this dress. Normally, I'm given new dresses twice a year. But this is special. I put on my corset and the dress over it. Constance fastens the laces at the back. It looks wonderful on me. I lift the hem as I parade around the room. The dress rustles delightfully. Then the bell sounds for the evening meal.

I descend the stairs on Constance's arm. We enter the Great Hall and stop, for a moment flabbergasted. There are so many guests: knights, noblemen, and guild masters. The kitchen boys run busily back and forth with jugs of wine. It's as if every important person in Flanders has been invited here tonight, and an uncomfortable feeling creeps up on me. Two kitchen boys roll in a small table on wheels, carrying large silver bowls with the steaming *blamensier*. Squire Godfried puts a bowl down on the table in front of me. I smile at him. As usual, I'm seated to my father's left.

My father rises and announces that his daughter is "ready for marriage." The knights, ladies, and other guests push their benches back and stand up, raising their goblets of wine. I stay seated and feel the life draining from my body. I watch my father, afraid of what he's going to say. He looks at me, grinning. I look away from him, at the guests.

One of them, Guild Master Slicher van Rijpergherste from Bruges, smiles broadly. He's the most prominent citizen of Bruges, who, among other things, runs a brothel by the Minnewater, where the ships are turned around and where my father has a lot of debts. Next to him sits Guild Master Frans Ackerman from Ghent, who calls the tune in the largest city of Flanders. Normally, the two leaders would drink each other's blood: their cities have been rivals for centuries. But tonight they sit together like old friends. My father may be the Count, but in reality they are the leaders of Flanders. It's only thanks to them that he's able to pay off his many bank debts, the result of his luxurious though unsatisfying way of life. Their presence tells me what my father has decided about my future.

"We drink to your daughter's beauty, My Lord Count," fawns Slicher van Rijpergherste. "The Lady

Marguerite will be as mature and beautiful as a bouquet of summer flowers."

He smiles. I merely nod and direct a haughty look at his son Roderik, who is sitting next to him. I remember once knocking out one of his teeth. I have indeed grown more mature. The baby fat has gone from my cheeks and my figure has become curvier. But I'm nowhere near as beautiful as my mother. I still have big feet, long fingers, bony shoulders, small breasts, and my father's foxy head. Sometime that autumn, Constance let it slip that I look more and more like my father. I called her a Provençal mountain goat, and it was weeks before we spoke to each other again.

"Your daughter's hand is no doubt much sought after among the great of this world," Frans Ackerman suggests, pouring himself another goblet of wine.

"The princes of England and France want to marry her," my father agrees, "so they can acquire my title and rule over Flanders after my death."

"Surely you are no longer wavering between your loyalty to France and your duty to England," Ackerman says teasingly. There's an undertone of mockery in his voice.

A momentary silence falls over the hall. Knight Craenhals rises and glares indignantly at the leader from Ghent. The Count, with a gesture, makes it clear to Craenhals that he should let the challenge pass. Ackerman certainly has nerve daring to say those words in a hall full of knights who fought in the war against England.

I've heard that, in a letter from his prison in London, the King of France has begged my father to marry me to his nephew Philip of Rouvres. The King of England has pushed his son Edmund of Langley. Both Philip and Edmund are my distant cousins, fourth or fifth, which is barely permitted by the Pope. If I marry an English prince, Flanders will become English after my father's death. If I marry a French duke, everything stays as it is, and that is not what Slicher van Rijpergherste and Frans Ackerman want. They are prepared to go to any length to prevent it.

"I have thought carefully about my daughter's marriage," the Count says, picking at his pointy beard. "What's more, I've come to a decision."

Everyone is watching my father. Everyone is holding their breath. But I know what he's about to say.

"She will marry Edmund of Langley, Duke of Cambridge, Prince of England, and youngest son of King Edward the third. The marriage will be celebrated this summer."

The hall is suddenly as silent as a tomb. Only the torches hiss.

11

THE WAR HAS BEEN DISASTROUS for France. The English won battle after battle. First at Sluis, then at Crécy, where my grandfather fell, and finally at Poitiers, from where my father came back a broken man. The English king is allied with Ghent and Bruges, because the wool that keeps the Flemish spinning wheels turning comes from the hundreds of thousands of sheep in England. They graze on the extensive meadows belonging to the Benedictine monasteries. The Flemish guild masters of Bruges and Ghent would sell their souls for a treaty with England. When my grandfather died, fifteen years ago, such a treaty seemed within reach. This is what happened.

My father was just seventeen when his father fell, killed by English arrows. My father became the Count of Flanders. Then Slicher van Rijpergherste and Frans Ackerman came to Male and informed my father that the guilds of Bruges and Ghent had decided that he was to marry Isabella, the daughter of the King of England.

My father refused. He said he had been brought up among the noblemen of France. He said he would never marry the daughter of the man who was responsible for his father's death. Not even in exchange for half of England. So the Flemish made him a prisoner in his own castle. They refused to set him free until he agreed to the guild masters' demand that he marry the daughter of the English king. He could go wherever he wanted, but was always followed by five men-at-arms in white hooded cloaks. These White Guards never let him out of their sight. Even when he had to relieve himself, they stood around the shithouse. All this drove my father mad and after five months of such imprisonment, he at last promised to do what they wanted. The guilds were delighted and sent couriers to England with marriage agreements full of wax seals, lead seals, and colored ribbons. Isabella of England prepared for the wedding. A ship was equipped for the triumphal crossing and the glad news buzzed all over Europe. The guild masters relaxed their attention. But during a hunting party in the forest of Ichtegem, my father dug his spurs into his horse and rode without stopping to Paris. The French king was delighted and immediately arranged a marriage with the Duke of Brabant's daughter. My father met my mother for the first time in Paris on the day of their wedding. She was a real beauty. Father thought God had chosen him because of his courage. He thought he would love his wife. He thought she would give him proud sons. He got everything wrong. A year later, I arrived in the world.

This time, the guild masters have no intention of letting the Count make fools of them. Particularly not Frans Ackerman, who has come to Male with a dozen bodyguards in white hooded cloaks. Ackerman is a handsome man in a tall red hat, a blue gown with gold embroidery, and shoes with curled-up toes. Like his little boy Roderik, Slicher van Rijpergherste has a short, thick nose and fat red cheeks. He carries on as if he's the most honest and the most unfortunate man in the world, but in reality he would marry his mother to the Devil if he could make money out of it. Frans Ackerman and Slicher van Rijpergherste beam when they hear my father say the name Edmund. They raise their goblets to my father and cheer. They drink to my health and my father's. Only a few of the noblemen raise their goblets. Some knights look as if they've been struck down by God's hand. I see Knight Craenhals gaping at my father. Jan van Vere seems too amazed to stand. I can picture how he looked that evening when he told all the people in the castle the story of Poitiers. How the English arrows blacked out the sky and how five hundred knights collapsed one after the other... How he saved my father from death and my father returned to Flanders dying of shame, never to be the man he had been... And now I was to marry England...

"Daughter, I'm more than proud of your coming marriage," my father grins. "You have my permission to show your joy." I stare straight in front of me, at the white flesh of the cooked chicken on my plate. I breathe deeply to stop myself being sick.

"Come on," my father prods me.

I raise my eyes and see everyone watching me. I see Slicher van Rijpergherste's fat face smiling so broadly it looks as if his chubby cheeks are about to split. I see Roderik staring at me, his face shining triumphantly, obviously having waited five years for this moment of revenge. I see Frans Ackerman sipping his wine, full of self-confidence. I see the knights looking doubtful, the ladies-in-waiting beaming, the guild members laughing. I see again my father with his foxy head, his short, graying beard, his hawk's nose, and his small mouth, so full of teeth they seem to be fighting each other for a spot. My goblet of wine trembles in my hand when I get up. I clasp it in my fist, the way I clasped Jan van Vere's whalebone sword. And I think of my mother who was so cruelly rejected by my father. I'm only allowed to see her at Christmas, and the rest of the year she sits there, talking to herself in that lonely convent cell. She keeps telling the angels on the walls that she'll soon be pregnant again and present my father with a son. And then I say it.

"I won't even think of it."

My father chokes on his wine and can't catch his breath. For a moment it looks as if he's about to suffocate. Squire Godfried gives him five careful slaps on the back, and my father spits vigorously on the floor—making a mess of Chaplain van Izeghem in the process. Only then can he find enough air to ask me, "What did you say?"

The eyes of all those present burn into my skin, and I clasp my goblet so hard my fingers turn white.

"Father, I don't think Edmund of Langley is a suitable husband for me, he—"

"You don't need to think, daughter. I'll do that for you."

At this, there's laughter in the hall, but my father isn't amused.

"She's right," Armorer van Vere calls out.

"The lady at least knows where her loyalty lies," shouts Knight Craenhals.

"You're raving, Lord Knight," Frans Ackerman shouts at him. "The Count has spoken wisely."

"Come over here and say that, weaver boy," Craenhals retorts. "I'd love to grease my sword with Ghentish guildsman's blood."

I feel the air gust over my face as my father brings his sword down on the table with a tremendous blow. The sword strikes so hard it stays stuck at an angle from the solid oak. Instantly, everyone stops talking. My father's eyes spew fire. The pages who were serving the food quickly depart.

"Your engagement, daughter," he pronounces slowly, "is hereby official. I have spoken with the English king in Kales, and we've reached an agreement. Edmund is coming to Flanders this summer and you will be betrothed at midsummer. I'll organize a tournament in honor of your engagement, though it's the guilds in Ghent who are paying for the tournament.

Everything has been decided."

Craenhals and van Vere sit down again. My father speaks with impressive authority. I can't think clearly.

My thoughts are scattered. Until I find the reply. "And my grandmother, your mother, the French king's sister…has she been informed of this?"

My father pales. Of course he hasn't informed the French court of his decision. He doesn't reply to the French king's letters, refuses to see his mother, and keeps as far away as he can from anything to do with France.

"Have you forgotten that you yourself escaped from a marriage to an English princess?" I say, shaking all over. "Have you become the guild masters' doormat today? Has the Lion of Flanders become the little lamb of Bruges?"

My father's hand comes out of nowhere. He grabs me by the throat and lifts me with one hand. My feet are off the ground. I can't breathe. I can no longer hear the people in the hall. Gurgling sounds come from my throat.

"Daughter," my father says with icy calm. "It isn't proper for a daughter to contradict her father. You will marry the nobleman I choose for you."

He puts me down and releases me. I gulp air. My heart hammers in my chest.

"Go to your room," my father shouts. "Go and learn to conjugate the verb 'to love' in English."

I leave the Great Hall, leaning on Constance Bouvaert's arm for support.

"Lady," she lectures, "your behavior is inexcusable. You have offended your father and—"

I tear myself loose from her arm and push her away. I stagger.

"Tell my father I'm staying in my room and will not eat until he changes his mind," I scream tearfully.

⊞ ⊞ ⊞

IT IS HOURS LATER. I have locked myself in Saint Anne's room. Godfried knocks on the door and I let him in. He brings me a bowl of reheated chicken breast with crushed violets, the *blamensier* I hadn't touched. I look at the dish, then at him.

"What can I do to please you, my Lady?" he asks.

"You can take a message to my father."

Then I open the shutter and throw the steaming chicken out the window. Immediately, the courtyard is full of the grunting and slobbering of excited pigs. Godfried is at a loss.

"But, what is the message?" he stammers.

"Tell him that tomorrow the pig shit will smell of violets."

He smiles and leaves the room.

The next day, I'm given wild goose, simmered in wine with eggs and garlic. The third day, a pie shaped like a birdcage, filled with stuffed blackbird with ginger and lime juice. On the fourth day, the kitchen offensive continues with baked pears in breadcrumbs, anise, eggs, and pepper. On day five, beaver is on the menu, cooked in pea stock with lemon peel and vinegar, garnished with roasted almonds. On the sixth day, it's a dish of roast venison marinated in honey, cinnamon, crumbled rye bread, diced bacon, marjoram, and a dash of white wine. On the seventh day, they give me wild boar's breast garnished with grapes, baked in batter, and served on a skewer, followed by a pastry of marzipan and preserved lemon peel.

And all through that week, the courtyard is filled with grunting and slobbering sounds. You couldn't get the pigs away from under my window with a burning torch. If pigs could talk, the story of that week would be handed down from generation to generation, from sow to piglet, to the end of time, as the Legend of the Seven Fat Days.

▣ ▣ ▣

ON THE SEVENTH DAY, after the evening bell has sounded and the fires have been damped, my father enters the room. He is very calm. I feel ill and feverish. The book with the story of the unfortunate Hellawes lies on my lap.

"Daughter, you have fought, but the struggle is too unequal."

"I thought a knight of Flanders always stood firm," I replied.

My father sighs.

"You're not a Count for nothing! Surely you can manage a few stupid tailors!"

He takes the book about Hellawes out of my hands. It is gilded, bound in red leather. He leafs through the book and looks at the miniature of the loveliest of women, who died of a broken heart.

"You're just like your mother," he says. "She's never had any idea of reality either. She lives in a dream."

He points at the window.

"Can pigs read, do you think?"

"Father, that book is worth thousands of Flemish pounds. Give it back!"

"Edmund of Langley wants to marry you. He is overjoyed to be coming to Flanders to announce your betrothal to the world."

"Father, I only want to commit myself out of love."

"Oh, daughter…"

"On the day I die, the day I surrender my soul to God and my body is laid in the cold vault with my ancestors, on that day I want to be able to say: I have loved. Even if it was only for one night, like Hellawes."

"Those books of your mother's," my father sighs. "You don't even know Edmund. You could get on together perfectly well."

"Like you and my mother?"

He groans.

"I don't want him!"

I feel dizzy and everything goes blurry for a moment. I feel my father's strong arms under my back. I look up into his face, which is bent over me. Very briefly, he even seems to be worried.

"You must eat some soup, daughter."

I have no words left. I'll make Edmund's life a misery. As long as it takes to make him leave Flanders. I'll make him so afraid of marrying me that he'll beg not to have to face the altar with me. I'll make him crawl to the stables to find the fastest horse to flee back to his estate in England. There, he'll tremble at the mere mention of my name. He will not bring me to my knees.

My father hands me a bowl of steaming corn soup with pieces of meat floating in it. I clasp my cold hands around the warm bowl. The smell of the soup makes my mouth water. I want to drink it, but my father holds the bowl firmly.

"Swear!"

I look into his cold blue eyes. My body begs for the soup. He pulls a pendant from his tunic. It represents the suffering Christ on the cross.

He presses the pendant against my lips.

"Swear you will marry him."

I will stand firm. He won't break me. And everything goes black. I faint against my father's chest. When I come to, he has put down the bowl and is shaking my shoulders.

"Swear," he shouts. "By God, the Son, and the Holy Ghost."

I break. Nod.

"Say it," he hisses.

I say it.

I kiss the cross.

I've been beaten.

12

*O*UR BETROTHAL, DEAREST FRIEND, I read in Edmund's first letter, *will take place in twenty-six weeks. My delight at this is beyond words. French and Latin are inadequate to express how much my manly heart longs for your womanliness. I hereby give you a pearl. That pearl is you.*

That's where the letter ends. I fold open the silken cloth and inside it nestles a white pearl. It's almost transparent. It's the most beautiful pearl I have ever seen. I read the letter again. Once. Twice. Five times. The cloth is embroidered with a boar's head. I slide the cloth through my fingers. And then I sniff it. It's perfumed with crocus blossom, the most precious flower in the world because saffron is extracted from it. Crocus blossom is used to make the most expensive perfume in the world. I hesitate. Is this Edmund? Does this romantic letter really come from the young Prince of England? I leave my room and examine the dust-covered English courier who has ridden all the way from Kales. I snip off a lock of my reddish-brown hair and fold it into a cloth of Bruges lace with a pattern of flowers. I write Edmund a brief letter in which I thank him for his chivalrous attention. My words are cool but friendly. The pearl's not a bad start.

Twenty-nine days later, the courier returns, even dustier than last time. I have to restrain myself from snatching the letter out of his hands. *Your words have touched me*, Edmund writes. *I stared at the lock of your hair for hours before having it sewn into my tunic. The lace cloth I have tied around the hilt of my sword. The London noblemen all notice your cloth and praise my honor and good fortune. I am proud of your gifts.* I open the silken cloth, which is drenched in the perfume of crocus blossom. This time, two gleaming black pearls lie inside, even more precious than the previous gift. Like the other pearl, they must have come from Zebergit, the island in the Red Sea.

I shall have a hat made, friendly and noble Lord, I write back to Edmund, *into which your pearls will be sewn. It will be a beautiful hat, which I will proudly wear on the day you stand before me.*

⊞ ⊞ ⊞

WINTER SLOWLY MELTS AWAY. Every day that goes by brings me a day closer to Edmund. They're dreary days, with hail, wind, and cold lashing the castle. Clothes and bedding feel damp. It's as if the world will never be dry again. I'm getting more and more impatient. I want to see Edmund. I want to touch him. I want it to be summer.

I pass the time with my fencing lessons. After the

first five lessons, in which all I was allowed to do was learn passes and moves, Master Tagliaferro finally lets me handle my rapier. In the middle of the hall hangs a doll made of old rags. With a rope, Tagliaferro makes the doll swing back and forth.

"*Contessina*," Tagliaferro asks me, "whom do you hate most in this world? Whom do you curse?"

I look him in the eyes while he adjusts the hilt of my rapier on my wrist. My arm is trembling.

"*Maestro*," I finally reply, "that's something I can't tell you."

"I don't want you to tell me," he barks. "I want you to think about that hatred. I want you to let all that hatred flow into the tip of your sword and then thrust your sword forward."

He makes the doll dance up and down in front of me. In my mind's eye, I see the battered little statue of Our Lady of Hate. I hear the wind scouring the moss-covered chapel. I see the spiders that have covered her head with cobwebs. I push off with my left foot, bend my right knee, and all of my body becomes one long sword. My right arm flashes forward. But the tip of my sword meets only with empty space. I've missed the doll by a wide margin. I take an awkward step sideways to regain my balance. Tagliaferro roughly shoves me sideways. With a thud I hit the floor, but I don't drop my sword.

"Is that hating?" Tagliaferro exclaims. "Is that all you're capable of, *Contessina*?"

I scramble up and stare at him.

"Again," he barks.

It's not until the seventh lesson that I manage to hit the doll on the first try. From the tenth lesson on, I never miss.

▨ ▨ ▨

EDMUND'S THIRD LETTER arrives on the day Hendrik and Godfried are knighted. The evening before, they went into the chapel and laid their weapons on the altar. They prayed all night, wearing only shirts. It's April, and there's still frost every night, so the chapel is freezing and in the morning, when the chaplain blesses their swords, Hendrik and Godfried are cold to the bone. My father knights them. They're fifteen years old and suffering running colds.

The third letter contains three dark-green pearls that look as if they might have come from the fabled fairy forests. Edmund writes that every shutter in Britain is closed against the rain, the cold, and the winter winds, but none of that worries him because his body is suffused with warmth when he thinks of me. With every letter and every pearl, my longing for Edmund grows.

It's May when the frosts finally stop and spring breaks out. Chaplain van Izeghem is surprised that spring has come. He keeps warning us that the end of the world is near, but no one believes him any longer. His habit is fraying and his sentences are becoming incoherent. His eyes glow like those of a mad dog, and the children in the castle are afraid of him.

I RECEIVE A FOURTH LETTER with four blue pearls from the Indian Ocean. The courier from Kales is covered in dust. I now have ten pearls, and my hands shake with excitement as I read Edmund's words: *I'm nearly dying with impatience to come to Flanders and drink in the sight of you. You are my Helen of Troy.* I write back to thank him and to warn him that I'm not like the princess of Sparta who fled to Troy with her lover and so unleashed a war. *I am only a Lady of Flanders,* writes my goose quill. *And if you imagine, noble Lord, that I resemble Helen of Troy, I am bound to disappoint you. No woman could fulfill your expectations.* I sign, *Your Marguerite.*

A FEW WEEKS LATER, when I come home from my fencing lesson, a carriage decorated with French fleurs-de-lis is standing in the courtyard. My grandmother has made the journey from Paris to Male to confront her son about my coming engagement to Edmund of England. I run up the steps to the Great Hall and see my grandmother standing face-to-face with my father. In my whole life, I've only seen her once or twice. She doesn't see me because she has her back to me. A few feet behind her stands a young man of about fifteen, nervously biting his fingernails. I've arrived in the middle of my grandmother's fiery tirade.

"…your loyalty," her old voice rasps, "lies with the French king…"

"Who's imprisoned in England," my father calmly adds.

"He is your sovereign, your ruler, your liege Lord," her voice croaks on. "And my brother. Your uncle!"

My father avoids her eye and stamps up and down in front of the empty fireplace.

"You must cancel the marriage and promise your daughter to Duke Philip of Rouvres and Burgundy."

"What do you know about the situation in Flanders when you live in your far-away Paris?" shouts my father. "The cities no longer need a count. They exist in their own right. They have their own militias and their own leaders. They're wealthier than the Pope. I am not necessary."

"That's nonsense," my grandmother almost screeches. "How can the greatest nobleman of Flanders not be needed?! The Flemish in the cities may call themselves free, but they are sheep that need a shepherd. And what can they do against the King of France? He only needs to flick his finger and his armies of knights will be here. They have obliterated the Flemish time and again."

"And the other way," the Count sighs.

"That Battle of the Golden Spurs," my grandmother says mockingly. "A year after the battle, the French armies were back to punish Flanders and take back all the captured spurs, which were on display in the church at Kortrijk. We even took the church bells, the symbols of their city's freedom."

"Sixty years ago," my father replies. "An eternity. The English are invincible. The wealth of the cities depends on English wool and they will use force to make me give in to their demands. Marguerite must marry England."

Silence falls over the hall. I see the young man behind my grandmother nervously rocking on his feet. I go closer and watch my grandmother. I'm struck by her resemblance to my father. She has the same cold eyes and hard features, but they're made more noticeable by the deep grooves etched in the yellowish parchment that must once have been her youthful skin.

"I am ashamed of you, my son," she hisses slowly. "These loins that have borne you are French, these hands that have cherished you are French, these lips that have kissed you are French…"

She's wheezing. Her bent body moves up and down. She pulls a dagger from her wide belt and uses it to cut open her dress and her corset. Her slack left breast tumbles from the corset. My father looks bewildered. The young man stiffens.

"This breast, too, which has fed you, is French…and because you will not submit to the will of your king nor to the will of your mother, I'll cut it off."

My father stares at her. She holds the dagger below her breast.

"I'll cut off this breast and throw it to the dogs."

I stare at my grandmother. Startled, my father looks at the knife below his mother's breast. That's when I realize that this woman of bones and perishing skin has never cherished my father. That her lips have never kissed him. That her breast has never fed him. This woman is as cold as ice. For the first time in my life, I feel compassion for my father. Because this woman, this mother, has never loved anyone. My father can't utter a word. My grandmother presses the knife against her breast.

"Well, son, what is your answer?"

"For heaven's sake, woman, get your clothes back on."

"I mean it!" my grandmother shouts. Her voice breaks. She tightens her grip on the knife under her breast and clamps her eyes shut.

My father stamps past my bent-over grandmother, out of the hall.

"Where are you going?" she croaks, opening her eyes and turning around stiffly.

"I'll go and get the dogs," my father says calmly.

A moment later, he's gone.

I follow him with my eyes. In the chess game of diplomacy, he's still a master. I turn back to my grandmother and catch her cold eyes staring at me. She has seen my glance of admiration. The young man moves toward my grandmother in an effort to support her. She waves her knife and the young man jumps back. With a vicious gesture, she puts the dagger away, pulls her corset closed, and comes toward me. She stands facing me. She sniffs. She looks me over from top to toe. I try to smile.

"Grandmother," I say politely, "I'm pleased to see you again. It's been so—"

"Make no mistake, child," she cuts me off. "You are

merchandise. And if you have ever looked in a mirror, you must realize that Edmund isn't marrying you for your beauty." That last word she mashes between the five teeth that remain in her sunken mouth.

"You're not missing out on anything, Philip," she hisses at the young man next to her. "Any gooseherd would have more charms than this bony thing."

My grandmother turns and walks away. Her shoes drag along the wooden floor. She's gone. Her words still echo painfully inside me. I feel my fingers trembling, but I clench my fists to stop it. I'm not a bony thing. Let the rattling old carcass herd her own geese. I watch Philip. I nod. He nods back. This is the French king's nephew. My other potential husband. He's wearing lovely silk clothes, a bronze chain, and a sheepish expression. He smiles cautiously.

"You want to marry me?" I ask him, my chin in the air.

"It's my uncle, the French king's wish," he replies tonelessly.

"But not my father's."

"I'm sorry for your sake," he frowns. "I understood from your grandmother, my great-aunt, that you would prefer to marry me."

"No, you have misunderstood. I want to marry Edmund. Anyway, you don't exactly look like a cheerful Charlie."

Philip of Rouvres, Duke of Burgundy, looks mystified.

"Charlie?" he repeats. The frown on his forehead becomes deeper.

"Yes, that's an expression we have for someone who's full of fun and exuberant—someone who enjoys life. All that frowning makes you look old."

"Whether I enjoy life or not is my business," he says curtly.

"So you're a frowner," I challenge him. "And why are you a frowner? Because you can't marry me?"

My chattering is making Duke Philip quite nervous.

"*Ma Dame*," he says. "You must forgive me, but I do not love you. My heart belongs to another. Someone of whom I dream incessantly, the thought of whom keeps me awake every night and whose name tastes like honey on my lips."

"Well, you're quite the poet," I say coolly. "And who may this honeyed lady be?"

"Are you mocking me?"

"I wouldn't dare," I answer.

"She's a noblewoman from Toulouse," he explains reluctantly. "Her name is Isabeau de Cahors."

"And she's already married," I complete for him.

"Yes, to the Count of Toulouse. He's nearly thirty years older than her."

"Oh well, all you need then is a little patience. He won't last long."

And, for the first time, Philip smiles.

"My Lord Philip. I don't want to marry you.

You don't want to marry me. Let's stop talking about marrying."

Philip smiles once more.

"I've spent two weeks traveling in a closed carriage with your grandmother," he says. "You can imagine what a pleasant experience that was. I wouldn't mind stretching my legs a bit and seeing some of Flanders."

Smiling, I move to the door. "I'll have a stallion saddled for you. Would you mind a fiery beast? You can work off some of your frowns."

Philip grins.

◻ ◻ ◻

THAT AFTERNOON we leave the castle of Male on horseback. Clouds are gathering in the spring sky. We're followed by Jan van Vere. We only go a short distance before I dismount from my ladies' saddle.

"Would it bother you, my Lord, if I remove my ladies' saddle?"

Philip looks puzzled.

"What do you mean?"

"I prefer riding astride a horse."

"Like a man?" Philip sounds shocked.

He does seem quite shrewd. I undo the straps, pull the saddle off Palframand, and carry it across to Jan van Vere, who remarks, "Her horse is used to it that way."

"You may go back to the castle," I tell van Vere. "I think Philip is man enough to protect me."

Philip can't believe his eyes when I lift up my skirts and throw myself across Palframand's back.

"But, *Ma Dame* Marguerite," he stammers, "this is highly unusual. If a priest were to see you like this, with a stallion between your, your…"

"Thighs," I supply.

"Yes, your thighs. It is heretical!"

"*Messire* Philip," I cry. "You carry on as if you were born before Charlemagne! This is the year 1361! The dark ages are past."

"But, the Church doesn't want—"

"My Lord Philip, I promise I will go to confession tomorrow. I also want to remind you that you have promised to protect me. So you won't look so good tonight at the castle, when you'll have to explain why you couldn't keep up with me."

"Couldn't keep up with you?" Philip asks.

"Oh, stop repeating everything I say," I cry. Then I move my hips forward, and Palframand, who recognizes my slightest hint, shoots away like an arrow. Philip has plenty of trouble making his stallion obey him. Which isn't all that surprising, since I've given him the most high-strung horse in my father's stable. Palframand seems to hardly touch the ground. My calves grip him tightly. He gallops like the wind. I can feel his muscles moving under his skin. His shoulders are pumping, foam flies from his mouth, and I make him jump a hedge in a wide arc. I slow Palframand and look behind me. Philip now has his stallion under control. He's obviously a good horseman. He digs in his spurs. I can hardly repress a laugh of delight.

"Come on, Palframand, let's see what you can do," I whisper, and my stallion storms ahead like a horse from the legends. I am Hippolyta, Queen of the Amazons. Present and past flow into each other as I feel Palframand's damp back under me and the west wind roars through my hair. The spring chill leaves me altogether. I slow my horse. He snorts and shakes his head. I look back and see Philip approaching in the distance, through the immense space of the polders where it is so flat that land and sky seem to be making love to each other on the horizon.

Philip slows his horse to a trot as he gets closer.

"Tired already?" he smiles.

I nudge Palframand and, at the same time, Philip digs his spurs into his horse's flanks. Both our horses charge forward neck and neck. They gallop as if the Devil is right behind them. I sniff the sweet scent of my horse. Philip does not yield. He stays level. In perfect movement and practically in time with each other, we jump a ditch and find ourselves in a plowed field. We let our horses gallop on. At times, I get ahead, at other times, Philip, and whichever of us is behind gets sprayed with mud. We come upon a chapel that I recognize instantly: Our Lady of Hate. I yell out to Philip that we should stop because we're riding into the Marshland. We rein in our horses. They steam. We look at each other. We're both covered in mud.

"You need a bath, my dear Burgundy," I laugh.

"As do you, my noble Flanders."

"You'd be better off going to a bathhouse in Bruges."

"A bathhouse? I bet you wouldn't dare to go there with me," he grins, looking at me challengingly.

"I'm up for anything," I reply.

"Good," he smiles. "But we should hurry—there's a thunderstorm coming."

And so there is. In the distance, above the dunes that separate land from water, I see a flash of lightning. My heart contracts. A rider in an open field is the highest point in a landscape, and my horse's tack, even without the saddle, is full of metal. We spur our horses in the direction of the towers of Bruges. We hit the road at breakneck speed. Two peasants hurry out of the way when they see us coming. Our cloaks stream behind us. The moment we get under the vaults of the Donkey's Gate, the thunderstorm breaks out above us. We're covered in sweat. And again, Philip and I are laughing together. With rain falling in buckets, we ride into the town. Our horses' hooves clatter in the empty streets. Everyone has taken shelter against the storm. We arrive in the vicinity of the bathhouse. It's in a neighborhood that Chaplain van Izeghem curses every week, because here morals are ignored and the stone tablets of the Ten Commandments are broken every night. It's a neighborhood where the Devil is never left out in the cold and where a young lady has no business. For a moment I wonder if this really is a good idea. I rein in my horse.

"Would you rather go back?" Philip asks. It's late in

the afternoon and rain pours down onto the streets of Bruges. The world is bathed in gray, but the sun shines out of Philip's eyes.

13

THE BATHHOUSE IS IN A LANE IN BRUGES that's jokingly referred to as the "Valley of the Virgins." On its sign board is a painting of a bath and written underneath, in graceful letters, is the name of the establishment, The Red Door. We dismount. Indeed, the main entrance to the house is painted red. An old man dressed in rags admits us. We hand him a few copper coins, and he leads our horses into the stable. We go up a few steps. At the door, Philip motions to me to go ahead of him, but I shake my head. I am *incognita*. Nothing must show that I'm a lady. He goes in first and takes off his hat just as the corpulent landlord, whose name is Colaard, comes to meet us. I hear vague noises from the next room. I don't feel so sure about this anymore.

The landlord greets us. He wants to take my cloak, but I step aside. The landlord looks a bit surprised, but Philip immediately produces a silver coin from his purse. The landlord smirks and leads us inside. I pull the hood of my cloak down carefully to hide my face. No one must recognize me here. I know this house is considered safe because city fines do not apply to it. After all, the bailiff, the representative of law and order in Bruges, has invested heavily in this bathhouse. He sees to it that no trouble occurs in his dubious inn and that important customers are left in peace. Any disturbances are stopped before they can begin.

Yet I shrink back at the sight of the disreputable-looking interior. It's a spacious hall, divided by a central aisle from which three-foot-high wooden platforms stretch to the right and left, each with a bathtub for two or four persons. Some are screened off with curtains. Behind the curtains we see the moving shadows of rough leatherworkers and drunken soldiers sitting opposite women. With slurred voices, they're calling for more food and wine. Steam rises everywhere. It's hot. Serving girls in long red dresses bring jugs of wine and boards of food to the tubs. In one of the tubs, I recognize Ursmarus van Coutervoorde, the captain of the Bruges militias. A little farther on, I hear a German complaining loudly that the wine tastes like turpentine. The captain shouts at the German to keep quiet.

"It's spring wine," shouts the captain. "It always tastes like that. Perhaps you should drink cider. That'd suit your sort better."

The German rips open his curtain, looking furiously at the captain.

"Are you saying I'm some sort of yokel? I come from Moselle, where they make the best wine in the world. We think cider is a French peasant brew."

"Gentlemen, gentlemen," the landlord intervenes, his arms raised. "Let's remain calm."

"Usmarus, love," the woman in the captain's tub implores. "Am I going to get any attention?"

The captain and the German give each other a final withering look, pull their curtains closed, and settle down into their tubs again. The landlord heaves a sigh of relief and lowers his hands. I hang on to the edge of my cloak. My face is invisible in the shadow of my hood. The landlord shows us to the alcove next to Usmarus van Coutervoorde's. It's a round tub, lined on the inside with linen, to guard against splinters. At the bottom of the tub sits an iron drawer filled with warm coals. I feel the water. It's lukewarm. The landlord pulls out the drawer and, after a short wait, returns with a coal shovel full of red-hot coals. He drops the pieces of coal into the drawer and pushes it back under the tub.

"Food will be brought in just a moment, noble Lord," says the landlord. "The water is still clean. It's only been used twice. Enjoy it."

Philip thanks him, and he leaves us alone. Philip closes the curtains around our alcove. We face each other. Philip gets undressed far too quickly. He nearly falls over as he pulls off his stockings. He jumps into the tub. On top of the tub sits a folding table, covered in linen. It divides the tub in two. Philip sits at the far end and has nowhere else to look but at me. I take a deep breath. I've never taken off my clothes in front of a man.

"Lord Philip," I say, "please turn around."

"I can't," he replies. "There's no room to turn around. I can't move."

With a sigh, I unbuckle the belt that holds my dagger. Then I undo my cloak and put it on the stool next to the tub. I loosen the cord that laces my dress and look at Philip.

"Take a deep breath," I say, "and stick your head underwater."

"For how long?"

"Until I say."

Philip does as he is told. Quickly, I clasp my long white undershirt between my thighs. Then I take off my dress, being careful not to loosen my undershirt. I drape the dress over the stool, once again ensuring that my shirt is still in place. It reaches down to my knees. All this time, Philip is keeping his head underwater. I wonder how long he'll be able to do it. I lean forward over the tub, my head in my hands. Time crawls past and finally Philip comes up out of the water, spluttering.

"Not bad," I say.

Philip looks at me in surprise.

"You'll be the death of me," he pants.

I lower one leg into the bath, again clasping the undershirt between my thighs. I let myself slide into the tub. The ends of my braids get wet. For a moment, the shirt balloons out of the water. I quickly push it back between my thighs. Neither of us says anything. Philip and I clean our arms with sweat scrapers. His feet touch

168

mine. A servant girl pulls the curtain aside and I hide my face behind my hand. She puts down a wooden bowl and a jug on the table tray between us. In the bowl is some bread, a few pieces of river fish, aged cheese, and dried walnuts. We're famished. I sniff the wine, and it's indeed watery spring wine. We eat some of the cheese and walnuts so our next mouthful of the thin wine has a sweet taste. Philip stares at my breasts, which have become visible through the wet shirt.

"You could look somewhere else," I say with a snarl I only half mean. I can't get angry. My whole body is still tingling from that horse ride.

"I'm sorry," Philip replies, "but my eyes are always attracted by beauty."

"Your great-aunt, my grandmother, called me a bony thing," I blurt out.

"That old bat," Philip grins. "To her, everything young and lovely is ugly."

"Lord Philip, stop trying to flatter me. And get your legs out of the way. You're taking up too much room."

I kick him under the water. He moves his legs out of the way, sniggering.

"I'm not being dishonest," he beams. "Not at all."

He tears a piece of bread in half and starts chewing. A silence falls between us. Somewhere in the hall, someone calls for more bread. A woman laughs a bit too loudly, the sound of her laughter tinged with wine.

"Won't your father get worried?" he asks.

"Yes, of course. Imagine if he knew I was sitting in

a bathtub with you. He'd rip out your belly button and hang you by your innards."

Philip smiles and dips his bread in the wine.

"Your grandmother was talking about you in the carriage. She told me you were a quiet girl. An exemplary young lady with impeccable manners. And now that I see you in the flesh in a bathtub—"

"I disappoint you?" I interrupt, taking another sip of wine.

"Quite the contrary, Marguerite, quite the contrary," he says softly, his eyes shining.

Another sip of wine gives me confidence and I look into his dark eyes. He's almost a man, with his broad shoulders and his provocative smile.

"Nothing your grandmother said could have prepared me for you," he whispers.

Another silence falls between us. I keep looking into his eyes. For just a few moments, I feel a link with this man. For just a few moments, it feels as if we are two halves of one story. A story of love and chivalry from one of Saint Anne's books. He is Tristan and I am Isolde. Then I feel his hand on my knee. I look at him in horror. Suddenly, the water feels cold. I push his hand away.

"Do tell me about Isabeau de Cahors," I say coldly, "the great love of your life, without whom your heart would stop beating."

Philip frowns. A gray sadness washes over him, when only a moment ago he seemed to radiate light. I want to get away from here. I want to go home. That's when I hear my name.

"Lady Marguerite, is that you?"

I look up and, through a break in the curtain, I see Roderik van Rijpergherste, the son of Slicher, the leader of Bruges's guilds. He looks impudently inside our alcove. I can feel myself blushing up to my hair. Instinctively, I push my shirt deeper between my legs. I curse silently. The servant who brought the food left the curtain open a little. Roderik pushes it all the way aside.

"And in the company of a noble Lord, too."

Roderik's voice is dripping with mockery. He's wearing a shirt that reaches down to his knees. He's on his own ground here, and I realize this bathhouse is his father's property. He studies Philip, as if he wonders who he might be. Then he looks at my breasts and says, "You have grown…well, a bit anyway…"

"I wish I could say the same of you," I blurt, sliding my glance down to the softer part of his anatomy.

"You know each other?" Philip asks, a little nervously and somewhat unnecessarily.

"Yes, I once smacked this lad with a whalebone. Couldn't do much damage there."

"You make a mistake by insulting me, my Lady," Roderik says, and I can see he's furious.

"And you would do better to leave before my knight teaches you a lesson," I snarl.

Roderik looks up uncertainly. "That little man is a knight?" he scoffs.

Philip gets up. Water drips off him. A chunk of bread drops in the bathwater.

"You are insulting me," he says slowly.

"I should hope so," Roderik smirks, shamelessly bending over our tub. "And I'm sure, Lady Marguerite, your father would be most interested to learn that you visited this establishment with a man who, I suspect, is not your fiancé."

I must stay calm. I must let it pass. I must remember it would be his word against mine and Philip's. No one in this bathhouse has recognized me. It's an empty threat. So what if he tells? In a few weeks I'll be married. I must let it pass. I must ignore his mocking eyes and stinging voice. But something about Roderik brings out the worst in me. He's a little man who thinks he's far better than he is. He thinks he's my equal. My body is a sword. I push off with my left leg so my right hand shoots up. I move like lightning and have Roderik by the collar before he has any idea what's going on. With a single movement, I pull him into our tub. The little table clatters aside. Roderik's fist connects with my cheek, but my fingers close around his throat. I push him under the water.

I can feel Philip pulling at my arms and the next moment the landlord Colaard arrives. He tries to pull us apart. The tub is getting crowded now and topples over. The lukewarm water washes over the floor. We fall headfirst onto the ground. The hot coals bounce over the tiles and the water hisses. The first to get up is

Roderik, who staggers backward and steps on the hot coals. He screams, pushes a curtain aside, and jumps into the nearest tub to cool his feet.

In that tub sits Ursmarus van Coutervoorde, the captain of the Bruges militias, in the company of a very charming and very undressed lady. The captain is far from amused when the young man jumps into his tub and, against the house rules, pulls down the sword that's hanging above him. Roderik jumps clear and knocks over a servant girl. Philip and I hastily gather our clothes, while the landlord tries to calm down the captain, who keeps on cursing.

The German merchant who had earlier complained about the wine now rips open his curtain and, his tongue tied in knots, asks who the blockhead is who's making that confounded racket. The captain yells he should keep his German gob shut or he—the captain— will personally come and hammer it shut for him. The drunken merchant throws an earthenware water jug at the captain, but it hits a passing servant boy right in the face. Two servant girls scream when they see the young man go down. Meanwhile, the captain of the Bruges guards hurls himself at the German troublemaker, who is screaming bloody murder.

What follows is pure chaos. There's a lot of shouting and screaming. A second hot tub crashes down from its platform. Someone is hit smack in the face with a fat roast chicken. A woman slips on a spilled bowl of fish. A naked man attacks another with a back scrubber, and naked women scramble away on hands and feet. Everyone in the bathhouse is dragged into the unlikely melée. Philip grabs me by the wrist and guides me through the fighting mob. Suddenly Roderik pops up in front of us, brandishing a coal shovel. He hesitates before hitting me, giving me just enough time to retrieve my dagger from my pile of clothes.

"My dagger loves soft flesh," I hiss at him, and he instantly drops the shovel. He can't get away fast enough. The landlord appeals for calm. He winces when a piece of furniture is reduced to kindling. Philip and I run out the door and into the stables. The old man in rags looks on with some surprise as we scramble into our clothes. I can't get my clothes done up, and it's Philip who stands behind me and expertly pulls the laces tight. It nearly squeezes the breath out of my lungs. We bump into each other. I sniff the scent of his hair. I look at him, push him against a beam, and kiss him. My lips grip onto his and our tongues find each other. My whole wet body presses against his. Then I push him away and turn around. I hurl myself onto Palframand. The old man in rags is still looking bewildered. The din in the bathhouse has reached its peak.

"What's going on in there? What's all the commotion?" the old man asks.

"Commotion?" asks Philip. "What commotion?"

I laugh as I urge Palframand out of the stables. Philip follows me, away from The Red Door. We ride our horses hard through the High Street toward the Cross Gate. It's nearly nightfall. Soon, the gates will be locked until the next morning. We just manage to leave the town in time. We ride to Male at full gallop without once slowing down. The towers of Male appear in front of us. We're still panting.

"I'm terribly sorry," I say, as our foaming horses start slowing down. "I shouldn't have allowed myself to lose control."

"There's no need to apologize, Lady Marguerite," he says. "You're beautiful when you lose control." He laughs, showing his teeth, which are spectacular. He still has all of them and they are all white. He wants to kiss me, but I spur my horse and tear across the drawbridge. The watchmen recognize me by the light of the torches. Philip follows without hurrying. I ride into the courtyard, jump from my horse, and kick awake one of the stable boys. In a daze, he jumps up. I hand him the reins. Jan van Vere hurries over from one of the outbuildings.

"*Ma Dame*, I was getting worried about the two of you," he calls.

"There was no need," I retort. "I have protected the Lord of Rouvres from all danger."

"The courier from Edmund is here," Jan van Vere says quietly. I look across and see the courier standing in the torchlight by the main building. His clothes are caked in dust. Suddenly, I'm ashamed of this afternoon. I'm angry with myself. Furious at my shameless behavior.

I've let myself go like a washerwoman.

"Marguerite." Philip hasn't heard anything. "I just want to say—"

"My Lord Rouvres," I interrupt him brusquely. "You've said quite enough this evening. I suggest, for your own good, that we forget what has happened today."

"But, *Ma Dame*—"

"And that you return to Burgundy with your aunt as soon as possible."

I turn and take delivery of Edmund's fifth letter. I sniff the letter, and the perfume of crocuses fills my head. Out of the corner of my eye, I see Philip walk his horse into the stable. I run to Saint Anne's room where I undo the velvet cloth. Inside are five red pearls and a letter. Edmund writes, *I am coming*.

And Philip? I've already forgotten him.

14

MY GRANDMOTHER RETURNS TO PARIS, but Philip of Rouvres stays in Flanders. He sticks to me like a leech. The moment I set foot in the stables Lord Philip is there, dying to accompany me. I ask him about his lady love from Cahors.

He says he doesn't think of her as often since he met me. Philip is not just in love with me, he's totally ablaze. Every single day, he sends me a poem, each more yearning than the last. I read all of them aloud in the women's room, to the great amusement of Lady Alaïs and my lady-in-waiting, Constance.

"Love, with a capital L," I recite, "is not granted to everyone. It is unbridled joy. It is rapture and bliss."

"Is there a difference?" Constance giggles.

"Every moment you are away from my sight," I continue, "is unbearable torture for me. I am your secret heart."

Alaïs can't contain her laughter. One of the washerwomen claps her hands.

"I only come to life," I read on, choking with laughter, "when you are near me. Every moment we are together is too brief for me even before it starts."

Alaïs bends over the chamber pot making vomiting noises.

"Even if a night lasts a whole week," I hiccup on, "a week a month, a month a whole year. Even if I live longer than anyone on Earth, I will still long for one more night with you."

We're shrieking with laughter. This is better than the *Roman de la Rose*. I can't go on. Alaïs takes the letter from me.

"A night," she continues, "so warm and endless you wish the sun would never rise again."

"Mercy!" I shout.

The washerwomen are rolling on the bed laughing.

"What does he think he would do with you on a night like that?" someone howls.

"Play *patience*," shrieks Alaïs.

Worst of all, Philip perfumes his letters excessively. One time it's orange blossom, another henna. Once, the whole letter has been drenched in so much almond oil, the ink runs. The poems are sealed. The seal in the red lacquer shows a prancing unicorn.

"You must admit he's subtle," smirks Alaïs.

For an entire week, he writes me poems about the garden of love, whose walls are so tall that only one mortal in a thousand will behold its fruits. But it's a garden he, Philip, will show me.

"Where is he going to find a ladder tall enough?" Alaïs remarks.

In the courtyard, the women can't stop laughing when they see him. When he asks me what I think of his letters, I tell him I've thrown them unopened into the fire to warm my feet with them. In his last poem, Philip writes that he wishes he were a sheet of parchment being consumed by the fire so he could at least once in his life warm my sublime feet. In short, the more poems I receive, the more I long for the Prince of England. For Edmund of Langley. My betrothed. The man who has won my heart with pearls. The man I'm going to marry.

⊡ ⊟ ⊡

IT'S MIDSUMMER. The twelve hours between sunrise and sunset are now at their longest. Each of the twelve summer hours takes nearly twice as long as each of the twelve winter hours. At the end of that endless day, which stretches my patience to the limit, Edmund arrives.

My father has seen to it that I look like a princess. Compared to me, the Queen of France looks like a bag of rags. I'm wearing a gown of gold brocade and Damascus silk and a robe of Armenian velvet, lined with the fur of white wolves from the North. The outside of my cape is embroidered with leaves, eagles, lions, and unicorns in gold thread. Twenty men and eight women have worked thirteen days to have the robe ready for the longest day of the year. A picture of Tristan adorns one of my shoes, Isolde the other. The hat decorated with the fifteen pearls given to me by the Prince of England graces my head. They're pearls that were gathered in the darkest depths of the world's five oceans. The last pearl, the most beautiful, comes from Zanzibar and represents the year ahead. The year I will turn fifteen.

⊞ ⊞ ⊞

A MIDSUMMER CELEBRATION is in full swing in the castle of Male. Many knights have heard about the tournament that will be held to mark my betrothal. The inner court-yard is full of activity. All the knights from Flanders and beyond who are taking part in the tournament have set up tents. It's a confusion of colored canvas, knights' standards, banners, and pennants. The entrance of every tent is marked with a coat of arms. I've decided that, after my marriage, my father's coat of arms, a black lion on a gold field, and my mother's, a gold lion on a black field, will be added to that of England. I'm dying to meet Edmund. My heart lies wide open.

More beautiful than I have ever been, I walk into the Great Hall of Male. At long last, I'm face-to-face with Edmund.

He is one of the most repulsive-looking people I've ever seen.

⊞ ⊞ ⊞

EDMUND IS EIGHTEEN YEARS OLD and looks as if he has just risen from the dead. His skin is as pale as a ghost's and covered in festering pustules. I gape at him. His small, almost childlike eyes inspect me from top to toe. They're the color of blueberries, and there's something mean about them, like the eyes of a wolf looking over its prey. He rubs his small mouth with his glove and sniffles long and loudly. His sniffling sounds like a rattling cough, and it makes my hair stand on end. In my imagination, the inside of his head is like a basin full of mucus. He's dressed too elegantly: a raspberry-red tunic with frills on the shoulders, black culottes bordered with moleskin, and boots made out of the skin of young wild boars.

He takes a step forward and I instinctively take a step back. Edmund of Langley sniffles some more and casts a sideways glance at my father, who's coming toward us. With large, fatherly hands, he takes Edmund and me by the arms and with a broad smile pushes us together. My face rubs against Edmund's tunic. He's drenched in cologne and smells like an over-ripe orchard. I look up into his dull watery eyes and feel two rough leather gloves around my hands. He brings his head closer in order to kiss me. I avert my head and the kiss lands on my right temple.

I look at my father, too shocked to say anything. Edmund stares at me and sniffles. And there we stand: the betrothed pair, two immovable cold stone statues.

"The pearls suit you," Edmund begins. His voice is loud and shrill.

I nod and give him a small bow in thanks. I'm having difficulty standing. This is the man with whom I must spend the rest of my life. I still can't utter a word.

"Can she speak?" Edmund asks my father.

I look up at my father. He must see the horror in my eyes.

"The Prince has brought a gift for you," my father smiles, trying to appease me.

Edmund sniffles noisily and offers me his arm.

I nod coldly, lay my arm on his, and let him lead me to the open window. I hear cries of astonishment from outside, so I quicken my step and, there, in the courtyard, draped in a black cloth, is a magnificent animal that seems to have escaped from the Garden of Eden.

"The Arabs call the animal a *zarafa*," Edmund explains. "A 'giraffe.'"

"I can see it's not a unicorn, my Lord Prince." I have at last found my voice. "Can it be ridden?"

"Yes, certainly," Edmund replies a little absent-mindedly. "I'm also told roasted giraffe's neck is quite a delicacy."

"I've heard," I say, trying to hide my contempt, "that English cooking leaves people dumbfounded."

"Indeed," boasts Edmund, who hasn't noticed the mockery in my voice. "Our cooks prepare dishes after my own heart. And after yours, I'm sure." Edmund winks, but my face is like marble. "You'll see," he brags, "it's nothing like French *cuisine*." He spits the word out like a piece of rotten fruit. "Those Frenchmen eat nothing but frogs, snails, and pigs' feet."

"And how might you prepare the giraffe's neck, my noble Lord? In mint sauce?"

182

For the first time, Edmund seems to think I may be mocking him. He stretches out his arm and calls, "Axe." A servant hands him a battle axe. The head of a wild boar is etched on the huge blade. I instinctively take a step back, and even my father looks surprised.

"Shall I slaughter the beast for you right now?"

"No," I say hurriedly, getting worried. "This animal is far too noble and unique to end up in a mint sauce."

"So the gift pleases you?" Edmund asks.

"Just as your letters did. Who wrote them for you?"

"My father's court jester," he replies without a moment's hesitation. "He's the funniest man in England. And he knows French quite well."

"The French was indeed very good," I agree.

"So the giraffe pleases you?"

"Certainly," I say, after a moment. "But can you tell me what the animal usually eats? Right now, it's eating Knight Craenhals's tent."

And indeed, the giraffe has ripped a banner from one of the colorful tents and is chewing it up in its pointy mouth. Johan Craenhals emerges from his tent, furious, and tries to push the huge beast away, as some of Edmund's servants come rushing up and tug at the ropes that are tied around its hind legs. The giraffe begins a terrible braying and beats its head about, making clots of milky white slime fly around. One of the clots plops down on Knight Craenhals's black tunic.

"Who is the owner of this beast from Hell?" he shouts, foaming with rage. "Who?!"

"It's mine," Edward shouts conceitedly. "Don't make such a fuss, man. I'll buy you a new banner."

"Are you trying to insult me, my Lord Prince?" shouts Craenhals, going red in the face. "Is this how you show respect for the knights of Flanders?"

Edmund pulls off his glove and throws it out the window, at Craenhals's feet.

"Shall I come and help you pick it up?" Edmund asks. "Or can you manage on your own?"

Knight Craenhals picks up the glove, makes a big show of rubbing it on his behind, and then holds it out to the giraffe. The animal sniffs the glove somewhat mistrustfully, then wraps its tongue around it and makes it disappear into its long, graceful neck.

"The beast really does eat anything," I can't resist saying.

Edmund is filled with rage.

"We'll meet at the tournament, princeling," shouts Craenhals.

"I didn't know peasants were allowed in,'" Edmund spits.

"My noble Lords," my father intervenes. "Save your spittle and your passion for the tournament. You can settle any insults there."

"My dear father and wife-to-be, please excuse me." Edmund bows. "I hope to get to know you better soon, over dinner." He strides away, followed by his knights. I am alone in the Great Hall with Constance and my father.

"You are incorrigible, my Lady," Constance complains. "You came very close to insulting him."

"And he us."

She seems startled by the tone of my voice.

"He's the Prince of England," Constance scolds me. "He's the best match in Europe and—"

"You're welcome to him!"

"Leave us alone," I hear my father say. Constance leaves with a bow. I face my father. The counts of Flanders look down on us from their warped painted panels.

"My daughter, you have sworn to marry the Prince of England," my father starts slowly. "With your lips on the cross."

I kneel in front of him, my folded hands raised high. He looks down on me.

"I beg you, Father, remove this man from my life."

He stares.

"He fills me with total disgust," I stammer, feeling tears streaming from my eyes. I have never allowed myself to look so vulnerable in front of him. "If you marry me to him, I shall dry up and die."

My father keeps staring at me.

"Or I'll go mad, like my mother."

The door swings open. Kitchen boys come in to light the fires for the evening meal. My father shouts at them to clear off. They hurriedly turn tail and run out the door. My father turns back to me.

"Are you betraying me, daughter?"

"Betray..." I stammer.

"It's that Philip, isn't it?"

"Philip?" I ask, not understanding.

"Do I need to spell it out, daughter?" He raises his voice. "You go and have a bath with him at The Red Door, you threaten Guild Master van Rijpergherste's son with a dagger, and you flirt with Philip in the stables."

"And what of it?" I shout.

"Are you still a virgin, daughter?"

For a moment I'm speechless. But only for a moment.

"Have you promised Edmund a virgin?"

"You haven't answered me, daughter!"

"Yes, Father, I'm a virgin. And I want to stay that way. I don't want to give myself to that man."

"Do you know how much I had to pay the guild master to keep quiet about your adventures in The Red Door?"

"That was just a game, the whim of a young girl," I cry. "I'm not in love with Philip. I don't want him. And I certainly don't want Edmund."

"So who do you want, daughter," my father roars. "You have more whims than a dog has fleas."

"This is not a whim, Father, please," I beg him. "Please believe me. Edmund will violate Flanders, the same way his brother, the Black Prince, violated France."

"Edmund will bring honor to Flanders after my death," my father insists. "A union of England and Flanders is the only possible future."

"So am I just the highest trump in your card game, Father?"

"Perhaps you want to go back to your little Knight of Sindewint? He has long since married a beautiful woman and he has two sons."

I shake my head. With both hands, I grip my father's ankle and press my face against it.

"Have mercy, Father," I beg. "Have mercy on your only daughter."

My father kicks my hands away from his ankle. I feel his shoe against my face. A stab of pain shoots through my head.

"You're a fickle creature," my father shouts. "You're untrustworthy, and you're my sole heir. You will marry Edmund."

He strides away. I remain on the floor, shaking and sobbing, while all the counts of Flanders look down haughtily on their last descendant.

15

THE MORNING AFTER MIDSUMMER DAY, I'm in Bruges, in the former hall of the Black Sisters. I'm looking at my small fencing master, ready to start my lesson. We face each other. I see my sword, sheathed in leather, stretched out opposite his. I think of Edmund. I think of my father. The next moment, Tagliaferro lashes out and knocks the sword out of my hand. It clatters to the floor.

"When I give a fencing lesson, *Contessina*, I expect concentration," Tagliaferro snarls.

He strokes his little beard with his left hand and regards me with his light eyes.

"*En guarde, Contessina*," he shouts.

"This is my last lesson, *Maestro*," I say tonelessly. "My husband-to-be arrived yesterday. I'm expected to be at his disposal. I will miss your lessons."

Maestro Tagliaferro shrugs and turns away from me, swishing his sword up and down. He's not interested in my waffling.

"You are having a fencing lesson, *Contessina*," he says indifferently. "That is what you pay me for."

"I'm not myself today," I reply.

"Then I will teach you to be yourself today."

"Be myself?" I ask suspiciously.

"Take your sword in your left hand, *Contessina*," he orders. "Take off the leather cover." I do as he tells me. I examine the sharp, cold steel of my rapier. The leather laces of the hilt feel strange in my left hand. The fencing master goes over to the wall and releases the dummy that hangs from a ring in the ceiling. The dummy swings from side to side. It has three red spots, where a single sword thrust is lethal. One red spot over the heart, in the middle of the chest, one red spot on the neck, and one on the forehead, between the eyes. He makes me stand with my back to the dummy. Then I must turn and, in a single movement, pierce one of the three red spots. It took me twelve lessons to hit the dummy in the heart with my right hand. But now I have to do it, in one perfect movement, with the arm that is not my sword arm.

"Ready?"

I nod. My hand grips the hilt of my sword as if I'll never let go of it. I can hear the dummy swinging behind me. I concentrate on the sound. I let my blood go cold. Everything seems to become still. Then I let all the hatred in my heart come to life, like an enormous red bloom. I feel the draft from the dummy on my neck and hear the rustling of the rope. I spin round, push off on my right foot, and bend my left knee. My whole body is one long sword. I thrust. I pierce the dummy's heart, pull my sword back. I pierce the neck, pull the sword back once more, and run the steel through the doll's forehead. Then I twist the sword out of the head and step back. I realize that I screamed with each thrust. Maestro Tagliaferro is taken aback at the ferociousness of my attack. I'm shaking on my legs, but I keep my balance. No one could push me over now.

"Your heart is on your left, *Contessina*," says Tagliaferro. "I can teach you nothing more."

"I'm glad to have learned where my heart is, *Maestro*," I reply, barely able to suppress the bitterness I feel.

"In any fight, you must be able to control the heart. You must be able to bring love and hate into balance and, most importantly, not to mistake one for the other."

"How could I ever confuse love with hate?" I ask.

"That is a question you will have to answer yourself when the time comes," he replies.

Master Tagliaferro is surely the strangest person I've ever met.

"You're a master of the art of fighting," I say, as we put our swords away. "Is there anyone who's better than you?"

"The only man who has ever beaten me in this hall," Tagliaferro says slowly, "is your father."

I can feel the blood pumping through my body. With a vicious thrust, I push my sword into its scabbard.

"What made you decide to teach me fencing, *Maestro*?" I ask him.

Very quietly he puts his rapier away in the rack against the wall. Then he turns to me.

"It was because of the first time I met you."

"When I came here with Jan van Vere?"

"No, when I was being covered in shit on the dike along the Reie. The boys ran away like hares. But you, you stayed."

"I was only nine," I say with surprise. "I didn't think you had recognized me."

He grins. "You had courage. You are a worthy Lady of Flanders," he says with a nod. It's the first time the master has paid me a compliment.

"That's not something I hear from my father," I say somberly.

"Your father," Master Tagliaferro begins, "is not—"

"You don't know my father," I snarl. My own voice scares me. It reverberates in the large, cold hall.

"No," Tagliaferro concedes. "That is true. I don't know your father."

Master Tagliaferro walks me to the gate and opens it for me. The paving stones are hot from the summer sun.

"I greet you, *Contessina*," he says with a nod.

"I greet you, *Maestro*," I reply.

And so Master Andrea Tagliaferro, too, disappears from my life.

▣ ▣ ▣

IT'S THREE DAYS AFTER MIDSUMMER. Evening. Everyone in the castle is getting ready to depart for Ghent and the tournament tomorrow. Philip of Rouvres comes to bid me farewell in Saint Anne's room. He is wearing his most handsome tunic. The book of Hellawes lies on my lap. Thank God, Philip has not brought a poem.

"I bid you farewell," he says.

"Already?" I let slip.

"I'm leaving for Rouvres."

"Aren't you staying for the tournament?"

"Every time I see you in the company of Edmund, my heart bleeds," he replies melodramatically.

I close my book with a sigh. I couldn't bear another bleeding heart. He sees my irritation.

"Why should I stay?"

"To teach English princes some humility," I blurt out.

For the briefest moment, Philip's eyes come to life, but they promptly turn dull again.

"You want me to fight against the prince who is to be your husband? What good can come of that?"

"But isn't it the essence of knighthood, my Lord Philip," I say slowly, "to love the woman you can't win? And to perform great deeds of courage for her?"

"Indeed, *Ma Dame*," Philip agrees. "But you will never love me. You've read my letters to all the women in the castle. You've mocked me. You mock everyone."

"It's just that you do not have a god-given talent for poetry, my Lord Philip, and I find it hard to take all that courtly nonsense about my person seriously. You exaggerate too much."

"Then my letters deserve only to be burnt," he says dryly.

"Oh, you poor thing," I sigh. "I haven't burnt them."

"What do you mean?"

"I mean that I haven't burnt them," I cry impatiently. I can't very well tell him I keep them in a box. He is, after all, the only man who has ever written me poems.

"Do you mean that?" he cries hopefully. I smile, and right away he is the perfect knight again.

"I shall win the tournament for you. I'll rip Edmund's harness off and use it for a scarecrow in my vineyard in Burgundy."

He heads for the door, but changes his mind. He turns back and kneels before me.

"I am your knight," he says with bowed head. Then he jumps up and leaves.

Duke Philip! He will never change!

◫ ◫ ◫

WE TRAVEL TO GHENT and the Gravensteen, the stronghold where my father tortures his enemies and has his coins struck. The Gravensteen is the best-guarded fortress in all of Flanders. A stock of precious metals is hidden in the strong room in the cellars behind an oak door with nine locks. The alloy for coins is produced there, and the waste water that results from the process is so toxic that it isn't discharged into the city canals, but dumped downstream in the River Scheldt. The face of each coin has an image of my father, the Count of Flanders. They're heavy silver coins and we call them Flemish pounds. Any coins that come back to the Treasury, my father has melted down and struck again with a lower silver content. The new coins are put into circulation with their old value, and he keeps the difference in his Treasury. My father is as sharp as the sharpest money changers!

That evening, a banquet has been arranged in the Great Hall of the Gravensteen for all the noble guests. My father, Edmund, and I are seated on an honor dais near the fireplace. The rest of the nobility are seated closer to us or farther away, according to their rank and importance. Furthest away—"below the salt," as we say—sit the people of lower orders. The main dish is cuckoo from Mechelen, cooked with cinnamon in a gingerbread crust.

Philip is cool and distant. He seems to have regained his aloofness. I smile at him the way I did when we turned half the bathhouse in the Valley of the Virgins upside down.

My father stands. He raises his goblet. It's made of maple wood, the noblest of all woods, and inlaid with gold. Holding it high, he addresses the gathering. He declares that he's looking forward to having the great honor and delight of witnessing all aspects of his future son-in-law's courage at the tournament. Edmund stands and raises his cup. He proclaims that he loves his future father-in-law like his own father and that he and the entire English royal house have never been so honored as they are today, the day of his betrothal and the day when, for the first time, the Dragon of Saint George and the Lion of Flanders are on the same banner. The Flemish nobles and the leaders of the cities cheer him. He trumpets that he will honor his future father-in-law even more by giving him every suit of armor he captures by his own hand from a knight in the tournament, to the greater glory of the many grandchildren I will give Flanders and England.

My father thanks his future son-in-law from the depth of his heart and loudly declares to all present that he already looks on him, Edmund of England, as the son he never had. He is certain that his daughter—*moi*—will be a fertile wife for Edmund and give him much happiness and joy, as well as producing many descendants.

Edmund grins broadly, and I notice one of the pustules on his face bursting spontaneously.

"I drink to your love and fertility," Edmund calls, full of self-confidence, raising his cup. "And to your body, whose many beauties will never cloy, and which year by year I will enjoy."

The nobles laugh and applaud. Edmund raises his cup to my father and, looking into each other's eyes, they drink a toast. I stand up.

"I am pleasantly surprised by your poetic skill, Knight of England," I smile.

"England *and France*," Edmund completes my statement.

"I, too, am looking forward to witnessing your

bravery in every detail," I pronounce, trying not to sound provocative. "But what is courage if it hides behind a steel breastplate, an oaken shield, a helm, two iron leg covers, and the hardened codpiece that ensures the English royal lineage doesn't come to an end?"

A wave of muttering slowly dies away. My father's eyes are fiery. Edmund goes red in the face. *Take up the challenge,* I cry inwardly, *so Philip can give you a beating of which, my Lord Consort, I will remind you for the rest of our married life. Every evening, if necessary.*

"Real courage," I continue haughtily, "is the courage to fight without armor, in your shirtsleeves. Are you a man of such courage, Edmund of England *and France*?"

I can see Edmund hesitating. I've got him, my blood shouts, I've got him. He's on the verge of yielding. But then my father's fist bangs the table.

"That's enough, daughter. You're talking drivel!"

And Edmund doesn't yield.

"Do you take me for a fool?" Edmund retorts. "Fighting in shirtsleeves is for peasants and serfs. A knight protects his noble body from all possible injuries. It's his privilege."

"Stop challenging my future son-in-law like that, daughter," shouts my father. "Who on earth would fight in a tournament without armor? It's sheer idiocy."

"It's a great pity," I continue, with a sigh. "I'd hoped that the man who loves me would prove that love through his courageous actions."

"I will prove my love in other ways," Edmund smirks,

to the great amusement of the audience. There is much cheering, clapping, and raucous laughter. I feel my head go hot and red. That's when Philip of Rouvres stands up. He waits for the laughter in the hall to die away.

"My Lady," he announces theatrically. "Your husband-to-be will fight with your veil for your greater honor and glory. But I will fight in my shirtsleeves for your love."

My father stares at him. I hear Edmund sniffing. I lower my eyes. This is not what I'd intended. This is not at all what I'd intended. A log shifts in the hearth. The wind makes the candles flicker, and in the kitchen, two floors down, someone drops a bowl. Otherwise, the silence is so intense it's as if the angel Gabriel himself were floating past.

16

THE CORN MARKET is a flat, sandy area between Saint Nicholas Church, where there's a large graveyard; the Church of Saint Pharahildis on Veerle Square; the city prison, which looks out on the Graslei; and the deep canal that runs from the top of Veld Street to Volder Street. All of Ghent seems to have gathered here. I see bowstring makers hawking their bows, barbers pulling teeth in the street, carters unloading their boats, prostitutes in their striped caps, weathervane makers hurriedly fixing a weathercock to a roof, layabouts pretending to be lepers or lame, and many other characters of low degree and even lower morals.

The prison warden has emptied the cells on the first and second floors and packed all the prisoners together in the ground-floor rooms. He's renting out the cells on the upper floors, as they provide an excellent view of the tournament. In the few windows of the residences, privileged spectators crowd together. But it's in the flat, sandy square, where on normal days grain is traded, that the crowd is so dense you could walk across the heads.

Such a cavalcade of knights has never been seen in Ghent. We're sitting on three covered stands in front of Borluut House, the stands a mass of colors, banners, and flags. The noblemen around me are magnificently dressed, and I have decked myself out like some forest goddess. My long crêpe dress is adorned with three small emeralds. Around my waist I wear a wide belt with a clasp showing a woman spearing a wild boar. Constance had urged me to dress in red, the color of passion and love, but I've chosen green, the color of youth and freedom and nature in the month of May. The color of hope, which I leave behind me forever.

The trumpets sound. My father pulls me up, and I stand next to him. The people of Flanders are looking at us.

"This tournament," my father announces, "is celebrated on the occasion of the engagement of my daughter, Marguerite of Male and Dampierre, future Countess of Flanders and Brabant, and of the domains of Rethel, Nevers, and Artois, and today the queen of love and beauty. She is promised to Edmund of Langley, Knight and Prince of England and Duke of Cambridge. I declare this knightly tournament open." Deafening cheers rise from the crowd.

One by one, the knights parade, in measured steps, along the arena. They're led by Johan Craenhals, First Knight of Flanders. His coat of arms, his blazon, is yellow, with a graceful white swan. Then comes Knight

Edmund. His horse is covered with a dark green cloth embellished with an image of Saint George, the most godly of all knights. On Saint George's left arm is a terrified-looking maiden and under his right foot an even more terrified-looking dragon. Edmund's weapons and his helmet—with a crest representing an eagle— are carried by liveried servants. There's cheering in the Corn Market as I dutifully tie my scarf onto Edmund's lance. The silk cloth is embroidered with the Lion of Flanders. Then Edmund raises his lance to the public so that everyone can see my scarf and know that he has conquered the heart of their future countess. People cheer till they're hoarse, but I'm silent. I have eyes only for Philip of Rouvres, who sits on his horse in his shirtsleeves. Philip of Rouvres receives louder cheers than any other knight.

Old Marshall Ingelram Noothaec controls the tournament. The wine-red color of his robes is a perfect match for his drinker's nose. The trumpets sound and Ingelram reads out the names of the forty knights and squires who will do battle today. Each one will defend his honor, his colors, and his blazon. Their horses are closely covered in leather to absorb blows, and the leather is then covered with elegant cloths with beautiful designs. The knights and squires glitter in the sunlight. They will do battle in a field that measures some two hundred feet by sixty feet, marked out by a wooden fence. Knight Edmund is the leader of the group of English knights, and Knight Craenhals leads their Flemish and

French opponents. Among the Flemish are Hendrik and Godfried, my comrades-in-arms from long ago. This is their first tournament.

Ingelram announces that this is a tournament *à plaisance* and rattles off the rules. Fighting is with blunt weapons, and only sideways sword blows are allowed. Those who break this rule will forfeit their armor and warhorse and be excluded from all future tournaments. He also announces that every lady has a scarf with her champion's colors. If the lady's fighter is suffering too much, she can throw her scarf to one of the referees so her knight is spared further blows and can leave the arena. A knight who has his helmet pulled off has lost the contest and must pay the knight who has defeated him. If one of the leaders loses his helmet, that group has lost and the battle is decided.

Five heralds blow their trumpets, and on that signal the two groups of horsemen turn to face each other, like living walls of iron and steel. Everyone is holding their breath. It's a sacred moment, a final moment of calm before the great storm. I'm so nervous I scratch my thumb open with the fingernail of my index finger. Fathers hoist their children onto their shoulders. Women climb onto chairs they've brought. Pickpockets scramble for the best spots and lower little blades from their sleeves into the palms of their hands. They'll strike the moment the battle begins. A young boy who's climbed up the back wall of the Spijkerhuis slides off the roof with a hoarse cry and falls on top of the stall where Jozefien van Merelbeke is selling fresh loaves of bread filled with rhubarb and mulberries. The stall's canvas roof breaks his fall and then rips, and he falls flat on his face onto the loaves. The little boy is stunned but quickly comes to his senses when Jozefien hauls him away from the table and boxes his ears. Dripping with mulberries and rhubarb, the boy runs off. The bystanders laugh, but then Marshall Ingelram shouts *Laissez aller!*

Visors are lowered. Lances are aimed forward. The ropes across the middle of the arena are cut, and forty pairs of spurs are dug into the horses' flanks. Two seas of grinding steel and savage spikes hurl themselves at each other. The whole marketplace resounds with the thunder of horses' hooves. Noblemen and commoners, porters and monks, whores and beggars shout themselves hoarse. The pickpockets' little blades do their work.

The day's first casualty is Hendrik, who aims his lance so low that it digs itself into the ground and shatters, hurling him through the air and onto the ground in front of the opponents' horses. The horses' hooves batter poor Hendrik's breastplates. With a scream, I jump up. The last thing I can see is the contest between Iwein van Ruwhoutbosch and Humphrey of Leeds, who are the first opponents to meet. Their lances graze each other's shield and they gallop straight into each other so that pieces of shield, lance, and shoulder plates are hurled into the air. Iwein's helmet, decorated with a frog's mouth, spins into the crowd. By then, so much dust has been kicked up that no one on either side of the arena or in the windows of the houses along the Corn Market can see what is happening. Everyone is holding their breath, and the only sounds that are heard are panicky whinnying, dull blows of metal on metal, and every so often a raw scream. My eyes search for a spot where the dust is less dense, but it's hopeless.

When, after an eternity, the dust begins to settle, half the knights have been unseated. Some are lying helplessly on their backs like overturned tortoises. Others have managed to get up and are slashing at each other with swords and shields. A servant running up to assist his master is trampled. Noble ladies in the galleries utter cries and drop their scarves to indicate that their knights must be carried off the field.

Philip, in his shirtsleeves, is still in the saddle. He has avoided the front line, but an English knight is coming at him. Philip dodges the mighty sword by letting himself fall sideways from the saddle while his horse pushes his opponent's mount out of the way. Philip is using his horse as a weapon. The English knight's sword slices empty air, and for a moment his horse is unbalanced, giving Philip time to get back into the saddle. He rams his shield against his opponent's neck, and the knight slides out of his saddle like a rag doll. It's a brilliant maneuver. I cheer. Philip may be a hopeless poet, but he's a brilliant horseman, and it is exactly because he's not wearing armor that he can move faster than his opponents.

For a brief moment he's the star of the tournament. Both commanders, Edmund of Langley and Johan

Craenhals, are still in the saddle, trying to get a view of the battlefield and barking quick orders. Edmund is clearly in a winning position. He gathers his knights. Eleven of them are left. Craenhals has only seven. I curse.

"Come on, Johan," I hiss. "For God's sake don't let a mob of island dwellers in armor get the better of you"

The next moment Edmund and his knights come thundering at the small group around Craenhals. It's a complete tangle. There's not even enough room for the knights to swing their swords. It's all pushing and shoving, tugging and hanging on. Knights drag each other off their horses and down into the mud, and among the stamping hooves they try to rip off each other's helmets. One horse crashes through the fence and falls onto its side into the crowd. A woman screams. A child cries.

Craenhals is forced into a corner of the fence by Edmund and one of his knights. He falls. A gasp of horror goes through the Flemish crowd. Craenhals scrambles up, his left arm hanging limply by his side. It must be broken or dislocated. But Craenhals doesn't give up. He takes his mace in his right hand and hits an English knight's horse with it, right on its nose. The horse shudders and crashes lifelessly onto its forelegs. The rider tumbles off. Craenhals isn't able to step out of the way, and the knight falls on top of him. They both fall against the fence, and Craenhals loses his mace. The Englishman attempts to pull the Flemish leader onto the ground by his left arm, while Craenhals, screaming with pain and without his sword, tries to beat him off with his right arm.

Edmund is just a few feet away, ready to pull off Craenhals's helmet. But just then, Philip spurs his horse and charges. He rides toward Edmund, and, like the good horseman he is, makes his horse rear. The horse's hooves strike directly in the center of Edmund's breastplate, throwing Edmund from the saddle with enormous force. Philip jumps off his horse, dodges a sword blow from an Englishman, and slips past him. He hurls himself at the Prince of England. If he can get Edmund's helmet off, he, my knight in shirtsleeves, will be the winner of the tournament. But something is making Philip hesitate. Next I see him fall, his hands clutching his stomach, his shirt staining red with blood.

I scream, shout his name, drop my scarf, and run off the viewing stands. A knight is pulling Philip out of the arena. It's Godfried, dear old Godfried, who has never said more than two words to me.

The next moment, Edmund picks up his blunt sword. Craenhals is still wrestling with his English opponent, covered in mud and straw, but he seems to be gaining the upper hand. Edmund sees the remaining Flemish knights rushing toward him on horseback or on foot to relieve their leader. He realizes it's now or never. Every second counts. He throws his sword away and jumps on Craenhals, who falls onto his back. Sitting on his chest, protected by his men's shields, Edmund wrenches the helmet with the lion's head crest from Craenhals's head.

Then he stands up and holds the helmet aloft.

"I am the king of the tournament," he shouts. The audience cheers wildly. Craenhals lies flat on his back, unable to get up. Edmund rips off his armored glove and stuffs it into Craenhals's mouth. The Flemish side has lost.

The servants carry their wounded masters to their tents, where they're looked after by surgeons. Broken arms and legs are wrapped in silk cloths drenched in egg white, which hardens when it dries and is then reinforced with splints. The knights' open wounds are washed with warm wine mixed with henbane and then cauterized with red-hot irons. I smell the stench of burning flesh. I run to Philip's tent. His white shirt is covered in blood. My father's personal physician, Wirnt van Obrecht, tears open the shirt and anxiously examines the wound. A single glance is enough for him to conclude, "It's a stab wound." The dagger has passed right through the side of his chest. The wound looks terrible—I can see a rib bone sticking out—but the physician turns to me and tells me it's not serious. The dagger has slid past the ribs and hasn't touched the lung. He'll live.

"It's no worse than a bloodletting," he shrugs. "It'll purify his blood." He turns away, leaving the patching up to his assistants. Philip looks anxiously at the needle and thread they hold ready. I take his hand. Our eyes meet.

"You are my knight," I say. He beams. Meanwhile, Surgeon van Obrecht is bending over another knight whose helmet is jammed on so tight it takes three men to wrench it off. It's Hendrik. He was the first to go down in the tournament, and his armor is covered in dents from the hooves of the horses that trampled him. And Hendrik, the knight from Ostend, doesn't make it. His face is blue. When the surgeon holds a small flask that spreads a foul vapor under his nose, nothing happens. The surgeon then slaps his face several times, but still Hendrik doesn't stir. He has suffocated inside his armor. He's the only fatality among the noblemen.

That evening, my father decides to have Hendrik's body lie in state in the Church of Saint Nicholas. The parish priest refuses at first, because a knight who dies in a godless tournament is not admitted into Heaven. But my father manages to persuade him with a modest gift to the church. The knights of Male hold a wake for Hendrik that night.

Edmund of Langley is unharmed and when the bolts of his armor have been unscrewed, he comes up onto the dais to receive his prize. He kneels before me, his future bride. I put a golden crown on his head. He stands and kisses both my hands. Then he embraces my father. The people cheer Edmund and me, the future Count and Countess of Flanders.

◫ ◫ ◫

THAT EVENING, Edmund knocks on my door and enters my room at the Gravensteen.

"You shouldn't be here," I protest.

"I wanted to be alone with my bride."

"Why?"

"To talk to you."

"We'll have the rest of our lives for that."

"Why are you displeased?"

"You won the tournament by treachery. You stabbed Philip with a dagger—"

"—but only wounded him," he confirms. "It was a mild punishment for the cowardly way he unseated me. He let his horse do all the work. He's no knight. He's a buffoon."

"You broke the rules of the tournament," I snap. "You ought to surrender your warhorse and armor. You stole victory."

"Your father doesn't share your opinion," is his calm reply. "He admires guile and cunning."

Edmund comes closer. I step back.

"You are indeed good in war," I say. "But I wonder what you're worth in love."

"What am I worth in love?" he muses. "In my time I've known countesses, milkmaids, ladies-in-waiting, and washerwomen, but there's no one I want more than you. I want your love."

"What for?"

"To have, of course," he smiles.

"To have me," I correct him. "And Flanders. I'm just a piece of land to you."

"You look at it the wrong way," Edmund gushes.

"If you have indeed known all the ladies you mentioned, my noble Lord," I say, "what makes me so special? I know what I look like. I'm not beautiful. I have ginger hair, my nose is too big, and my face is common as common. I bloody well look like my father. That's why men lie to me. They say they think I'm beautiful. But they're lying. Just like you."

"You are the most eloquent woman I know," Edmund says softly. "I like women with character."

I look at him. He's almost sweet. But something about him is false. If I were Eve, the first woman God created, then he is the serpent and his love the apple I have to bite.

"I would appreciate it, my future husband," I say slowly, "if you were to show a single quality that would make it possible for me to love you."

He comes closer, examining me from top to toe. He can't stop himself from smirking. His lips stay together so I can't see his teeth. His gentleness disappears as he looks at me.

"You will love me as I am, I promise you," he whispers, and I feel his warm breath on my face. He licks his lips and smiles. His hand scrapes along my cheek. I turn and try to go to the other side of the room. But he is quicker and cuts me off.

"You will please me," he says.

"We're not married yet," I reply.

"As good as."

With his left hand he pulls one of the pins out of my hair, making it cascade down. I'm frightened. He grabs a lock of my hair and holds it under his nose.

"You smell of love, woman," he whispers, putting his

hand on my breast. I slap his hand away, grab a stool by one of its legs, and prepare to thump him.

"We're not married yet," I scream.

Edmund doesn't come closer. He keeps grinning.

"I'm glad you want to fight. Scratch me. Hit me. I'd be delighted. I'll enjoy breaking you," he grins. I see his hunger for me in his glittering eyes. I shudder.

"I'll make you kneel before me," he hisses. "I'll make you crawl. I'll make you beg. I'll squeeze all your womanly spirit, all your Flemish pride, all your French airs out of your body until you lick my fingers like a dog."

"How dare you speak to me like that," I stammer, shaking uncontrollably.

"Oh, I'll break you. I can't wait to break you."

He smiles, bows low, and leaves the room.

17

I N MY DREAM, I'm running through the fields. My clothes get caught on thorn bushes. I look around, fearing robbers and the wandering souls of unbaptized children. I'm walking into the Marshland. The marshes surrounding me are teeming with living things. I'm crossing the little wooden bridges that link the dikes and finally I see the chapel. Our Lady of Hate.

The statue is almost unrecognizable. Damp and time have nearly eaten it away. But it's still there. I pray to Mary for Edmund's death. I beg God to let him catch leprosy or intestinal colic or blood boils or brain worms or any other fever or disease that will eat away his body and make him pray for mercy to all the heathen gods of old England.

I pray for hours, and days, weeks, and years seem to pass by. I dream of my mother giving birth and of my father being told that his child is lying crossways and that only God can help him. I see my father marching along the battlements while the people of Male stream into the freezing chapel. I see his face become expressionless when he thinks of the witch Morva, and I see her, although I've never known her. I see her woolen cap and the hole where her eye should be. I see my father pushing the shivering chaplain toward the altar. And I see him dragging the surgeon Wirnt van Obrecht out of the kitchens. He leaves me alone with Morva. I feel her bony fingers turning me in my mother's belly. I see Morva using her five lower teeth to bite through the navel string that links me to my mother.

I wake up screaming. It's pitch dark around me. I wonder how far the night has advanced, just as my mother wondered when her pains started during the night I was born.

I get up shivering, put on my undershirt, and throw a cloak over it. I walk through the deserted Gravensteen and climb to the top of the central tower. Everyone is asleep, even the watchmen around the pitch barrel, whose fire is nearly out.

The sky is clear. A star falls. I wonder if it's Hendrik riding to his final resting place. I look at the stars, but it feels as if all the stars are looking at me. I wonder why I dreamt about my birth and about my father who gave me life. Now he's taking that life away from me. Why did I see all those images in my sleep? What does it all mean? I'm looking at summer the way my father was looking at winter. That was where he found the inspiration to do what no one else would do: fetch Morva. But what can I do?

And then, suddenly, in the house of the Dominican Fathers, next to the unfinished Church of Saint Michael, the bells start ringing for lauds. The sign for the monks to start their day of prayer, as it is everywhere in the world of monasteries and clergy. And then I know.

I run down the steps as fast as I can. I need three things: a quill, a sheet of parchment, and a messenger. It takes me half an hour to write my letter and seal it with my signet ring, which shows the Lion of Flanders clasping a lily. Anyone would immediately recognize it.

Then I go to find Godfried. He's the silent one, the boy who, an eternity ago, with Willem, Hendrik, and me, set fire to haystacks. It was he I saved from Andrea Tagliaferro, who wanted to cut off his ears. His eyes look small and dark, because he has kept vigil over his friend Hendrik's body all night in Saint Nicholas's church. I ask if he'll travel to Avignon and back for me within twenty days to deliver this letter and bring me back an answer. He has to be back before the day of my wedding. I tell him my life and my happiness are at stake.

"To Avignon?" he says incredulously.

"Yes," I say. "Within twenty days."

He looks at the name on the cover of the letter, and his eyes pop.

"The Pope?" he stammers.

"His Holiness, Urban the Fifth."

Godfried immediately understands. He kneels before me.

"For your happiness, my Lady," whispers the boy

who never talks, "I'm ready to ride to the depths of Hell and cross swords with Satan himself."

An hour later, Godfried is ready to leave. He's dressed in leather trousers and shirt, with a dark tunic and a long hooded cloak. His clothes have little color so in case of danger he can easily hide. They're light so his horse can go as fast as possible. He holds the reins of a second stallion, which he'll use when his first horse becomes too tired. I give him a purse of gold coins and my long dagger, inlaid with agate and engraved with the motto of Flanders: *Ic houd stand*—I stand firm. When the cocks crow and the town guards unbolt the Ketel Gate, Godfried spurs on his horse.

❏ ❏ ❏

EDMUND STAYS ON IN FLANDERS. He visits every town in the county and is received everywhere as the future of Flanders. He is taken out hunting and drinks himself stupid at the banquets. I'm obliged to follow him everywhere. He can hardly keep his hands to himself. Any excuse is good enough to touch me, and he can't stop running his greasy fingers through my hair. Every time he wants to tell me something, he does it with his lips against my ear and I feel his hot, putrid breath on my face. What makes my skin crawl the most is feeling the tip of his nose in my neck, when he tells me in a whisper how many days are left before I'll be his in the eyes of God and all the saints who guard the portal of the Church of Saint John. On that day he'll be allowed to share my bed and do whatever he likes with me. My father has had Philip moved to the infirmary at the Norbertine Monastery in Grimbergen near Brussels. He says that Philip will recover faster there, in the hills of Brabant, surrounded by the most caring monks. But everyone knows my father just wants to keep Philip as far away from me as possible.

⊞ ⊞ ⊞

ON MY MAP OF HIS ROUTE, I check every evening how far Godfried has gone. I figure that he can comfortably make between fifty and a hundred miles a day. After all, he's riding for me, the heiress of Flanders.

As my wedding day approaches, I become more and more nervous. The ladies-in-waiting can't keep away from me. My skin is cleansed and my fingernails cleaned. My eyelashes and eyebrows are plucked and the hair along my hairline pulled out to make my forehead more elegantly high than it's ever been. My wedding gown is a wealth of blues, because blue is the color of fidelity.

The day before my wedding, I abandon all hope. I quarrel with Alaïs, who has come with her Knight of Gavere to congratulate me, and I mistreat Constance when she tries to tell me exactly what to do during the wedding night and what precautions I should take to prevent becoming pregnant too soon. Constance tells me I must do my duty. My fingernails have been cut so short I can't even bite them.

But on the evening before the wedding, when the pigs are being slaughtered for the banquet and the road between the Gravensteen and Saint John's church is strewn with red flowers, Godfried finally returns. I race down the stairs when I see him coming through the castle gate.

His horse is steaming. Foam drips from its mouth. Godfried's tunic is gray with dust. His lips are cracked. His face is deeply lined. He seems to have aged years in those few weeks.

"Lady Marguerite," he groans. "The world is dying. Wherever I went, the people were sick. It's the plague. It has returned."

"Have you got the letter?" I interrupt him.

From his leather shirt, which smells of decay and exhaustion, he produces a velvet wallet embroidered with a scepter, a crook, and the letter P, the emblem of the Pope.

"I had to wait a whole day outside the gates of Avignon," Godfried says hoarsely. "The people were fleeing the city to the North. The guards were forbidden to allow anyone to enter the city. I had to bribe them with the money you gave me. I presented the Cardinal with your dagger, and finally I was admitted to the Pope."

"And," I ask impatiently, "what's in the letter? Did the Pope say anything?"

"The Pope," Godfried says in confusion, "sat in a hall between three burning fires that were intended to keep the plague out of his palace. They had cut holes in the ceiling to stop the thick smoke filling the apartment. The Pope was sweating like mad among those fires while the whole palace was sweltering under the Provençal sun.

Your letter was first fumigated over one of the fires and then handed to the Pope on the end of a stick. He broke the seal, read your letter, and sighed. He told me to come back the following day. I tried to sleep in the stables with my horses, but in the city people were groaning and wailing. I heard doors being nailed shut and funeral bells ringing. I have never been more tired in my life, but I couldn't sleep. Everywhere around me, Death was doing its work."

Godfried has never spoken so many words at one time. He's still holding the wallet and I want to take it from his hand. But he won't let go, as if that wallet contains life itself, and so I tear it from his hand. He has trouble standing up. I stroke his cheek and tell him he'll always be my knight. He smiles faintly, and I rush inside the Gravensteen.

With thumping heart, I run up the stairs and swing into the Great Hall. There, my father and Edmund are playing chess. Edmund is seated and my father is on his feet, pacing in front of the chess board with its red and white chessmen. When Edmund sees me, he smiles broadly.

"My bride," he exclaims, holding his arms wide.

My father looks up and studies me. He sees immediately that something is going on.

"Your daughter is becoming more beautiful every day," Edmund says to my father.

"Let's finish our game first," my father says worriedly. "You're still under check."

"Ah, I concede the game, Father. I can't keep my head on the game with your lovely daughter so close."

My father groans and casts an uncertain look at the letter I have in my hand. Edmund approaches and stands before me with the broadest smile he can manage. It gives me a wonderful view of the black and brown ruins that pass for his teeth.

"I have a letter for you, Lord Father," I say, walking past Edmund to my father. He hesitates to take the letter from me, and keeps looking at the chess game, touching the white queen, made of walrus tusk.

"Do play on, son-in-law," my father grumbles.

"It's a letter from the Pope," I say.

"I'll read it tomorrow," he says, waving the letter away.

"I think it's urgent," I raise my voice.

My father looks me in the eye. Edmund comes to stand next to me, putting his arm around my shoulder.

"She's just bringing you a letter, Father," Edmund explains, stating the obvious.

"Son-in-law, you're not checkmate yet," my father almost whines. "Your bishop is about to take my queen."

Edmund examines the game and smiles.

"I concede victory, Father," says Edmund, toppling his red king.

My father groans. Without taking his eyes off me, he accepts the velvet wallet. He removes the letter, breaks the seal, and unrolls the letter.

Edmund slides his hand over my behind. I ignore it. I hardly feel it. I keep looking at my father's eyes reading and re-reading every line, every word, every flourish of the letter. As Edmund looks on, it slowly dawns on him that this letter might have something to do with our marriage. My father turns to the hearth. For a brief moment, I fear he's going to throw the letter into the fire. He must realize that I've done this. That I have broken the promise I swore to him and to God.

"Father," Edmund asks, his hand on my waist, "is everything as it should be?"

My father doesn't say anything. He turns around. I take a step back, afraid he's going to knock me down with the flat of his hand, like he did after our prank at the windmill. But he doesn't. He looks at me, his face as immobile as marble. I lower my eyes, like a dutiful daughter.

"What is it, Father?" asks Edmund. The Prince of England reads the letter. I see his eyes moving feverishly back and forth down to the end of the roll.

"I don't understand," he stammers.

"Will someone please tell me what the letter is about?" I say in a voice as innocent as a dove's.

"The Pope," my father grumbles, "the shepherd of mankind who holds the keys to the Kingdom of Heaven, informs me that the marriage of my daughter Marguerite of Flanders to Edmund of England cannot proceed. It appears he has discovered, upon a thorough examination of the many branches of the family tree of the world's great nobility, that the two of you are cousins. Far removed, it's true, but not far enough. Four removed, he's worked out, and that's forbidden by the Church and by God. Rules are rules, and the Pope has ordained that the marriage cannot be valid. Hence Marguerite of Flanders is not permitted to enter into holy matrimony with Edmund of Langley, Prince of England. Signed Urban V, Pope by the grace of God."

Silence falls in the hall. Edmund's lip trembles. My father looks at me.

"Oh, but that's terrible!" I shriek.

18

ON MY WEDDING DAY THAT ISN'T, a west wind scatters all the petals strewn between the Gravensteen and Saint John's church. I'm in the gallery that overlooks the Great Hall and I see Guild Masters Slicher van Riijpergherste and Frans Ackerman arrive. Ackerman is accompanied by two men in white caps, the captains of the Ghent militias. Slicher van Rijpergherste looks around nervously, but Ackerman radiates self-confidence. My father is seated on his chair, which is upholstered in deer skin. He receives the guild masters without any men-at-arms at his side.

"My Lord Count," Ackerman begins, without even bowing, "the whole city is abuzz with rumors about the break between your daughter and the Prince of England. Why has the Pope forbidden this union?"

"Because my daughter and Prince Edmund are blood relations of the fourth degree," my father replies dryly.

"Why did the Pope send you this letter? Who has prompted him to do this?"

"Gentlemen, you don't actually think I informed the Pope of my children's kinship," my father roars, getting up. "You're surely not thinking of accusing me in my own fortress."

Ackerman hesitates. Meanwhile, Guild Master van Rijpergherste has turned pale at this exchange of harsh words. He had no doubt urged Ackerman to take a proper diplomatic approach to the matter.

"Do you swear, my Lord Count, that neither you nor your daughter had a hand in this?" Ackerman shouts threateningly.

"I'm not accountable to you," my father shrugs. "The Pope is as wise as all the muses. He is God's voice."

"But we, Lord Count," says Slicher, taking a careful step toward my father, "we are the voice of the Flemish people. And what shall we tell them when they ask us to explain what has happened? How can we assure them that you haven't broken your word?"

"Because I tell you so," my father parries easily.

"Don't give the angry mob an excuse to kill," Ackerman enunciates carefully. "Because they will. Just as they did in Bruges during the Red Night, sixty years ago."

At this point, the guild master from Bruges turns to his colleague from Ghent, his arms raised. He urges him to remain calm and show restraint, but Ackerman will have none of it.

"Master Ackerman," my father begins. "Continue like this and you'll finish up like your predecessor, Jacob van Artevelde, who was butchered by his own people in Ghent."

His words are ominous, but Ackerman won't budge. Slicher van Rijpergherste looks terribly uncomfortable. Ackerman's captains have their hands on the hilts of their swords.

"The people are muttering. They suspect, Lord Count, that you want to sell Flanders to France," Ackerman says without batting an eye.

I see my father's fox face hardening. The scar around his eye flares red. He takes a step forward and hits Ackerman across the face. Blood spurts from his nose. I shrink back. The two captains are about to draw their swords, but my father already has his sword in his hand, its tip at Ackerman's throat. It's all happened in a flash. The captains take a step back.

"Gentlemen, gentlemen, please," groans Slicher, sweat pouring down his round face. "Let us please discuss the matter calmly."

The soldiers of the guard come running, but my father gestures for them to stay back. He's in complete control of the situation.

"I swear, Master Ackerman, I had nothing to do with the papal letter." My father looks Ackerman right in the eyes. "It was my wish, too, that Flanders and England should be united. I wished to give my daughter to Edmund."

My father speaks slowly. He almost seems to be enjoying the confrontation. The captains keep their hands on the hilts of their swords. Only when the soldiers of the guard come closer with their long lances do they let go. Slicher is so tense he can't stop stamping his feet.

"The Pope is the French king's puppet," Ackerman hisses. He's not daunted by the tip of my father's sword.

"He is still the bridge between God and humankind," my father says calmly. "And aren't we all puppets in God's hand?"

"Not us Flemings," Ackerman cries.

My father raises the hilt of his sword so the sword tip rests in the hollow of Ackerman's throat. The sword must weigh at least five pounds, but his hand is steady.

"You Flemings buy wool from England," he says. "Not from the English king, not from the English nobility, but from the Benedictine monks who keep tens of thousands of sheep on their estates. If you go against the Pope's will, you will no longer be able to obtain wool from the Benedictine monasteries."

Ackerman's face is contorted. My father knows the man came here full of fury and frustration. Not with strong arguments, nor with sanctions to force him to his knees. The matter was lost before it was even discussed. Slicher stands rigid and stares at Ackerman and the Count.

"You would kiss the Pope's cape and dry his feet with your own hair if the Benedictines would sell you their wool more cheaply, you money-grabbing weaver," my father concludes, slowly lowering his sword so its tip now rests on the collar of Ackerman's tunic.

"It occurs to me, my Lord Count," Ackerman says, pushing the sword aside with icy calm, "that your daughter is uncontrollable."

"My daughter submits to my will."

"Your daughter makes a laughing stock of us," Slicher finally intervenes.

My father sighs. I take a step back, into the shadows of the gallery.

"She's a horse without reins," Slicher asserts. "People say she's crazy. All of Flanders is gossiping about her—about her jewels, her clothes, her vanity, and her arrogance. They call her 'Princess Pearl.' She needs a strong man. A man like Edmund."

"If she were of common descent," Ackerman adds, "she would have long since been put on display in the marketplace wearing a muzzle, like a scold."

"But I'm not of common descent," I shout, stepping out from the shadows. All heads turn to me. "I'm your future Countess. After my father's death, I will reign over Flanders. No matter who I marry, I'll still be your Countess."

I must have spoken with great authority, for the guild masters and the captains are struck dumb. Even my father is silent for a moment. Then he smiles broadly.

"My friend Ackerman, I hereby exempt you from

the tax I imposed to finance the wedding and the tournament," he says generously. Ackerman relaxes. Slicher laughs with a hiccup.

"I'll keep you to your promise, my Lord Count," Ackerman says coolly. He slides his hand along his still bloody nose, indicating he won't forget the insult. Then he gives a little bow and turns. Slicher follows, reassured. He walks away from the Count backward, bowing three times before he reaches the door. I see my father looking in my direction. He nods. I take a step back, into the shadow.

⊡ ⊡ ⊡

LATER THAT MORNING, I look for Godfried to ask him to ride to Grimbergen and tell Philip the news. But I can't find him. His page tells me he left early in the morning to go to the Church of Saint Jacob. It's the church all pilgrims visit before they set off to the South on pilgrimage, wearing the emblem of a scallop shell. I wonder why he chose that church. I run from the Gravensteen, through the deserted streets, across the Friday market to Saint Jacob's.

Inside the church it's chilly and dark. Only a few candles are burning, and there's no sign of Godfried. I walk through the empty nave to the aisles. The sound of my steps dies away with a hollow echo in the large space. In the aisles, where sunlight barely seeps through the stained-glass windows, there's no one.

Then I hear bolts being drawn. When I'm close to

the altar, I turn to see four shadows gliding along the stone floor. Their steps are barely audible. Their leather shoes seem to float above the flagstones as they come at me, fast, unstoppable. Their cloaks flare out and under them I recognize English uniforms. Fear crackles inside me like chestnuts on a hotplate. The men grab me, and before I can scream, one of them clamps his glove over my mouth. I'm pushed onto the floor in front of the altar. I feel the cold of the stone floor penetrate my clothes and my body. One man holds my wrists and two others grab me by the ankles, spreading me out as if I'm a criminal about to be quartered in the market square.

Then the fourth man approaches. He takes off his hood and fear roars through my head as I recognize his face. I see eyes full of hatred. Edmund's eyes. He bends down, grabs the hem of my dress, and rips it in a single movement. I want to scream and yell. I bite into the glove, but it stays immovable over my mouth.

"I know what you're thinking, this is a church, this is holy ground, but you can't humiliate a Prince of England like that," Edmund rages. "I'm going to have you, no matter the consequences in this world or the next." Madness glows in his eyes. He lifts up his skirts, kneels, and pulls me toward him. I throw myself about violently as panic rages through my body like a hundred hornets. I try to wrench my ankles and arms loose, but his accomplices hold me in an iron grip. I can't control my tears and over the glove I can see Edmund smirking.

I see his awful teeth. I hear my own panting, and my choked moans. I feel his hands. They're pushing my thighs apart. There's nothing I can do.

But then Edmund hesitates. His lips clamp shut. He's looking at something or someone coming from the side. The man who's holding my wrists and mouth sees it, too. Edmund stands up and draws his sword.

Now I, too, discern a shape in the half dark of a side chapel. It's Godfried. He's unarmed. He's wearing only a blood-soaked shirt. I see how Edmund and the others hesitate. Only then do they see Godfried's face. It's covered in large, bluish boils. One of the boils has burst and seeps yellow pus and blood.

"It…it's the p-p-plague…," stutters one of the soldiers holding my ankles. Godfried lowers his shirt from his shoulders and I see that his whole body is covered in boils, pus, and blood. Edmund's sword is trembling in his hand, and when one of the soldiers lets go of my ankle, I kick out, using every ounce of my strength. My shoe hits the soldier's face, and I hear his nose break. My legs free, I hurl myself backward. The third soldier lets go of my wrists. Edmund looks at me and back at Godfried, who is coming at him like a ghost out of Hell. The three soldiers run away. Edmund's sword remains pointed at Godfried for another moment, but then he turns and hurries after his men. Godfried looks at me.

"Godfried," I stammer, instinctively stepping back.

"My Lady," he says, stretching his hands toward me.

He's a living corpse.

"I'll get the surgeon," I mutter and run.

"Marguerite," he groans.

I don't dare look back.

□ □ □

LESS THAN AN HOUR LATER, Surgeon van Obrecht emerges from Saint Jacob's church with his two apprentices. They have wrapped Godfried in a sheet. I hear him moaning deliriously as the apprentices carry him away.

Before it's even midday, one of the two apprentices becomes ill. He dies the next morning, a few hours after Godfried. Then the fire bells are rung.

Godfried has brought the plague to Flanders.

19

*L*ORD, REMEMBER US *in your goodness.*

The plague is more virulent than ever. The city of Ghent, which just two days ago was celebrating, seems to have collapsed into itself. So Chaplain Johannes van Izeghem was right. The end of the world has come. The gruesome prophetic Book of the Apocalypse has been opened, and the Four Horsemen of Doom have come to exact payment from humankind. The rider on the white horse is God's punishment for people's sins. On the red horse sits War. The rider on the black horse is Hunger and the rider on the gray horse is the most feared of them all. That rider is Plague. Death comes among us like black smoke, like a specter that knows no mercy for children, youth, or beauty. The people of Ghent are afraid to come out of their houses for fear of being infected. The magistrates don't dare go into the streets to record the last wills and testaments of the dying. The priests refuse to leave their churches to hear confessions. People scrape grit from the walls of churches and wear it on their breasts as protection. They say Our Fathers and Hail Marys. They burn candles before the statue of Our Lady. Every saint's help is invoked. Everyone begs God for mercy. Nothing helps. God's patience is exhausted. The plague spreads like an uncontrollable fire. The children are the worst affected. Mothers leave their sick children to their fate. The wooden cranes on the docks, which are worked by children, come to a halt. Kitchen Master Aelbrecht loses one kitchen boy after another. But it's not only children who die. Roderik van Rijpergherste succumbs. As does Constance, my Constance. She's taken to a plague house where, surrounded by the wailing and lamentation of other victims, she must wait for her death. I couldn't even say farewell to the woman who tried to be a mother to me.

People avoid each other. Charity is dead. The bells toll day and night, because the grave diggers want to receive their payment while they still can. My father prohibits the grave-diggers guild from ringing the bells. He forbids people to dress in black, even widows, and the announcers of death notices are silenced. The people of Ghent say there is a Plague-girl, who, in the shape of a blue flame, rises from the mouths of the dead and flies through the air to infect the next house.

I can still see the cart full of children's bodies standing outside Saint Nicholas's churchyard. A mob of starving dogs circles the cart. A black dog gets hold of a dead girl's leg and tries to drag her off the cart. The grave diggers shout, but the dog ignores them. Only when one of the grave diggers starts throwing stones at it does the animal finally let go. It runs off whining but stops about thirty feet away and stalks around, not daring to come closer. The graveyard is now overcrowded. The bodies are in shallow graves, and every night the rats root around in the loose soil for anything edible. My father approaches the grave diggers and orders them to burn the cart and the bodies. He commands the priest to give the children absolution for all their sins.

"But they're already dead," the priest objects.

"So what? All of us are already dead," the Count of Flanders exclaims. "We've just been granted a stay of execution."

The priest blesses the cart and sprinkles the children's bodies with holy water. An hour later, a black, stinking smoke rises from the graveyard. The wind blows the soot through the city. The fine, dark ash sticks to my skin. I rinse my hands and face again and again, afraid the thin soot of Death will contaminate me, too.

◫ ◫ ◫

MY FATHER DECIDES I am to marry Philip of Rouvres. We leave the infected city of Ghent. While whole families are locked in their houses, the shutters nailed down so they must die in misery and loneliness, the monks sing *Hallelujah* and the Archbishop of Flanders celebrates our marriage in the grand Church of Saint Walburga in Oudenaarde. Away from Ghent. The wedding guests wear masks to ward off the evil vapors of the plague.

I, too, hold a white mask inlaid with jasper over my face. Ten servers walk about swinging censers in which alumroots smolder to keep the plague out of the church. Our marriage itself seems to be tainted by misfortune. I look at Philip's red mask and his dark eyes moving behind it. The nuptial blessing is pronounced. We are man and wife. Philip lowers his mask. For the first time since the tournament, I see his face—but I see a stranger's face, as if our afternoon of delight was only a dream. Now that the end of time has come, now that the world is on fire and the horsemen of the Apocalypse are among us, those few brief moments of carefree adventure I shared with Philip seem foolishly childish.

He bends toward my mask to kiss me. His mouth distorts in pain. The wound in his side has not yet healed. His lips come closer. But I turn my head away, afraid he'll infect me. My father is seated behind me on a chair covered in purple velvet. He has great trouble sitting still. He's one of the few who don't wear a mask.

Followed by a long retinue, and accompanied by the singing of fifty children, we proceed to the church portal. There, under an arc of saints, the people of Oudenaarde throw a cloud of petals over us. My father stands behind me.

"Now you can no longer hit me," I whisper to him from behind my mask.

"Your husband will take care of that," he says.

"He wouldn't dare," I hiss back at him.

"Every stubborn she-ass deserves a whipping," is his

reply. "And if he doesn't have the gumption, I will."

"Father," I say calmly, "if you as much as touch me just once more, I'll hack off your head."

Before he can reply, Philip takes a step forward.

"You are my father now," he says, lowering his mask and spreading his arms to embrace the Count of Flanders.

"You're forgetting the plague, son," my father warns, taking a step sideways. Philip lowers his arms.

"I wish you much luck with my daughter," my father says to Philip. "You'll need it."

◫ ◫ ◫

MY DEPARTURE FROM FLANDERS is a flight. Our carriages rattle away from Oudenaarde and from Flanders. We journey to France. Philip and I travel in two separate carriages. But the farther south we go, the more terrible the world looks. Fields lie deserted, houses have been destroyed, and in a valley lie hundreds of carcasses of cows, sheep, and people. The soldiers of our escort keep scarves over their mouths, and I keep my face pressed into a cloth drenched in lavender water, but none of it can suppress the overpowering stench of Death. We see men and women roaming about like lunatics. No one is sowing. Fields are not cultivated. Everywhere, weeds overgrow fertile ground. All is lost.

◫ ◫ ◫

THE CASTLE OF ROUVRES is a hunting lodge. It stands at the end of *Le val sans retour*, the Valley of No Return. You can see the lodge from a great distance. The valley forms one single forest. Summer has gone, and the whole region seems dull and dry. The lively green of advancing summer has given way to the wilted yellow that announces autumn. The lodge, which sits on the hunting grounds of the dukes of Burgundy, is surrounded by woods. No peasants or serfs are to be seen, and only a handful of game wardens, servants, and soldiers are in the castle. Behind it, a waterfall forms a stream that, beneath the dense undergrowth of the adjoining forest, disappears into the ground after a short distance. It's deathly quiet around the gray castle of Rouvres, as if the spirits of the forest have the whole area in their grip. I have arrived at the end of the world.

▣ ▣ ▣

OUR ARRIVAL stirs the castle into life. The dust covers are pulled from the furniture, the beds cleared of fleas, the floors covered in fresh hay, bats chased from the rafters, and the light blue shutters thrown open to the autumn sun. In this lost valley, Philip assures me, we're safe. It's our refuge. We're free from the jostle of people and the bustle of towns. This is where we'll stay until the plague passes. We take off our masks. I take deep breaths of the free air of Rouvres.

Philip tries to cheer me up by taking me on horseback rides. We gallop through the woods as gusts of wind rip the last leaves from the trees. Deer and roes leap away when we approach. All around us in the undergrowth, there are noises of animals hastily looking for cover.

"I would give a fortune to see you laughing again, my love," says Philip.

"You were the one who couldn't laugh," I reply. "Weren't you the gloomy Duke who pined away inside the cold walls of his somber castle?"

"But that was when I didn't know that you existed," Philip smiles.

"For God's sake, Duke, the whole world is dying, and you talk about laughter," I respond and spur my horse. He follows me.

"I love you because you're the most amusing person I've ever met," he calls from high in the saddle. "You can be cold and cruel, you can be as obstinate as a donkey, you can be surly and tiresome. But when I'm with you, I feel life streaming through me. There's a fire inside you and its sparks refresh me. You have an inextinguishable glow—"

I slow my horse. I feel infinitely tired and terribly old.

"Stop it," I sigh. "You're still an appallingly bad poet."

We rein in our horses. Philip isn't sure what to do. We look at the forest. We hear the rustling of the wind.

"When I was little," I say after a while, "my mother said that, like her, I was guarded by twenty-six angels. That was the privilege of a Lady of Flanders. But I think the angels have forgotten us. I'm like my mother. I, too, will end up inside the four walls of a convent. She talks to the ghosts from her youth. She looks outside with eyes that no longer see. She eats with a mouth that no longer chews. Every day, she's given poppy juice to dull her senses and prevent her fits of madness. And that is someone with twenty-six angels."

Philip takes his time before replying.

"My love," he says finally, "you're not going into a convent. And forget about those angels. You are the angel. Do you remember that first afternoon we spent together? That ride, getting away from the thunderstorm! And the kiss you gave me! I felt I was born that day... Aren't you the woman who kicked over the bathtub in the Valley of the Virgins, and didn't you give that lout... What was his name again...?"

"Roderik van Rijpergherste," I supply despondently.

"...a kick in the head!"

"He's dead, dead of the plague, because of me," I cry.

"What do you mean, because of you?"

"I've broken my sworn promise," I hear myself screech. "All of Flanders is now infected. And it's all my fault."

I'm out of breath from screaming. I can't get enough air. I grab hold of my horse's mane. I feel myself sliding from my saddle. I feel the ground slap into my back. It's as if God is punishing me here, on the spot, by drawing the air out of my lungs. I see clouds and the sky through the browning tree tops and then everything goes black. Is this what dying is like? I keep seeing the cart full of dead children outside Saint Nicholas's church, the dogs circling the cart, the black dog biting into the dead girl's leg. I see the girl's long blonde hair gliding over the bodies and I see her face, pale as the fog… It's my face, but not quite. My nose becomes smaller, my features grow softer, and my hair turns blonde. I no longer have my father's fox head… I have become beautiful. I've stopped breathing. I feel the dog tugging at my leg, again and again. This time, there's no one throwing stones at the dog. I see my lips moving and I hear myself screaming.

Then I see the treetops again, and Philip, who's pulling me away from the stinging nettles by my legs. I take great gulps of air.

"I thought I was losing you just then, my love," says Philip, rubbing my hands with a wet cloth to soothe the stinging of the nettles. I'm still gulping in the fresh autumn air.

"How can you think it's all your fault?" Philip asks.

"I sent Godfried to Avignon to ask the Pope for an *interdictum*, a letter in which he would prohibit the marriage. I broke my sworn promise," I whisper, not daring to look at him. "But in Avignon, the plague was raging and Godfried brought the blue flame of the disease with him to Flanders. Everything is dying in Flanders, and it's my fault."

"How could a young girl like you spell the end of Flanders?"

"They say the plague is a girl," I whisper.

"You are not the end of Flanders, you are its future," is Philip's reaction.

I sigh. He doesn't understand.

"It's not your fault." Philip takes my hands in his. "It's not your fault. The plague was already in Avignon and is spreading everywhere. In Flanders, too. God is punishing humankind, not a fifteen-year-old girl."

"I'm not even fifteen," I say.

"The plague's not here, my love." Philip strokes my hair. "We're safe here. Here, in my hidden valley. We have escaped Death's clutches. You broke your promise to God by not marrying Edmund. But when you made that promise, you had never even seen Edmund. You couldn't know what he was like. I know what he is like. I've felt the dagger he stuck into me. How could God not forgive you? How could God not want your happiness?"

Philip is silent for a moment. I feel his fingers under my chin. He turns my head to face him.

"And your happiness, my love," Philip whispers, "is me."

"Oh, stop it," I push him away. "Stop being so manly. Don't go on and on with your silly talk."

I get up and painfully mount my horse.

"So what should I do," Philip shouts, his arms spread. He's desperate now. "What must I do to win your love?"

I push Palframand toward him. My horse nearly bumps his chest. I bend toward him and kiss him on the mouth.

"To win my love, you have to shut up," I smile.

He's silent. At least for the moment.

"I wouldn't mind another kiss," he murmurs.

"Only if you can gallop faster than me and get to the castle first," I reply, pressing my boots into my horse's flanks with a loud hoot. Palframand storms away. Philip runs to his stallion and drags himself into the saddle. It flashes through my mind that he's quite far behind. It's as if life is waking up inside me. My belly becomes warm. My breasts are tingling. I bend low over Palframand's back so he can gallop as fast as he can. The dark thoughts blow out of my head. As I gallop along, I pray. *God, grant me happiness*. I keep repeating that until we storm into the courtyard of the castle. The two girls tending geese scamper away. The geese honk and flap in a panic. One of them lands in the horse trough. I push Palframand close to Philip's stallion. Our horses rub against each other. There, in the courtyard of the castle of Rouvres, amid the squabbling of a whole herd of furious geese, I give him a second kiss. The kitchen master has been lighting the fires. He calls out that he'll organize a feast for tonight. And I decide to give myself to Philip that evening.

▣ ▣ ▣

GOD, GRANT ME HAPPINESS.

I pluck my hairline and my eyebrows. I wash my hair in rainwater in which floats a handful of rosebuds and some sprigs of marjoram. I put on a clean white undershirt and an under gown over that. It has so many ribbons and ties that Philip will have his work cut out for him when he undoes it tonight. *God, grant me happiness.* I pin up my hair and hide it under a butterfly hat decorated with the blue pearl of fidelity. When Philip removes it tonight, my hair will cascade over my shoulders like a waterfall.

I choose a cherry-red gown with wide sleeves and drench it in a bath with cloves, jasmine, and musk. Then I dry the gown in the evening sun and put it on. The gown sticks to my skin. *God, grant me happiness.*

I fasten a black ribbon below my breasts to push them up. I rub flour on my throat and the top of my breasts to make my skin even whiter than usual. I examine myself in the metal mirror and try a few dance steps. Keeping one foot on the floor, I spin around. My gown spreads like an opening flower. Even before the evening bell rings out, I walk along the top of the wall that links the towers of the castle.

And there I see Philip. He's looking at the setting sun, his hands leaning on the crenellations. He hasn't noticed me yet. *God, grant me happiness.* On tiptoe, I approach. The hem of my gown rustles on the stones. I'm now just a few feet from him, but he still hasn't noticed me. I'll put my hands over his eyes and surprise him. I'm nearly by his side. He turns and sees me. He gags.

The sound comes from deep inside him. I see he's having great difficulty standing. He spits out black slime that clings to his clothes. A wave of sickness engulfs him. He gags again and looks at me wild-eyed. "My face," he howls. "Look at my face."

I see the purple spots on his face and take a step back. My movement tells him everything. The plague has followed us.

God will not grant me happiness.

20

THAT VERY NIGHT, an isolated shelter is constructed. It's still dark when the inhabitants of the castle accompany us with torches to a clearing in the woods. The soldiers, servants, and game wardens keep a safe distance. Every time I turn to ask them something, they hurriedly step back. Small flasks of poppy juice for the pain are handed to us at the end of a stick.

Philip has difficulty walking upright. His face is dark and swollen. In a matter of a few hours, the purple spots have grown into egg-shaped boils. Pus drips from his right ear. He's shaking with fever and seems unable to see properly. I hold his hand to guide him to the shelter. Occasionally, his muscles spasm and he shivers.

The shelter is a cube-shaped wooden structure with two compartments. One for Philip, and one for me, the woman he has kissed and who has breathed the same air. The woman who, beyond doubt, is also infected. The woman who has been granted a slightly longer stay of execution. The woman who has been punished by God because she broke the oath she had sworn on the cross to marry the Prince of England.

Before first light, a priest comes. We're numb with cold from staying outside all night. Dew covers our hair. We both go to confession in front of the shelter. Philip is so weak he can't even cross his hands. I help him. Our four hands are crossed together for the priest who grants us forgiveness for all our sins. I see his right hand blessing us. *In nomine patris, et filii, et spiritus sancti.*

We enter the shelter. Through separate entrances. The last I see of Philip before he crawls into the shelter are his swollen lips, which seem to be shaping my name. I enter on the other side. Across the middle of the shelter there's a partition. Behind that wall is Philip. Philip's servants hurriedly nail up the two small entries into the shelter. We are now cut off from the outside world. This shelter will become our coffin. The gown I put on for love will become my shroud.

"Marguerite," I hear Philip whisper. I hear his clothes rub against the partition. "It's not fair," he groans. "It's not fair."

What can I say to him? That God does not wish our happiness? I hear him talking deliriously all morning. He's beset by terrible fever dreams. Only toward evening does he seem to rest easier. He's drunk some of the pain-killing poppy juice. He's breathing heavily, but talking calmly now.

"I'm only fifteen," Philip says. "A man shouldn't die at fifteen."

He tells me his life story. Everything he can remember. His first wrestling lesson, his mother who sang the old songs to him and cared for him on her own after his father was kicked to death by a horse just a month before he was born. His mother died a year ago. He tells me about the region where he grew up: the Auvergne, south of Burgundy. It's a country of extinct volcanoes, where shepherds sing their sheep to sleep. The mountain people learn from an early age to whistle on their fingers, and their whistling can reach across huge distances to warn of a coming thunderstorm or to wish each other luck. They have an alphabet of whistle-signals that only the native mountain people know how to decipher.

The mountains are high and craggy, and that is where people feel closest to God. There is a convent there, which is known as "Our Lady of the Snow," but the shepherds call it the "Convent of the Heavens." Philip tells me that once, as a little boy, he rested there after a long mountain walk with his mother. The nuns gave him goat's milk with honey. He had never before drunk anything as delightful.

Philip asks me if I love him. How could I possibly say anything but "yes," in those moments of total darkness, in those hours of utter despair, in that night when all Philip can do is waste away and die. And, on that last day, I know that I do love him. I feel myself one with him, my knight in shirtsleeves. The two of us will journey to Heavenly Jerusalem, where we'll gallop again through meadows full of flowers. I promise him that, together, we'll make roses rain down on Earth.

Philip dies as the first rays of sunlight poke through the chinks in the shelter. I tell the men who come to bring me food at midday through the small hatch in the shelter's wall. They slide the dish of food inside on a breadboard. They say they don't dare touch Philip's body. They'll wait. Until I die, too.

Now, my hope is that it'll happen quickly. I wait impatiently for the plague. Every hour, I check my skin in the half dark to see if any lumps have appeared. Every time my stomach gurgles, I bend over, ready to gag. At every cough I expect to spit out slime.

Three days pass and nothing happens. I'm so cold I completely wrap myself in my gown. All this time, Philip lies behind the partition. The entire shelter smells of decay. I lie down on the ground and no longer touch my food. I pray to God for deliverance, but nothing happens. I only get colder.

On the fifth day, the door is thrown open and a man pushes a burning torch inside. I look up, and by the light of the torch the man examines my face.

He turns to the outside and says, "She doesn't have the plague."

On hands and knees, I crawl out of the shelter and my eyes are blinded by the fierce light. Under my fingers, I don't feel grass, but snow. Winter has come.

▢ ▢ ▢

I WANT TO LEAVE for the South that very day. I will take

nothing with me. In the castle, I'm bathed and then two of Philip's servants escort me out of the castle on horseback. They'll take me to where I've decided to end my days. I want to be small, like an insect, and hide in the cracks of a stone. I no longer want to be part of this life full of suffering, pain, and fear. I want to be invisible. While we ride through the snow-covered valley, the shelter is set on fire. I look back one final time and see the black smoke billowing above the white forest. We ride for five days, sleeping in deserted inns. Animal skulls have been nailed to the doors to ward off evil. On the morning of the fourth day, high up on a mountain that rises from the landscape, I spot the convent Philip told me about. The convent of Our Lady of the Snow. The Convent of the Heavens.

Philip's servants leave me inside the entrance. I come face-to-face with the convent's Mother Superior. She's a thin woman of about forty, the lines of her jawbones clearly visible under the pale skin and blue veins of her face. She has a strange thick lower lip and sharp eyes that see everything. I'm still wearing my cherry-red gown. I tell her I want to enter the convent. That I want to share the life of the nuns. That I don't intend to return to a world that is coming to an end. I want to tell her my story, but she raises her bony hand.

"Every woman here," Mother Superior tells me, "has a story that may be even more painful than yours."

I don't know what to say.

"Tell your story to Our Lady in the chapel," she

continues. "We live in silence."

I'm led to the bathhouse, where I take off my gown and undershirt. Shivering with cold, I'm washed by two nuns. They cut my long, reddish-brown hair short with a large pair of blunt scissors. My gowns are burnt. My jewels are a gift to the convent's treasury. I put on the wimple and the white, undyed habit of the Sisters of Our Lady of the Snow. On my feet, I wear simple sandals. They guide me to the chapel and I kneel before the altar, behind which stands a remarkable statue of Our Lady, sculpted in jet stone. Above the altar, the chapel's only stained-glass window takes pride of place. The window shows Our Lady surrounded by images of the most important moments in her life. The nuns call the window the *glass bible*. The image of Our Lady is dressed all in blue. For a suffering woman, it's the color of pain and sorrow.

This is where I want to be. In the Convent of the Heavens. Far away from people. Far away from everything. Surrounded by silence. Here, I will no longer have to struggle through the rough waves of life. Here, I am a sister among sisters. I want to exist only for God. That is my destiny. It's not my task to love, bear children, and continue the House of Flanders. No longer will I live in the outside world, full of pain, fear, and death. I'm safe here, in this house in the clouds, inside these sacred walls, in this profound silence. I'm now close to Heavenly Jerusalem, close to my mother's spirit, and close to Philip. I will wait here patiently until I can join them. Here I will die and be carried, wrapped in a white sheet, to the resting place at the foot of the mountain. On these graves there are no names, because all sisters are equal in the sight of God.

▣ ▣ ▣

AS TIME PASSES, Flanders will forget me. Only later, much later, if the world still exists, the oldest survivors, toothless and brainless, will insist they once knew me. The bride of Flanders who disappeared into the mists of France. Chaplain van Izeghem was more than right. Woman leads man into confusion. She is a constant source of trouble, a perpetual state of war, a daily devastation, and a house filled with storms. And what is true for most women is doubly true for me. I, the heiress of Flanders, am guilty through and through. I am being punished for my frivolity, for my vanity, and for my broken promises. I, the Lady, born between the fingers of Morva, the witch of the Marshland. I am cursed. I am the Devil's plaything.

21

THE HORSEMEN come during a snowstorm. One dark morning, when it's hard to say whether it's day or night, their arrival is announced by a long drawn-out whistle from a shepherd in the valley. Only toward the end of the afternoon, while we're eating our evening meal by the last of the daylight, does one of the sisters announce that she's spotted the horsemen from the tower of the gatehouse. Mother Superior tells us to continue with our meal and then prepare for vespers. We go to the chapel by way of "Paradise," the inner courtyard surrounded by its four cloisters and facing the chapel. There we say vespers as we watch the world grow dark through the blue-stained glass. After our prayers, one of the nuns comes to tell Mother Superior she's seen torches on the path on the west side of the mountain. The east side of the convent, which is perched against the clouds and overlooks a ravine, has few windows. It's a massive structure of natural stone and hard timber. It's a fortress. But the horsemen come closer. They dismount and lead their horses to the door of the convent by the light of their torches. Mother Superior reassures us. No one knows who the horsemen are. They may not have bad intentions. Yet we all pray for protection. For a long time, we hear nothing more, except the winter wind scouring the walls. The silence goes on so long that some of us begin to think the torches were never there, that the horsemen were a mirage. We get ready for the final prayer of the day, gathering in the chapel to say compline. We cross ourselves with holy water and kneel on the floor. We reflect and pray in silence. But at that very moment, in the middle of the holy contemplation of the evening prayer, a fist hammers on the convent gate. The sisters get off their knees, panic stricken, murmur Hail Marys, and slide rosaries through their fingers. Again, I hear the fist hammer on the gate. Mother Superior marches to the gate. We follow. We stand behind her while she slides open the eye-level peephole. The man outside can only see her eyes.

"Lady," the man at the gate says, "we ask that you open your gate for us."

We can barely understand his words because of the howling wind.

"My Lord," Mother Superior says firmly. "No man has set foot under this roof for two hundred years. Except, of course, the local priests, who come to administer the last sacraments to our sisters. And as far as I can see, you are not a priest."

"Of course I'm not, woman," the man shouts, trying

to make himself heard above the noise of the wind. "I am the Count of Flanders, and I've come to get my daughter."

The sisters look at me. I lower my eyes. I take a step forward, but Mother Superior raises her bony hand. The other nuns pull me back.

"The woman you consider your daughter no longer exists," Mother Superior replies. "Only the brides of the Lord live here."

"Woman," the man shouts impatiently. He can still barely be heard above the howling wind.

"I want to see my daughter, whether she's dead or alive."

My heart contracts. I cross myself.

"My Lord of Male," Mother Superior replies. "Your daughter has given her life to God and she doesn't ever want to see you again."

She has spoken forcefully, but I can see her thick lower lip trembling. She closes the peephole. For a short while, there's silence outside and I imagine my father must be cursing by a whole gallery of saints. The nuns hold each other's hands. They surround me as if to protect me from calamity. All we hear is the whistling of the wind and our own breathing. The silence goes on for so long that we begin to wonder if the horsemen have gone back to the valley. But we know it isn't so. It would be madness to try to descend the mountain in this wind and darkness. But still there's silence. Until suddenly we hear a thundering blow and see the gate shaking on its hinges. The nuns scream. I feel my skin tighten. Then there's a second blow. I wonder what they're using to ram the gate, and remember there were boulders lying by the path. If three men lifted one of those and ran at the gate with it, it would create this sort of din. Mother Superior looks as if she can't believe what's happening. As if she's convinced that all that thick timber, all those iron nails, all those steel reinforcements will keep the men out of her convent. At the next blow, we hear timber cracking, and Mother Superior shouts that we should move away from the gate. But there's no escaping from this house built on the edge of a ravine. Our habits rustle and our sandals squeak as we run into the passages of the convent. There's another blow, and still another.

The battering resounds throughout the convent, as if someone is trying to shake awake those walls that have been asleep for centuries. Hollow echoes thunder through the rooms. We flee along black-and-white-tiled floors, through halls with painted ceilings and multicolored mosaics. We run outside through the cloisters that surround the Paradise Courtyard. The cold wind hits us in the face and pulls at our wimples. Snow stings our noses. We hurry into the chapel—it's as far as we can go. Behind the altar wall lies the abyss. Not in a hundred years has so much noise been heard here.

We huddle together before the black Virgin. Her features are finely drawn and her hand is raised in a blessing for those who kneel before her. But the black

Virgin does not reassure the sisters. They ask me what sort of man my father is. Is he a follower of God or of the Devil? How dare he desecrate a convent, one of the most grievous deadly sins? Someone says the heavy wooden gate will stop him, but I know that not even a dozen gates would stop my father. He wants to take me back to Flanders. But I will stay here, among my sisters, close to God. No one can go against the Lord's will, not even my father.

The battering continues, but with each blow, the hope in our hearts grows stronger. Perhaps the gate is too strong after all. It's made of heavy wooden beams and what could a handful of armed men achieve against that? Nor does the convent have windows for them to come through. But above all, we put our trust in Our Lady to protect us. We pray constantly in front of her jet-black image. Vapor rises from our mouths as we pray. The gate will hold. Here we are safe. Then we hear the splintering. It's as if the whole world is being torn apart.

"Let us be," we hear Mother Superior shout in the distance. "This is the house of God." Which, all things considered, is a useless thing to say to someone who's battering down your door.

"Woman," comes the reply, and my heart skips a beat when I hear my father yell, "I've come hundreds of miles to see my daughter, and see her I will!"

For a moment we hear no more voices. Only the clinking of swords against armor and the sound of the convent cell doors being thrown open and shut, one by one. We look at each other. Are all the sisters here with us? Or has someone hidden in the kitchen or the bathhouse? The answer comes right away. A loud scream rises from the direction of the bathhouse, where half-deaf Sister Anna-Francisca is peacefully enjoying her monthly bath. Sister Anna-Francisca is a veritable fortress of a woman. She has a copper washbasin in her hand and she uses it to instantly put the intruders to flight. The door slams shut, and the soldiers march closer and closer. I'm standing behind the altar among my sisters. With my hands crossed, I look up to the statue of the Holy Virgin. The soldiers' steps gain speed as they get closer. It seems as if we can hear them breathing on the other side of the chapel doors. The double doors swing open. They bang into the walls. Winter blows in. My sisters and I shrink back. Our bodies press together.

One man steps forward, and I immediately recognize my father. His clothes and hair are dripping from the snow. The sleeves of his hauberk glitter with moisture. His cloak, its hem covered in mud, drags along the floor. From his belt hang a one-and-a-half-size sword and a rapier. I recognize the knob shaped like a marguerite daisy. It's my rapier.

"Sisters," my father calls. "We don't intend you any harm. I've come only to fetch my daughter." Silence falls in the chapel. The candles hiss. The soldiers remain by the door. Just then, the alarm bell sounds. Mother Superior has run into the gatehouse and started ringing the bell. Its sound will reverberate all over the valley and warn people that the Convent of the Heavens is in danger.

Angrily, my father looks back and two of the soldiers run off, toward the gatehouse. I detach myself from my sisters and take a step forward. My father looks at me.

"Sister," he calls, "I want my daughter." He hasn't recognized me. I pull off my wimple and see him looking, full of horror, at my shorn hair.

"What have you done?" he stammers.

"This is where I belong, Father." I hear my voice echoing through the chapel. My father is silent. "I'm doing penance for my frivolity, my vanity, and all the evil I have caused. My life now belongs to God and to these Sisters of Divine Mercy. God has called me to Him, and I ask you to respect His will."

"Daughter, God will call you to Him when I tell Him to," my father blasphemes, and the nuns cross themselves. "As long as you live, you are my daughter and you have duties to fulfill."

"I'm no longer your daughter," I spit back. "Thank God."

My father growls. All this time, the bell has continued to ring. One of the soldiers he sent off to the gatehouse has returned.

"My Lord, the abbess has barricaded herself in the bell tower," he stammers.

"What's stopping you from ramming the door open

and ripping the rope out of her hands?" my father shouts. "Must I do everything myself?"

The soldier nods and runs back.

"Leave the abbess in peace, Father," I say. "You don't stand a chance. All the people of the valley will have heard the bell and will be on their way here. What can you and your six soldiers do against them?"

My father comes closer. The rapier on his belt bumps against his leg. We face each other barely three feet apart. I can smell the wine on his breath. His eyes are wild and his short beard hasn't been trimmed for days. His clothes stink of horse sweat.

"There are two ways to come with me, daughter. The hard way and the easy way," he says, trying to keep his voice calm.

"This is sacred ground, Father," I shout. "We're in the house of the Lord. If you commit violence here, you offend your Creator."

His hand lands on my cheek with tremendous force. For a moment, I'm stunned and then my father grips me by the wrist. The nuns scream. I let myself go limp and try to kick his legs, but nothing helps. He drags me over the chapel floor. I'm screaming. The nuns cross themselves and their wailing echoes along the vaults.

"I curse the day your seed begot me," I rage. "I curse Flanders and your ancestors. I'm ashamed before God and the world to be your daughter."

My father drags me all the way to the entrance of

the chapel. He looks down at me on the floor, between his legs. Panting, I cross my hands as if for prayer, and for a moment he thinks I'm about to beg. Instead, I hurl my joined fists upward. I strike something soft, and my father doubles over with a long, drawn-out moan. The next moment I rip the rapier from his belt. The soldiers behind him come rushing forward but hesitate when they face the tip of my sword. My father lifts his arm, tries to say something, but all that comes from his mouth is an incoherent gurgle. Meanwhile, the bell keeps tolling and the soldiers are getting nervous. I feel the leather straps of the hilt of my sword in the palm of my hand. The knob of the hilt rests on my wrist. My sword does not tremble. That gives me courage. We hear splintering and screaming in the distance. The bell stops tolling. The men have overpowered Mother Superior.

"You have just proven, daughter, that you weren't meant to be a nun," my father says, sounding more like himself. "You're just like me. You're a fighter."

"I am not like you," I fume, pulling my sword back and raising it high behind me, ready to bring it down with a devastating swing on anyone stupid enough to come too close. One of the soldiers looks as if he may try to disarm me, but my father holds him back.

"You have my blood. You have the blood of the counts of Flanders. You are a warrior," my father shouts, coming forward threateningly, ignoring the sword I hold in readiness. For every step he comes forward, I take one back.

"You aren't meant to dry up in a convent on top of some godforsaken rock. You are meant to be the Countess of Flanders. To put the guild masters in their place and to tell the stupid French knights how to fight a war. You shouldn't be here. I know you!"

"You know nothing about me," I shout back. "You've ignored me all my life, you drove my mother to madness, you took Willem away from me, you forced Edmund on me… Has there been one moment, one single moment in your life when you thought not of yourself, but of me?"

"It has made you what you are today. Only one person will be able to rule Flanders when I'm no longer there, and that person is you. You're made of iron, and I have forged you."

"I'm not made of iron, I am made by God. This is where I'm at home. Here. I would rather die than go with you."

My father stares at me. A panting young girl with a sword.

"So be it," are the last words my father utters. Then he draws his sword.

22

ANDREA TAGLIAFERRO GAVE ME FIFTY LESSONS, but I suddenly realize that I have yet to face a naked sword. Tagliaferro taught his lessons with swords tightly covered in leather cloths. Those weapons would at worst inflict a bruise. But now I'm confronted with a sword whose edge and tip are so sharp they would penetrate cloth, skin, flesh, sinews, and muscles at the slightest touch. I'm about to die. Here in this chapel, under the eye of God and his servants. There's no point in fighting. *I must drop my sword*, I decide in a flash, *I must go with him*. I'm about to do so when I see something flicker across his face and his sword comes flashing at me in a sideways swing. I instinctively do what Tagliaferro has taught me. I parry the blow by taking a step back and deflecting his sword with a vertical swing. Fast as lightning, my father changes his movement and the tip of his sword flashes right at my forehead from below. I parry that blow, too. A right-hand swing, a left-hand swing, and another right-hand swing follow. I parry all three. When his sword tip comes straight at my breast, I parry that, too. Every time our swords touch—the narrow rapier I took from his belt and the heavy battle sword in his hand—sparks fly.

Then everything becomes quiet. My father takes two steps back. Our first skirmish went so quickly, I haven't had time to think. My arm was guided completely by my instincts, strengthened by Jan van Vere's instruction and the fifty lessons on the wooden floor of Tagliaferro's school. I see the soldiers stare at me with open mouths, and behind the altar the nuns, too, are struck dumb. I feel every muscle in my body. I curl my toes in my sandals, I rotate my ankles to warm them up, I loosen up my wrists. I stretch out the fingers of my sword hand and clamp them firmly around the hilt.

"You fight well, daughter," my father grins.

"And you're fighting like a clod," I shout. "Is that the best you can do?"

"You think that the fire that burnt inside you has been extinguished. You think you'll never love anyone because your Philip has left this world. But it takes more than that to put out the fire inside you, young Lady of Flanders."

"Oh, shut up," I screech. "How would you know what I want and what I feel? You know nothing."

"You," he shouts, pointing his huge sword at me, "you want to crawl away, like a rabbit into its burrow.

You want to hide from the sun like a bat under a roof. You want to escape from the world, but the world doesn't want to escape from you."

"Stick the world where it fits, Father," I shout and attack. I make short, rapid passes. My feet glide over the tiles and my right arm slashes forward. The tip of my sword flashes at my father's belly. It misses his hauberk by a thumb's width and he hurriedly takes a step back. He's taller, stronger, better trained. But I'm smaller, so can move faster, and I have a lighter sword. I rain blows on him. My right arm hacks, swings, and thrusts, but each time he deftly parries my attacks. Yet he can't find a way to set up a counterattack. Finally, he jumps away and turns, his sword stretched out in a defensive stance. My habit is stuck to my skin with sweat. The nuns and the soldiers have become very quiet. They understand they're witnessing a rare fight. My father is good, very good. He has never lost a man-to-man fight. He is the only person Andrea Tagliaferro has ever considered his superior. I realize he has allowed me to attack to wear me out. But my blows have come dangerously close to his body. One miscalculation on his part and the point of my sword would cut clean through his hauberk. But there's something else. Something I would never have thought. Something that, perhaps, I've always feared. Something I would never dare admit to him: I'm enjoying this fight.

My father attacks. His long sword flies at me with incredible speed. His ability to handle an unwieldy sword at such speed amazes me. I barely dodge the blow, and I know the pain will come even before I actually feel it. The sword point cuts right through my habit and scratches my side. The pain slices through me. I scream. I curse. I stamp my feet. My white habit is red with blood. I feel the wound screaming inside me.

"Shall we leave it at this, daughter, or do you want more?"

I bellow like a wild beast and run at him. I don't even bother to hold my sword in a defensive position to stop a thrust from the front. I know he'll hesitate to cut me down as I storm at him in my total rage. And, indeed, he hesitates. With a circular sideways movement, I hack at his side. He parries at the last moment. I spin around and thrust at his thighs. Again, he parries and counterattacks with a sideways lunge at my shoulder. It's a predictable thrust and I don't parry it. Instead, I dive under the swishing sword blade and see the surprise in my father's eyes. I thrust upward at his chest and feel my sword rip the side of his tunic to shreds and graze his hauberk. If he hadn't worn that hauberk, my sword would have tasted flesh. Now he knows I'm truly dangerous. He won't take a single risk from here on. At the beginning of the fight, he saved his strength and restrained his movements, but now he goes all out. He counterattacks. What an unimaginably good fighter he is! Every attack is carried out with precision. He fights at a speed that continues to amaze me.

But I keep parrying his blows with my light rapier. I dodge, step back, step sideways, go up the altar steps (scattering the nuns), and stand my ground. I realize my father doesn't want to kill me—he wants to disarm me. I move back toward the altar as our swords clang together at dizzying speed. I bump into the statue of the black Virgin and it falls to the floor with a heavy thump. The sisters scream. I jump down off the steps. I am totally exhausted. My arms tremble with the effort. My legs wobble.

My father comes slowly down the steps. He knows he has me. But there's one thing he doesn't know: my heart is on my left side. I see the point of Tagliaferro's sword between my eyes. I remember him saying that a fight isn't won through force but through cunning. But can I still be cunning? With my side bleeding and an opponent who has never been beaten? And then I know.

I take three steps back, dragging the end of my sword along the floor. With my left hand, I feel for the wall. One of the sisters screams. I feel the wall at my back. I breathe heavily. I groan. I have nowhere left to go. My father comes at me. He stretches his sword out before him. He's on his guard. I look toward him, clenching my teeth and distorting my face. He knows that I have come to the end. He knows that I am gathering my last strength for a final desperate attack. I raise my sword. I make my arm tremble. I want the sword to strike him with a sideways blow, a blow that's easily parried. My sword flashes toward him. I see that he's in position to parry, but at the last moment,

I throw my sword vertically into the air.

My father must have been surprised when his sword slashed through empty air instead of hitting the steel of my rapier, but I don't see his look of surprise. Everything is happening too fast. The next moment I've caught the hilt of my sword in my left hand. I push off on my right foot, bend my left knee, and my whole body becomes one long sword. The point of my sword cuts through fabric, hauberk, skin, flesh, blood vessels, and ligaments. The point meets bone. I have pierced my father and withdraw the sword.

My father screams with pain. Blood gushes from his right shoulder. The ringlets of his hauberk have ripped apart, and the purple flesh has torn away. The point of his sword lands on the tiles, but his right hand is still clamped around the hilt. He doesn't drop it. With his left hand, he takes the sword from his half-paralyzed right hand.

The soldiers come running to support him. He pushes them away with his shoulder. He clasps the sword in his left hand and points it at me. Blood keeps gushing from his wound. The injury is probably not fatal, but it will rapidly weaken him. I can hardly hide my triumph. I want to shout out my victory. My father, beaten by his own daughter. The man who has never lost a man-to-man fight. I feel sweat prickling on my face. A tiredness as heavy as lead is slowly making my muscles go stiff.

"I think you should go now, Father," I gasp, feeling the throb of the wound in my side. I press my habit against it to staunch the bleeding.

"And I used to think Tagliaferro made you pay far too much for his lessons," he mutters.

"Tagliaferro? How did you know I—"

"As I told you before," he says, biting back the raging pain, "I know everything about you. And I know you can't win this fight."

My father hauls himself back into position, his sword in his left hand. His tunic is soaked in blood. For the first time, I tremble. And then his sword comes. They are violent, hacking blows, and I parry them as best I can, realizing that my father's heart, too, is on his left side.

I look into my father's cold eyes, and he looks back. We watch every flickering expression, every movement of the pupils, while our swords touch each other almost automatically. The swords have become an extension of our bodies. My father's blows are becoming harder and harder. I know what he wants to do. He wants to use his battle sword to break my much lighter rapier. But time after time, I deflect his blows. Then comes his great swinging blow—a blow I couldn't detect in his eyes. Suddenly, his sword isn't where it should be and even before panic can seize me, the flat of his sword batters my left temple. It's as if I'm hit by a stone. I fall to the ground, drop my rapier, and vomit uncontrollably.

I'm stuck to the tiles. My body soaks up the coolness of the floor. I try to move my arms and legs to push myself up. But they don't respond. I manage to turn onto my back and try to raise my head. The whole chapel is shrouded in a red mist. I see two soldiers pressing a cloth against my father's wound. The nuns are clustered near the altar but don't dare come to me. I can feel my fingers again. I try to lift myself but fall over once more. My father comes toward me, and I wonder what awaits me. The final blow?

He grips me by the wrist and drags me up. My feet can hardly support me. I'm so dizzy I fall against his chest. I don't want to faint. I want to be awake. And yet... The darkness of oblivion encircles me. It covers my body like a stone shroud. I taste my father's blood on his tunic. Blood sticks to my short hair. I try to push myself away from his chest, but all strength seems to have gone from my arms.

"I'm lost," I mutter, coughing up spit and bits of vomit.

"I have to think of my reputation, daughter." My father grinds out the words. "It's bad enough that you've ruined my shoulder."

"Your own fault," I mumble feverishly.

My right hand clings to my father's tunic. For a moment I feel as if I'll fall over backward. But I hold on. My hand doesn't let go of the tunic.

"There's so much fire and so much life in you," he says, biting back the pain. "Don't throw it away. Grab hold of your life. It won't be easy. There will be sickness, death, and war. But there will also be beauty. Somehow."

Then I fall into an ocean of black. My fist has dug itself into the tunic. I hear the fabric rip. Then nothing.

23

MOTHER SUPERIOR HERSELF takes care of me. I'm knocked out with poppy juice and brandy, but I still scream my soul out when the wound in my side is cleaned with altar wine and then sewn up with catgut.

For five days I stay in a darkened convent room. My entire head is still buzzing from the blow of my father's sword. I have a huge lump on my left temple. My side is burning. Despite blankets and a fire, I shiver with cold and fever.

Only on the sixth day do things begin to improve. Mother Superior comes and sits with me. She tells me my father is being nursed in the valley. A surgeon has taken care of his injuries. My father has bitten through a lot of pieces of wood in the process.

"The surgeon says his right arm will never be the same again," Mother Superior tells me. I watch her bony face and full lower lip. I feel her thin fingers that hold my hand. Her sharp eyes are set deep in their sockets.

"Your father refuses to return to Flanders lying down in a carriage," she says while cleaning my wound. "He wants to return home upright in the saddle. The surgeon is of the opinion that his wound is nowhere near healed."

Mother Superior carefully dabs at my wound. I make a huge effort not to scream with pain.

"Your father has had a gown delivered to the convent," she says.

"I don't want to see it. I won't put it on until I leave."

"I insist, sister," Mother Superior continues, "that you don't return to Flanders till after the end of winter."

"If it ends. The chaplain of Male says it'll never end. This is the last winter. This is the end of the world. Snow, cold, and ice will persist till the day of the Last Judgment."

Mother Superior doesn't seem to have heard me. She bandages my wound with washed silk and then helps me pull a shirt over my shivering body. It's cold in the convent, even though the thick layer of snow on the roof prevents the water inside from freezing.

"Winter will end, sister," Mother Superior assures me.

"I'm sorry I have caused you so much trouble," I sigh.

"What I'm sorry for," Mother Superior replies with a smile, "is that I didn't see the fight. The sisters can't stop talking about it."

"And I thought this was a silent order," I joke.

She strokes my cheek.

"Rest now, and try to think of spring. It will come," Mother Superior whispers.

She gets up. The door of my convent room closes.

The next day, I gingerly walk to the chapel. With every step, the wound in my side pulls. The lump on my head has turned purple. I step into the cloisters that surround the Paradise Courtyard. The winter air tingles in my nostrils. The courtyard is still under a thick layer of snow. I look up and there's not a cloud in the sky. I stare into the blue, and all I can think about is summer.

I see the colors of late May. The grass rustling under our toes. The warm silt we dip our feet in. The wide, flat polder, the windmills, the dikes, the cornfields, the great granaries, and the little villages on top of their sandhills. I'm impatient to see my Marshland again. My land of swamps and creeks. I want to see the Northern Sea again and sniff the salty breeze.

I can't wait to leave the Convent of the Heavens and step into the world. I want to hear the clatter of hooves on the paving stones in Bruges and the creaking of the signs hanging outside the trading houses. I even want to smell the sulfur the leatherworkers use to burn the pigskins clean. I want my life back.

◨ ◨ ◨

THREE WEEKS PASS. We've just said matins. I take off my habit and put on the green gown my father had delivered. Soon, my father's soldiers will be here to get me. In a few moments I'll be mounting my horse. My hair has already grown a little.

I say farewell to the sisters and to Mother Superior. I can already smell the world outside.

The bolts are slid aside. I open the convent gate and see the horses.

They're snorting.

They're stamping their feet.

Marguerite of Male, 13th March 1361

AUTHORS' NOTE

About the real Marguerite

MARGUERITE VAN MALE, whose portrait appears opposite, lived between 1348 and 1405. She is no more than a paragraph in most books covering European history. This paragraph usually reports her marriage, in 1369, to Philip the Bold, Prince of France. The union brought Flanders under the yoke of the dukedom of Burgundy and bore in itself the seed of five hundred years of foreign domination; Marguerite was the last heiress of the Counts of Flanders.

Marguerite lived during the Hundred Years' War. She was an eyewitness to the second plague epidemic, which was called the Great Children's Plague, and received offers of marriage from both the English and the French courts.

If we are to believe the chronicles, she had a fiery temper and was far from attractive. She was always decked out in the most exquisite dresses, was wild about jewels, and had a stormy relationship with her father.

Not much is known about her personal life, and the history books often contradict one another. Even her date of birth is a point of contention. We have given our fantasy free rein to clear up the fog around her childhood and to make of her a girl of flesh and blood, who has to compete against the fierce and violent male world of the Middle Ages.

Marguerite van Male was buried in the convent church of the Collégiale Saint-Pierre in Lille, France. We visited the crypt of the convent church one winter's day, but it was completely underwater at the time. The chief archaeologist of the city told us later that the convent church had been gutted during the French Revolution and all the gravestones had been taken away. Marguerite's gravestone probably now serves as part of an open hearth or mantelpiece somewhere.

Was the real Marguerite exactly as she appears in our book? Did she ride like a man and swear like a trooper? Perhaps.

A Sword in Her Hand is a novel in which historical truth has been complemented and slightly adapted by our imagination.

And so in our novel, history, even though real, becomes to a certain degree legend again.

About the writing process

WE ARE OFTEN ASKED, How does it work with two people writing, and who does what? You could say that Jean-Claude is the storyteller and Pat is the researcher. Jean-Claude sketches out the storyline and writes the first version of the chapters, while Pat delves into books and whole libraries to furnish the world of the story.

In the second phase, we rework all the scenes together; we bring them to life with details and knead them into a dramatic whole. In the final phase, we read the book out loud together until the entire tale sounds good and gains a little bit of melody.

During the Middle Ages, troubadours told their ballads by the blaze of the fire and by the light of many far-too-expensive candles. They gave color to gray winter nights and brought romance into the monotonous lives of castle folk.

A Sword in Her Hand is such a ballad.

Jean-Claude van Rijckeghem & Pat van Beirs

ABOUT THE AUTHORS

JEAN-CLAUDE VAN RIJCKEGHEM AND PAT VAN BEIRS have written a lot together: young-adult novels, the script for the historical graphic novel series *Betty and Dodge*, and the Cannes Film Festival prize-winning screenplay for the hit film *Aanrijding in Moscou* (*Moscow, Belgium*). Jean-Claude is also a screenwriter and film producer who has contributed to the screenplays of such successful films as *Man zkt. Vrouw* (*Man Seeks Woman*), *Kruistocht in Spijkerbroek* (*Crusade in Jeans*), and *De Bal* (*The Ball*). Pat works as a translator of animated feature films, including *Chicken Run*, *Monsters, Inc*, *Atlantis*, *Wallace & Gromit*, and *Finding Nemo*.

ABOUT THE TRANSLATOR

JOHN NIEUWENHUIZEN is an award-winning, Australian-based translator of Dutch and Flemish literature. In 2006 John was shortlisted for the Marsh Award for Children's Literature in Translation (UK) for *The Book of Everything* by Guus Kuijerr, having previously won the Mildred Batchelder Award (US) for *The Baboon King*. In 2007 he was awarded the NSW Premier's Translation Prize and PEN Medallion.

More award-winning historical novels from Annick Press

MIMUS

by Lilli Thal

translated by John Brownjohn

New York Public Library's Books for the Teen Age

THE DARK MIDDLE AGES jump to life in blazing color as Lilli Thal conjures up a world of adventure, humor, and imagination.

Two mighty kingdoms have been engaged in endless, merciless war. A promise of peace lures King Philip to the castle of his arch-enemy, King Theodo, but he is captured and thrown into the dungeon. Soon Philip's son, 12-year-old Prince Florin, is lured to the castle, where the same horror awaits him.

On a whim, King Theodo decides to make the crown prince his second fool, trained by Mimus, an enigmatic, occasionally spiteful, and unpredictable court jester. But events ultimately turn for Florin and the other captives, and it is Mimus's intervention that helps make it possible.

PAPERBACK $12.95 | HARDCOVER $19.95

Praise for *Mimus:*

Winner of numerous awards, including the Society of School Librarians International Honor Book Award and ForeWord Magazine's Book of the Year Award.

"This is a sophisticated and engrossing historical tale by a writer who brings exceptional attention to detail, character development, and theme."

—*Booklist*, starred review

THE APPRENTICE'S MASTERPIECE: *A STORY OF MEDIEVAL SPAIN*
by Melanie Little

IT'S THE SPANISH INQUISITION and agents of oppression grow deadly for two teens.

Fifteenth-century Spain is a richly multicultural society in which Jews, Muslims, and Christians coexist. But under the zealous Christian Queen Isabella, the country abruptly becomes one of the most murderously intolerant places on Earth.

It is in this atmosphere that the Benvenistes, a family of scribes, attempt to eke out a living. The family has a secret—they are conversos: Jews who converted to Christianity. Now, with neighbors and friends turned into spies, fear hangs in the air.

One day a young man is delivered to their door. His name is Amir, and he wears the robe and red patch of a Muslim. Fifteen-year-old Ramon Benveniste broods over Amir's easy acceptance into the family.

Startling and dramatic events overtake the household, and the family is torn apart. One boy becomes enslaved, the other takes up service for the Inquisitors. Finally, their paths cross again in a haunting scene.

Melanie Little has crafted a brilliant story in verse about one of the most politically complex and troubling times in human history—the Spanish Inquisition. Drawing on intensive research, Little creates memorable characters and potently captures the turbulent events of the period. It is the work of a master.

PAPERBACK $12.95 | HARDCOVER $19.95

Praise for *The Apprentice's Masterpiece:*

"The subject and the history are enthralling ..."

—Booklist

"This riveting story is peopled by flesh-and-blood characters..."
—School Library Journal

"The brief narrative poems are small gems of insight and emotion ...and resonate with contemporary connections."

—VOYA

"The riveting personal narratives (are) carried forward in remarkable free verse that draws the young reader into a story with obvious parallels in modern life."

—Globe and Mail

"This sophisticated, unbending novel packs an impressive amount of information and intelligent insight into the small space juvenile historical fiction allows ... moments of lyric expression shine out like small jewels."

—Toronto Star

DARK HOURS
by Gudrun Pausewang
translated by John Brownjohn

DARKNESS AND TERROR VISIT CHILDREN who are entombed following a bombing raid.

On Gisel's sixteenth birthday, her world, like the war effort, begins to crumble. Her father is still away serving in the German army when the advancing Allies force the rest of the family to flee their home. Gisel, her three younger brothers, and their pregnant mother board a crowded train. But when their mother goes into labor, the children are separated from her at the next station.

Before they know what's happening an air raid siren sounds, and Gisel barely manages to hustle the children into a trackside lavatory. When the bombs hit, the children are trapped. As they await rescue, Gisel's only adult communication is with a dying soldier buried on the other side of the wall who offers guidance on how to survive.

Dark Hours is a suspenseful and dramatic novel about the injustice of war, its impact on ordinary people, and the hope that resonates in the human soul.

HARDCOVER WITH DUSTJACKET $21.95

Praise for *Dark Hours:*

New York Public Library's Books for the Teen Age
Tayshas High School Reading List, Texas Library Association
Independent Publisher Book Award, Silver

"... a page-turner... will appeal to those who enjoy stories about intense experiences. Pausewang paints a realistic picture of a teen in extraordinarily trying circumstances ..."

—VOYA

"Well written with suspense and powerful sentiments ..."
—School Library Journal

"... a compulsively readable story ... Celebrating courage, endurance and the final victory of hope, this is children's anti-war fiction at its finest."

—The Independent (UK)

"Add this to the usual list of World War II books to freshen and broaden your readers' views on the war."

—schoollibraryjournal.com

A fantasy novel based on historical fable

AFTER HAMELIN
by Bill Richardson

AFTER HAMELIN picks up the story where the Browning poem and other tellings of "The Pied Piper of Hamelin" leave off. The story is told with a sense of adventure and humor, and the author uses inventive wordplay and uninhibited imagination to spin a narrative tale through strange lands inhabited by characters both good and evil.

Penelope is now 101 years old, but as a child she was struck deaf on her eleventh birthday, the day the Pied Piper stole the town's children. Spared that fate, she accepts the quest to find the evil piper and bring the stolen children back. She tracks them through dangerous terrain, into the belly of a mountain, to a lost city. Before their adventure is over, Penelope and her companions use their wits and talents to rescue the missing children—standing against human, animal, and supernatural forces in order to triumph.

PAPERBACK $8.95 ($12.95 CDN) | HARDCOVER $19.95